LOVE
Unbound
DANIELLE BAKER

Dedication

TO MY MOTHER; MY BIGGEST FAN
Who has shared in all my joys and sorrows,

my trials, failures, and achievements,

whose love, courage, and devotion

have been the strength of my inspiration,

and who never gave up on this dream

of mine, even when I was in

doubt that I would get here.

I love you.

CHAPTER 1

She stood in the barn, running the brush over the smooth back of the tall horse standing in front of her. Dust motes danced in the rays of sunlight filtering in through the windows high above her. The musky scent of hay and grain and her own sweat mingled in the air.

A shadow fell across the center aisle and she turned. Her heart instantly began to pound at the sight of the man standing in the doorway. The cowboy's face was deeply shadowed by the wide brim of his black cowboy hat. Tight fitted jeans hugged his thighs and the apex of them. The toes of his dusty boots peaked out from beneath the hem of his jeans, a black t-shirt defined the muscles of his chest, arms, and shoulders deliciously, and a leather vest hung open over his chest. Leaning with one broad shoulder against the wood frame, he folded his arms over his chest and crossed his booted ankles. He watched her from beneath the brim of his hat and her breathing began to accelerate. She wished she could see his eyes!

"Don't let me stop you," he murmured low, his voice drawling and sexy, and she could barely make out the movement of his lips.

Turning back to the mare, she continued to run the brush down the animal's side. Her senses seemed to be on overdrive, because she heard it when he shifted away from the door and slowly sauntered over until he was standing inches away from her. She could smell his masculine scent, sweat and man, and his sweet breath as it hit the back of her neck. Her long hair was pulled into a single braid down one side of her neck.

She was feeling lightheaded, his nearness was so intoxicating. She had watched him for months, working on her father's ranch. He was handsome and mysterious. They had never spoken, but she knew he had been watching her, too.

She wore tightly fitting jeans that were tucked into a pair of clean cowboy boots. A plain white t-shirt with a deep V that revealed her generous cleavage fit snuggly to her body. She had worn it on purpose, in the hopes that she would see him during her ride.

She could feel his body heat radiating against her back, he was standing so close behind her. She swallowed hard just as she felt his work roughened fingers touching the soft skin at the nape of her neck, playing with the thick braid of hair. With a slow swipe of his strong hand, the braid was moved aside so it fell over her right shoulder, resting on the curve of her breast. There it trembled, as her heart was racing in her chest. The fabric of her shirt fluttered with each quick breath she took.

The hand at her nape cupped her slender throat and her eyes slid closed as her head fell to the side, into his hand. His other hand slipped around her, pressing his palm flat against the taut muscles of her abdomen. Without words, he urged her back against his front. She sucked in a startled breath as his lips found the exposed skin of her left shoulder. An unfamiliar but delicious ache began in her lower belly, where his hand was pressed. Rolling her hips backward, she gasped and he groaned against her throat. The cowboy hat was knocked off his head and it landed in the hay at their feet.

His breathing was becoming choppy as his hand skimmed up, over her ribcage, to cover one breast. Her head fell back and a soft moan escaped her slightly parted lips. His mouth loved her throat, kissing and suckling, as his hand cupped and massaged the tender breast it held.

She could feel the hardness of his erection straining against the fly of his jeans as she pressed her rounded bottom to his front.

He pulled away and a mew of disappointment slipped from her lips. It was fleeting, as he took her hand in his and turned her toward him. His aquamarine eyes were bright as they stared down at her. He reached for the brush she still had clutched in her other hand and tossed it aside. He looked over her shoulder and then back down to her. Pulling her with him gently, he guided her toward an empty stall in the back of the barn. Her heart thundered in her chest, terrified and excited at the same time.

He backed into the stall, her hand still enclosed in his. They were very secluded in the back of the barn, the high walls of the stalls giving them much needed privacy from anyone that might come looking for her. He released her hand and turned, taking down a blanket from one of the pegs and lowering it to the bed of hay on the ground.

Turning back to her, he tipped her chin up with one finger and lowered his mouth to hers.

His lips brushed over hers, once, twice, then pressed and stayed. She gasped, and his tongue darted into the honeyed cavern, tasting all of her. One hand caught her braid and held tight, holding her to him. His kiss was intrusive and intense, and she reveled in it.

She heard more than felt when his fingers began to undo the buttons of her jeans. He surprised her by gathering her into his arms. His mouth continued its onslaught on her senses and she didn't realize he was lowering her to the blanket until he leaned away to pull her boots off her small feet. She lay, reclining on the hay, watching through passion clouded eyes as he stripped her of her jeans. She blushed and whimpered softly and he was there, shushing her with his mouth.

The rasp of the zipper on his jeans being lowered was a strangely sexy sound. Flinging the leather vest off, he lowered his jeans on his hips and she gasped at her first sight of his hard length. Parting her thighs, he slid one finger into her silken warmth and groaned gutturally, his eyes blazing into hers. Lowering his body over hers, he captured her mouth with his again; one arm supporting himself up, the other sliding beneath her hips, angling them to meet his. She felt the tip of his steely strength probing gently, and she breathed huskily, "Free, oh yes, Free..."

"Jodi... Jodi..." he whispered roughly against the underside of her jaw even as he pressed inside her. "Jodi..."

Jodi Kendall's eyes flew open. She sat at the kitchen table, fingers poised over the keys of her laptop. Unsure what had drawn her out of her daydream, she let out a shaky breath and lowered her face into her trembling hands. His voice had seemed so real, as if he were mere feet away, instead of thousands of miles.

"Penny for your thoughts," she heard from behind her, and her heart stopped, for she would know that Texas drawl anywhere.

CHAPTER 2

Jodi whipped her head around and her heart thundered back to life with a vengeance, nearly knocking the breath out of her. She wondered hazily if she was still daydreaming, not completely believing her eyes. The setting sun was directly behind him as it descended beyond the trees across the field, casting him in shadow.

"Free," Jodi finally managed to whisper between dry lips.

He smiled, that slow, lazy grin that she remembered so well. He was propped up against the doorjamb with one of his wide, hard shoulders. He crossed sinewy, tanned arms over the broad expanse of his chest. His hips were narrow, his long legs crossed at the ankles. It was eerily close to what she had just envisioned in her daydream. He exuded a carefree laziness that only native Texans could manage.

"Yep," Freeman Thorp husked in that slow Texas drawl that he'd been born with. It still made her go weak.

She stood, nervously straightening the white shirt she wore. Her heart was pounding beneath her breasts.

"You're back," she said lamely, cringing internally. Why, after all this time, was she still so awkward around him?

He pushed himself away from the door and came toward her. That slow, rolling of his hips that all cowboys seemed to have mastered was blatantly sexual, even though it was unconscious on his part. The jeans that he wore were worn and faded and fit his long legs, his hips, his backside… his sex. They fit snug to his hips, emphasizing the lazy roll of them. A wide brown leather belt was strapped around them, accentuating how narrow they were. A plain black t-shirt was stretched over the impressive expanse of his muscled chest, hard back, and corded shoulders. He wore a black felt cowboy hat that sat low on his head. His jaw and upper lip were covered in a dark but well-groomed beard, no longer clean shaven like he'd always been before. She liked it, a lot. Jodi's fingers itched to touch it, to see if it was as soft as it looked. His aquamarine eyes were bright as he stared at her.

Watching him now, he made her weak, and it made her angry that he still had so much influence over her. Damn him.

He stopped a foot away from her. He was close enough that she could smell him, his body wash, cologne, whatever it was. Cedarwood and citrus. He smelled dangerously sexy.

He's so tall, she thought breathlessly as she looked up at him, a long way up. He was six feet, three inches of Texan.

Bad boy Texan.

"Yeah," he husked. "I'm back."

Long, black lashes spiked away from those incredible eyes. Briefly, she wondered if they looked that way when wet, too. A straight, narrow nose flared slightly over lips that could almost be classified as too thin. But those lips were very kissable. They were soft and warm and she remembered how they felt on hers.

With her heart thundering, and her mind continuing to haunt her with that delicious memory, she lifted her sapphire blue eyes to his, but his hot gaze was on her mouth. She blushed lightly and nervously wet her lips with the tip of her tongue.

His eyes snapped away from her mouth and she blushed again. What is wrong with me! she groaned at herself internally. Straightening her shoulders, she resolved to not let him see the effect he still had on her. He cleared his throat roughly and swiped the hat off his head and set it on the counter next to him. Jodi watched as the fingers of one strong, tanned hand ran through his dark hair, pulling the shaggy strands away from his eyes.

"You look good, kid," he said softly, slowly. "You've changed."

Her eyes narrowed with irritation at being called "kid" at the age of twenty-five. She had changed in more ways than he knew.

Cocking her head to one side, she raised her eyebrows slightly and said, "Yeah, seven years away will do that to a person."

Free's eyebrows shot up in surprise at the sharpness in her voice and she took perverse pleasure in it. She kept her shoulders straight and stared up at him, refusing to let him fluster her. She wasn't the same innocent eighteen-year-old she had been the last time he'd seen her.

"You've changed too," she said quietly, softening her tone slightly. Jodi had thought he looked good at twenty-seven. He no longer had a boyish look to him. Now, everything about him screamed male. He had filled out, hardened.

He nodded his head, his gaze intense, but didn't say anything. His stoic silence annoyed her immensely, and she turned away from him before he could see it. She crossed the kitchen to the refrigerator and asked him over her shoulder, "Would you like something to drink?"

"I would love something to drink," Free said, then laughed and held up his hands in mock surrender. "But I was just at your parents, so please, don't try to feed me!"

Jodi laughed heartily, knowing exactly how her mother is. She nodded and smiled over her shoulder at him as she opened the refrigerator, and said, "Mom probably thinks you're too skinny."

"That's exactly what she said," Free chuckled. Jodi held up a pitcher of lemonade and a beer, to which Free motioned to the beer. She brought two back and he sat down at the small kitchen table as she lowered herself into the seat opposite him. He glanced down at the laptop that still sat on the table, and she reached over to flip it closed, not ready to share what she'd been working on. Free's gaze lifted to hers, and they stared at each other for a long time. It had been so long since she'd seen his face, heard his voice.

Tearing his eyes from her face, he took a long drink of the beer as he looked around the small kitchen. She watched his eyes as they took in her simple home. It was decorated in muted tones of gray and white, with natural wood accents. "I like this place, Jodi. How long have you been here?"

"Just a few months," she evaded, taking a sip of her own beer. Starting over with a clean slate, everything was simple, minimalistic. She watched him for a long moment, then asked quietly, "Did you come here just to talk about my décor?"

Free chuckled, and Jodi couldn't help but notice the subtle laugh lines that appeared around his eyes when he smiled. At thirty-four, he looked better than ever, and she hated it.

"No, I didn't come here to talk about your home décor," he murmured, taking a long pull off the bottle of beer. He set it down and folded his hands together and rested them on the table in front of him. The way he stared at her made her heart flutter. Damn him for having this effect on her after all this time! Walls she'd carefully built around her damaged heart seemed to be paper thin where Freeman was concerned, and she immediately steeled herself against him.

"Then why did you come here?" she asked bluntly.

"I just thought I'd stop in to see you," he said slowly, eyeing her warily.

"After seven years?" Jodi asked sharply, drawing her eyebrows together and narrowing her eyes on his. "You were gone so long I figured you'd forgotten me, so why now?"

Shaking his head in confusion, his eyes drilled into hers as he said a quiet, "Of course I didn't forget you, I could never forget you, Jodi—"

"Then why did you leave? Why did you stay gone for *seven years*?" she demanded, crossing her arms on the tabletop in front of her.

Thrown off by the bitterness in her question, his head snapped back and he looked away guiltily. "I had to, Jodi."

"But why?"

"I just did, okay?" he said tersely.

Jodi's lips pursed in irritation again. She shook her head before snapping, "I think I deserve an explanation after… what happened. Whether you like it or not, I'm not a child anymore and I refuse to be treated as such."

"Jodi, dammit," he said through gritted teeth. His eyes swung around to hers and she was immediately mesmerized by the heat radiating out of those turquoise depths. "You're smart enough to know why I couldn't stay here and be around you every day. But if you want me to say the words, here they are; all of a sudden, all I wanted was to kiss you every chance I got. I couldn't stop wanting to do… things… with you whenever I saw you. Especially after that kiss. You were *seventeen* for christsake."

"I was eighteen, Freeman," she snapped, though hearing the words come out of his mouth made butterflies take flight in the pit of her stomach.

"Barely!" Free shouted, then blew out his breath in frustration, closing his eyes tightly. Opening his eyes again, he took another long drink of the beer before looking back at her, his aquamarine eyes burning with intensity. "You were a child. And I was way too old to be doing things like that with you. It was wrong. If your dad had found out—"

"I am twenty-five years old!" Jodi exclaimed, splaying one hand over her chest. His eyes dropped to where her hand was, and she felt more than heard his groan.

"But you weren't then!" Free argued, then rolled his head across his shoulders in frustration. When he brought his eyes to hers again, Jodi could see the torment in them. "Whether you realize it or not, what I did to you that night… wasn't okay." Jodi watched him for several seconds, their eyes never wavering.

"You didn't do anything to me that I didn't want," Jodi whispered, her eyes never leaving his.

"That still didn't make it okay," he whispered back brokenly. He dropped his gaze and snapped, "Stop looking at me like that, dammit."

"Like what?" Jodi snapped back.

Ignoring her question and standing, striding away from the table, he muttered, "I left to keep you away from me. To keep you safe. I was supposed to protect you from guys like me."

"I didn't need a babysitter!" Jodi said heatedly, standing too. "I can take care of myself, thank you very much."

"Like you did with Will?" Free shot at her and planted his hands on his hips.

Jodi forced herself not to lose the temper she unfortunately shared with her hot-headed father. When she spoke, she strained to keep cool and collected. "I am not a child anymore, Freeman, and I won't be treated as such. I have made plenty of mistakes, yes. Like any other human on the planet. He was a college-aged prick and I was an idiot for not seeing it until it was too late." A character flaw that seemed to have followed her into adulthood, she thought to herself wryly.

"That's why I left!" Free said heatedly and scrubbed his hands over his face in frustration. "I made a mistake, too. When I caught you in that car with him, I lost my temper because I was crazy with jealousy, not only because I was being protective. What he did was… inexcusable, but at least he was *age appropriate*, Jodi." His eyes drilled into hers hotly. "Then I kissed you and I never wanted to stop. I left seven years ago because I needed to protect you from me. I'd made a mistake and I needed to fix it."

Jodi's breath blew out in shock, hurt making her angry. "So kissing me was a mistake?"

"I didn't mean it like that," Free muttered and flung one hand out in aggravation. He blew out his breath and squeezed his eyes shut, shaking his head. "Dammit. This definitely isn't the way I wanted this to happen."

"You had to know if you showed up here, we were going to talk about this at some point, Free," Jodi whispered, crossing her arms over her stomach in an effort to hold herself together. "You can't kiss someone like that then leave for years."

"People do it all the time, kid. They're called one-night stands." He cringed as the words left his mouth, as if regretting them instantly.

"I wouldn't know; you left before that happened," Jodi muttered bitterly then snapped, "and quit calling me kid!"

"It's a damn good thing I did leave!" Free shouted, spreading his arms wide. "Your dad would've skinned me alive and probably would have you in a damn chastity belt for the rest of your life!"

Through her frustration and anger at him, Jodi couldn't help but laugh at the mental picture he'd painted. Her laughter melted his anger, too, and he chuckled.

"I missed you," Jodi whispered earnestly after a long moment. Her heart pounded against her ribs so hard it hurt. Her confession had taken all her courage.

Free sighed and smiled sadly at her. "I missed you, too."

"Are you home for good?" she asked quietly.

"I'm just home for the wedding," he said softly. He picked up his cowboy hat and fidgeted with the brim. "I'm the best man."

"Oh," Jodi said, disappointment making her heart sink to the pit of her stomach. "So, you'll be headed back to Texas soon then?"

He nodded brusquely before sighing heavily, and murmured, "I uhh— I really need to get going. I haven't even seen Shane yet."

"Yeah, of course," Jodi said and smiled, though it was forced. She hated that they had already had a fight. Jodi walked him to the door and followed him out onto the covered front porch. He took a couple steps down the porch stairs and stopped, turning to look at her. "It was nice to see you, Free," she said awkwardly, one corner of her mouth tilted up in a half-hearted smile.

She had stopped at the landing of the stairs, and they were almost eye to eye. He took one step back up and her breath hitched, those damn butterflies taking flight again at having him so close. He stood so that his face was just a few inches above hers, and mere inches separated them. She swallowed hard; her eyes never leaving his.

Reaching up, he brushed the soft curls framing her face. His fingertips skimmed the soft skin of her cheek and she closed her eyes, leaning her cheek into his open palm, the movement involuntary on her part. She let out a soft, almost silent sigh and opened her eyes to look into his.

His eyes searched hers for a long moment before he dropped his hand. "Bye. Thanks for the beer."

"Bye," Jodi whispered back as he turned and sauntered down the remaining steps, pulling his cowboy hat back onto his head. She touched her cheek where his hand had been. He climbed into what she recognized as Shane's white Chevy Silverado and the engine rumbled to life. He waved out the window as he pulled out of her driveway. Covering her aching heart with her hand, she swore succinctly under her breath before turning to walk back into the house.

CHAPTER 3

Freeman Thorp climbed into the cab of the truck that Shane had left at the airport for him when he'd arrived and started the engine, waving, all while watching Jodi out of the corner of his eye as he pulled away from the house. In the rearview mirror he watched as she finally turned and walked back into the front door, closing it behind her.

The truck bounced and rumbled back down the long, dirt paved driveway. A wood rail fence lined one side of the drive, and he followed it back to the road. Turning left, he started down the familiar roads toward his brother's home.

Free scrubbed one hand down his face, the other draped loosely over the steering wheel as he drove. He still didn't know what had possessed him to seek her out. When his brother had asked him to come home and stand as his best man in his wedding, Free had told himself he would avoid Jodi Kendall like the plague.

That had lasted all of a handful of hours after making it back to northern Michigan and the place he'd called home for over a decade.

He had hoped she would have forgotten about what happened, hoped that she would laugh it off as a silly teenage crush that she'd outgrow with time, hoped that she would be happily married, something, *anything* to absolve himself of the guilt he'd carried for nearly a decade. That hope had been dashed the second he'd seen her, more beautiful and impossibly stubborn now than she'd been before, with those damn blue eyes that never failed to stir up those old feelings.

The last time he'd seen Jodi was still burned into his brain, a memory he had tried desperately to erase, but couldn't. As he drove the familiar roads, the memory of that night taunted him, as it had for so many years...

"What the hell is going on in here?" Free had snapped, flinging open the car door and hauling the idiot college kid out by the fabric of his jacket. Jodi had clutched the torn shirt over her exposed breasts, tears streaming down her face. Her hair was a tangled mess from where Will's hands had grabbed handfuls of it. Her lips were swollen and bruised. Free was shaking with fury as he watched Jodi scramble out of the passenger seat. The headlights of the car shone brightly, illuminating the field beyond. It was unusual for a vehicle to be out in this part of the property and he had been curious enough to check it out, and he was sure glad he had. Free glared into the younger man's pale blue eyes. "Well? What the hell are you doing?"

Will, Jodi's tool bag of a boyfriend, shrugged arrogantly. "Just getting what I've paid for over the last six months."

"*What you paid for?*" The words came out as a feral growl, fury emanating off Free in waves, and he watched as fear flashed through the twenty-year-old's eyes. Leaning close, he hissed through clenched teeth, "Get in your car, and don't come back here, do you understand? She doesn't owe you shit, you little prick."

Free shoved the kid away from him and got perverse pleasure seeing him scuttle back to his car. Jodi still stood on the other side of the vehicle, trembling and trying desperately to keep the tattered sides of her shirt over her chest.

Free came around the back of the car toward Jodi as Will slammed the driver's side door closed. Rolling down the window, he spat at Free's feet and snarled, "Good luck. She's nothing but a dick tease."

Free lunged for the door handle but Will saw it coming and peeled away, his tires flinging mud and dirt behind him. "You always had it bad for that dirty cowboy anyway!" Will shouted as he sped off down the dirt trail.

Free swore under his breath as the taillights of Will's car disappeared through the trees. Jodi was trembling, her arms wrapped tightly around herself, so he took his flannel shirt off and draped it over her shoulders. The late October evening was deceptively cool. She slipped her arms through and pulled it closed, crossing her arms over her stomach. Her head fell back and she released a shuddering sigh, and he watched as tears continued to leak down her cheeks.

"Are you okay, Jodi?" he asked quietly. "Did that bastard hurt you?"

Jodi shook her long dark hair, opening her eyes to look at him. "No," she whispered, "I'm okay, I promise."

But tears continued to fall, and a broken sob escaped her. Before Free could stop himself, he had gathered her tightly into his arms and held her against his chest, allowing her to cry openly against his shirt front. Her arms went around his waist, and he felt her fingers curl into fists into the fabric of his shirt against his back. His hands smoothed her mess of dark curls, and he whispered soothingly into her hair.

"Shh," he murmured, his heart aching at the pain he could feel radiating off of her. He had known Jodi since she was a little girl, had watched her grow. He hated that his feelings of anger and protectiveness were accompanied by a jealous rage at having found her in that douchebag's arms. He'd done everything he could to not notice how beautiful she had become in the last two years. She was still a teenager and he hated that he wanted her.

Jodi's tears seemed to finally slow, and eventually she pulled away. She hid her face from his, swiping at the tear tracks down her face. "I'm sorry," she whispered hoarsely.

"Shh," Free said quietly. "Come on, let me get you home."

"No!" Jodi cried in panic, her blue eyes wide. "Please, don't make me go home yet. I don't want Mom and Dad to see me like this. They'll ask questions. I don't want to tell them what happened—"

"Okay, okay," Free rushed to say. "Let's go back to the apartment then, let you clean up, I'm sure I have some of Shane's old t-shirts in the closet that might fit."

Jodi nodded, calmed slightly, "Thank you."

Free led her toward his waiting truck, holding the door open for her and helping her up into the seat. His shirt fell open for the briefest of seconds and he glanced away quickly, self-loathing eating at him even as he wished he could look. Her father would murder him and bury him in the back acreage if he ever knew the thoughts Freeman was having about his oldest daughter.

He rounded the hood of the truck and climbed in behind the wheel. It was a short trip back to the main property. The large ranch house stood a hundred or so yards away from the pole-barn, where Levi Kendall had built an apartment loft for Free and Shane years before.

When Free had first shown up as a teenager himself, younger brother in tow with nowhere to go, Levi had taken them both in, and started him out as a ranch hand. After years of hard work and earning the older man's respect, Levi had promoted him to project manager for the prestigious building company he owned and had built from the ground up.

Free helped Jodi out of the truck and she followed him up the narrow staircase to the one room loft. It wasn't fancy, but it was cozy and offered enough privacy for the twenty-seven-year-old. His brother Shane had long since moved into an apartment with several buddies closer to town.

Free crossed the small kitchenette to the open floor style bedroom that also served as his living room. It had once had two small twin mattresses, but when Shane moved out they had swapped it for a queen sized, which Free had been grateful for. It took up the majority of the floorspace, but he didn't care. His tall frame needed the extra room.

He opened the tiny closet and dug around until he found one of Shane's old t-shirts that would be small enough to fit Jodi. When he turned around, she was standing at the edge of his bed, her hands still clutching the sides of his flannel shirt closed. The light from the kitchen cast a halo around her. He handed her the shirt and said gruffly, "Go ahead and get cleaned up in the bathroom, sweetheart. I'll start some coffee."

She nodded and entered the bathroom, closing the door behind her. Free busied himself in the kitchenette, preparing a pot of coffee. She had still been trembling, whether it was from the cold or adrenaline he wasn't sure. He had just poured two cups when she walked out of the bathroom. She must have showered because her hair was wet, and he could smell his body wash on her. She was wearing his younger brother's shirt, but she had pulled the flannel shirt back on. The sleeves were far too long, and she had the cuffs tucked into her palms.

"Come on, come sit and have some coffee before I get you home," Free said and smiled gently as he crossed to sit on the couch. He was struggling to remain aloof. "Are you sure you're okay?"

"I'm better, I promise," she said and came to sit next to him on the old, faded couch. He swallowed hard as she settled into his side. Did she even know what she was doing to him? She looked up and smiled, her sapphire blue eyes capturing his gaze. "Thank you,

Free. I don't know what I would have done if you hadn't found us."

"Can you tell me what happened?" he asked, giving in and draping one arm across her shoulders, allowing her to settle into his side. This was harmless, right? Big brother protecting his little sister? Comforting her?

Totally harmless, he could definitely do this.

That was, until Jodi took a drink of her coffee and shrugged, and his totally harmless thoughts went straight to hell when her breasts bounced and then settled against his chest. He bit back a groan. "I told him I wanted to break up. He told me I couldn't break up with him until he got what was owed to him after all that time dating."

Free snarled, his fury with the stupid college kid back in full force. "So, he felt you owed him sex for having dated you for six months? He's lucky I didn't kill him." Then, remembering what Will had shouted as he'd left, Free asked quietly, "What did he mean earlier?"

Free immediately regretted asking and silently begged her not to answer that question. He didn't really want to know. He watched as a blush crept up her cheeks and his heart pounded in his chest, fearing what he had already had an inkling of.

Jodi closed her eyes and took a deep breath before answering softly, "He was always jealous of you. He knew... he knows I..." Jodi peeked up at him through her lashes and whispered so quietly it was almost a breath, "I've liked you for a long time. He always thought I wouldn't have sex with him because I was... because I wanted you."

"Oh Christ," Free groaned and let his head fall back against the cushion of the couch. It was worse than he'd imagined. "No, Jodi. You don't know what you're saying. You can't say stuff like that to me."

Jodi shifted her weight and set her coffee cup on the table beside her, turning until she was facing him. "Yes, I do. It's the truth." Her breathing was shallow and fast, coming in puffs against his face. She was so near, all he had to do with lean forward and press his lips to hers. She licked her lips and his cock tightened: his mind doing terrible things to that mouth. "I think you like me, too. I've seen you watching me. I watch you, too, Free."

"Jodi, stop," he begged wretchedly, hating himself even as he reached out one traitorous hand to tangle it in her curls. "Stop me before I do this. Please. This is wrong."

She shook her head emphatically, shifting her weight again, staring into his eyes. "No."

Free groaned and swore, tugging her forward until their lips met. Her hands came up to press against his chest, catching herself as she fell toward him. Free moved his lips over hers, pressing hotly until hers opened for him. His tongue sank into her mouth, and they kissed voraciously. He guided Jodi over him until she straddled his lap, the junction of her thighs cradling his hardness. "Oh!" he felt the influx of air against his own lips more than heard her soft gasp.

Their mouths melded again, and his hand tangled more securely in the hair at the nape of her neck, guiding her head to one side to deepen the kiss.

Jodi's hands flattened on the slope of his chest before her fingers curled into the fabric of his shirt, and when she settled onto his lap more firmly, Free groaned gutturally, pulling her snuggly against him even as he rocked his hips upward.

Just then, the door of the apartment opened, and they heard a startled, "Holy shit!"

Free jumped like a gun had gone off, pulling his mouth from Jodi's and looking around her toward the intrusion. His twenty-one-year-old brother, Shane, stood in the doorway, eyes wide. Shane's eyes bounced between his and Jodi's for a half a second before muttering, "Uhh, I... sorry," and closing the door quickly as he walked back out.

Jodi lowered her forehead to Free's shoulder and panted. Free let the back of his head rest against the couch cushion for only a heartbeat before he grasped her by the upper arms and moved her off of him roughly, standing and striding away from her. His body was on fire, and all he wanted to do was to keep going. But he was grateful his brother had walked in when he had.

This was wrong.

He leaned with his hands braced on the counter and hung his head between his shoulders, his chin nearly touching his chest, taking in lungful after lungful of air.

What had he done?

"You need to go," he barked roughly, not turning around. "Now."

"Free—"

"Go, Jodi!" he shouted, angry at himself that he'd lost all control like he had. He knew better! She was still a child! He heard her footsteps as she crossed the small apartment in a hurry, and then cringed when the door slammed as she left. He heard her sobs as she raced down the stairs, fading as she crossed the wide yard to the main house.

Tormented, he whispered brokenly, "I'm sorry…"

Still lost in thought as he drove through the darkening back country roads, he remembered how he had packed his bags that night so many years ago and was gone the following morning, giving no one a heads up except Shane and Levi. Both tried to convince him to stay, but he couldn't, not after that. He couldn't look Levi in the face, knowing how he'd betrayed his best friend, his mentor. Once he'd known what Jodi tasted like, there was no going back. He'd had to go. So he'd loaded up his meager belongings and driven to Texas. Running as fast and as far as possible from Jodi Kendall.

CHAPTER 4

Free pulled into his brother's driveway and parked the borrowed truck, then carried his one bag into the house, still preoccupied by thoughts of Jodi. Everything about her still tormented him. Her hair, her smell, those damn blue eyes. She called to him like a Siren and he was powerless against whatever intoxicating brand of magic she wielded.

He called his brother to let him know he had made it in, but it went to voicemail. When they had spoken earlier, Shane had told him that he and his fiancé would both be working late, but that a spare truck would be waiting for him at the airport terminal when he got in. He had said to go inside and make himself comfortable whenever he got into town. Finding a fresh case of beer in the fridge, he popped the tab on one and downed half the can in one swallow. He heard the door open and close and grinned when his younger brother walked into the kitchen. Shane smiled widely as he crossed the kitchen.

"Get over here and give me a hug, you bastard," Free laughed, his eyes crinkling at the corners he was smiling so broadly. The brothers embraced hard, and Free clapped the younger man on the back. "Good to see you, man."

"It's been way too long," Shane agreed and walked to the fridge to grab a beer for himself. "Want another?"

"Sure," Free said and finished the first. Shane tossed him the can and they migrated to the living room where they sat on the couch. "I can't believe you're getting married, Shane."

"Sometimes I can't really believe it myself," Shane laughed and opened his beer. "But she picked me, and damn am I glad she did."

"The last time I saw Cassie she was still in high school," Free muttered and shook his head in wonder.

"You've been gone a long time," Shane said and raised his eyebrow pointedly. Free sighed heavily. It was the running topic of the day apparently. The two brothers were quiet for a long moment, then Shane grinned slyly. "You already went to see her, didn't'cha?" he asked. Free didn't have to ask who he was referring to. When Free ignored the question and continued to stare out the front window Shane chuckled and shook his head. "She's damn pretty, isn't she?"

"I always thought she was," Free mumbled and finished his second beer. "But yes, I saw her. That woman makes me insane. Still just as stubborn as ever."

"She learned from the best," Shane laughed as he stood. He disappeared into the kitchen for a moment and returned with two more beers. "You definitely taught her everything she knows about getting under people's skin."

The older man rolled his eyes.

"She's gonna be at the wedding," Shane said with forced casualness.

Free uttered a vile, four-letter word and took another sip of the cold beer. He nodded somberly and said, "I figured as much. Jodi and her parents have always been more like family to the both of us. I think you would have broken Seren's heart if they weren't invited."

"Levi and Seren basically adopted us," Shane chuckled, taking a drink of his beer. "Jodi… she's the sister I didn't have. I couldn't believe it, but Levi and Seren gifted Cass and I our honeymoon. Jodi and Shaun are throwing Cassie's bachelorette party this week."

"They're good people," Free murmured appreciatively. "I don't know how we deserved to stumble into a family like that."

"Sheer dumb luck," Shane laughed out loud, shaking his head. Then, studying the label on the can of beer much too casually to be casual, Shane said, "You know, from what Cass said, Jodi doesn't have a date."

Free looked over at him. "Are we supposed to have dates for this?"

"I mean, you could always go stag and try to bag one of the single bridesmaids?" Shane muttered, shrugging his shoulders. "Or you could ask out the girl you've wanted for almost a decade…"

Free scowled at his brother. "The situation is the same as it was seven years ago."

"I don't think I will ever understand your logic on this, you dumb bastard. She's not eighteen anymore, man. Your argument doesn't have any footing," Shane muttered darkly.

"It's not just her age, Shane. It's more than that," Free snapped and blew out a sigh of frustration, squeezing his temples between his thumb and middle finger. This day was giving him a headache. "If Levi had ever found out I was lusting after his teenage daughter, he'd have skinned me alive. After all that he had done for us, taking us in after Mom died, building us that apartment, giving me a damn good job. I'm nine years older than she is for Christ sake. It didn't matter that she was eighteen, it was still *wrong*. I felt like a Grade A asshole. I betrayed that trust and respect he had given me. He's always been one of the best friends I've ever had, and it still eats at me, Shane. I was old enough to know better, she wasn't. I had to leave before I did something I knew I'd regret."

Free watched as Shane took another drink of his beer. Shane nodded grudgingly. "Okay, I'll give that to you. I just think it wouldn't hurt to give it a shot."

"What would be the point of that?" Free asked, settling back into the cushions of the couch. "I'm only home for the wedding. I'm leaving in a week."

"You could always move back home," Shane suggested quietly. When Free gave him a withering sidelong glance, Shane shrugged, like it had at least been worth the shot. "Maybe you could stick around a little longer. My regular worker who was supposed to watch the farm while Cassie and I are on our honeymoon broke his leg last week, so I need someone to take over until we get back. What do you think? It would be a huge favor for us. As long as you don't have anything pressing waiting for you in Texas."

"Of course I can help out, whatever you guys need," Free said and smiled. "It's good to see you. I missed you."

"Yeah, we all missed you, too. Next time don't stay away so long, please."

"Sure thing," Free said and stood, stretching. "Mind if I shower? My body is stiff as hell from being cramped on an airplane all day."

Shane stood too, pointing him down the hallway as he headed toward the fridge. He tossed a fresh can to Free, who caught it one handed and raised it in thanks. "Last door at the end of the hall is the guest bedroom, towels are in the hall closet. Cass will be home shortly, you hungry?"

Free shook his head vehemently, and at the same time both men laughed and said, "Seren." Free chuckled and headed down the hall, depositing his suitcase on the full-sized bed in the center of the room. Unzipping it, he fished for his toiletries and a set of clean boxer briefs and a pair of well-worn flannel pants. He stopped at the closet to grab a towel, and then disappeared into the bathroom. He opened the beer Shane had tossed him, then turned on the taps of the shower, letting the water heat up.

Stripping down, he let his clothes fall to the floor and took a drink of the cold beer. He was glad he was in for the night; he'd had enough to drink to give him a decent buzz.

As he stepped into the shower, closing the glass door behind him, he rolled his shoulders as he stood beneath the spray of hot water, letting the tension leave his stiff muscles.

Scrubbing the grime of travel off his body, Free's mind wandered back to the first time he'd noticed Jodi as more than just his friend's daughter. Jodi was oftentimes found hiding in the hayloft of the barn, where she could read without one of her four siblings finding her. Levi and Serenity had both warned her not to go into the loft after Levi had discovered a support beam that needed replacing. It was a large project, and Levi had hired out extra help for the following week. Free had walked into the barn that afternoon, striding to the back to gather tools. The stalls directly below the hayloft were empty of animals; instead, they stored some of the larger farming machinery and extra equine equipment. Levi had made a living for himself and his family by boarding horses, and it kept Freeman busy.

As he gathered what he needed, Free stopped and straightened quickly, as an ominous creaking sound caught his attention. The creaking got louder, and Free bellowed, "Oh shit!" as he realized the noise he heard was the wooden beams of the hayloft giving out, groaning as they shifted. He turned tail and ran toward the barn door, stopping again when he heard a startled scream come from far above him.

He knew what it was instantly, turning and cursing her beneath his breath even as he vaulted up the wooden stepladder to the loft above. "Jodi! Where are you?"

"Free!" he heard her scream, and suddenly he saw the top of her head over one of the lofts half walls. There was another wooden stepladder that led to the portion she had been hiding in, about seven feet above him. One section of the loft gave way, tumbling to the floor of the barn below, the snapping of the wood beams deafening. Jodi screamed again, losing her footing as the loft beneath her feet started to fail.

Free ran to the stepladder that was built into the wall, but as he started to climb, the supports below him gave out and he fell back, landing on his back with a thud. He groaned in pain, his shoulder throbbing where he'd landed on it. There was now a large hole in the loft flooring between them, and the wall that had the ladder was leaning at an angle. He stood and braced his legs to fight against the unsteady floor beneath his feet. "Jodi!" he shouted, and she turned, her eyes wide with terror. "I'm going to catch you! When I say jump, jump toward me! I'll catch you!"

Jodi shook her head in panic, eyeing the seven-foot drop to him and the ten-foot drop to the barn floor. "I can't!"

"I will not let you fall! Trust me, Jodi!" Free shouted again, reaching his arms out. "Come on, jump, Jodi!"

As the flooring beneath her feet gave way, Jodi screamed and jumped. Free caught her, but the force of her leap pushed them both backward and he lost his footing. Tucking her into his chest, they rolled to the edge of the loft and tumbled down. He squeezed his arms around her, praying they didn't land on any machinery or broken wood beams as they fell through the air. He felt more than heard Jodi's scream into his chest, and the next second they had landed, thankfully, in a pile of hay that hadn't been taken care of yet.

The impact knocked the breath out of him, but he didn't let himself linger on that, instead he rolled them until she was beneath him, his hips to one side of her, one of his thighs covering both of hers. Leaning on his elbows, his panicked gaze ran over her, checking for any blood or obvious injuries. Free couldn't stop his hands from brushing the hair away from her face. Hay was now stuck haphazardly in her wayward curls.

Her sapphire eyes stared up at him, her breathing rough through slightly parted lips, making her chest rise and fall where it was pressed tight against his own. His heart was pounding, adrenaline coursing through him. "You okay?" he breathed.

His fingers were still stroking her hair, their eyes searching the others. Jodi nodded and let out a long, shuddering sigh, and Free's eyes dropped to her lips. The sudden, indisputable urge to press his lips to hers made his heart hammer in his chest, and his eyes flew back up to hers, his hand stilling. She was still staring at him. He'd never noticed before that she was no longer the awkward child he'd met years ago, when Levi had taken him and Shane in as teenagers themselves. She was turning into a beautiful young woman. Never before had he thought about kissing little Jodi Kendall.

Lord was he thinking about it now! He couldn't stop thinking about it.

She shifted beneath him slightly, her hips pressing against the juncture of his thighs, and he clenched his teeth as a pleasurable groan rumbled in his chest. He was growing hard thinking about her body pressed so close to his, and how badly he wanted to cover her mouth with his so he could taste her.

What the hell was wrong with him!

Free heard shouting and the thunder of running feet moments before Levi, Shane, and another farmhand appeared in the doorway of the barn. Free rolled off Jodi quickly, his eyes bouncing from Levi to Jodi. He wouldn't blame Levi if he kicked in his face right then and there after finding him lying on top of his teenage daughter.

"What the hell happened in here?" Levi barked, his own sapphire blue eyes taking in the scene before him. "Were you up in that loft when it came down?"

Hinged at the waist, Jodi sat up. Tears filled her eyes as she nodded forlornly. "Yes. I'm sorry!"

"You could have been killed! We told you it wasn't safe up there!" Levi bristled, though Free knew the anger in Levi's voice was born of fear. Free was thankful the older man couldn't read the thoughts he was currently having regarding his sixteen-year-old. "You could have gotten yourself and Freeman killed!"

"I know, I'm sorry," Jodi whimpered and looked around at the carnage that used to be the loft. Dust and dirt clouded the air around them as everything settled. Free stood, brushing hay and dirt off the legs of his jeans brusquely, willing his rampant erection to go down. Shane reached down and helped Jodi stand. Free couldn't meet her eyes.

"Thank you," Levi said earnestly and extended his hand to Free, and he stared at it for a long second before grasping it firmly. "It sounded like thunder from the house. We came running as soon as we realized it was the barn. I'm just glad you were here to get her out, Free."

"Don't thank me, Levi," Free mumbled, taking several steps back. "It was pure instinct."

"Thank you, Free," Jodi whispered. At the sound of her voice, his eyes raised to hers. There were still pieces of hay sticking out of her curls and his palms itched to reach out and find each one. Her gaze dropped to his lap and he watched as a blush tinged her cheeks. He was still half-cocked, and as her eyes raised to meet his again, he watched as she licked her lips. He swore viciously in his mind, tormenting himself thinking about her mouth again.

He coughed roughly, half turning away from her. "Of course, kid."

Her eyebrows bunched together briefly, and her lips tightened in what he knew to be irritation. Free knew that look well. He didn't dwell on why she would give him that look now, though.

Levi then ushered her out of the barn, and she turned her head to look at him once more as she walked away. Free met her gaze for the briefest of moments before he turned away from her.

For weeks after he had avoided her. He couldn't be near her without imagining her mouth under his, her breast cupped in his hand, her body entwined with his. He was like a teenager again, unable to control his body. He became moody and damn unpleasant to be around.

"Jesus, Free," Levi had shouted one afternoon, months later. They were working on a new build across town. Jodi had been haunting him all day and he missed the nail he was hammering and got his finger instead. He cursed loudly and crudely. "Do you need to get laid or something?"

Free snarled an unintelligible response and threw the hammer he'd been using down. He ducked through the bare support beams and headed toward the door and to his truck. "I'll be back in an hour," he said tersely to Levi. The older man raised an eyebrow and shrugged, waving the younger man off.

Free drove angrily and pulled into the driveway at home, grinding the gears and parking abruptly next to the barn. He stomped up the stairs and into his and Shane's loft and went to the fridge, slamming three beers in rapid succession. His lower body ached with a need that he knew was not going to be quenched. At least not how he would like it to be. Palms flat against the counter, he leaned on them, bowing his head. Teeth clenched tight, he swore viciously again and straightened. Releasing the buttons of his fly, he freed his painfully erect cock from the tight confines of his jeans. Baring his teeth in intense pleasure, and hating himself as he pictured Jodi, his hand gave his loins the relief they so badly needed.

He'd sought out as much unsavory company as possible as Jodi continued to mature. He certainly developed one hell of a reputation with the ladies; he used them for what he couldn't—wouldn't—take from Jodi.

And then he'd kissed her and it had taken every ounce of willpower he possessed to stop himself from continuing until he had been buried inside her.

Free groaned now, the hot water of the shower beating down over his skin as he thought back on those months of torment. He cursed Jodi for still having such a hold on him. Hating himself now just as much as he had before, he did the same thing he had all those years ago, using his hand to find relief from the burning desire he had for Jodi Kendall.

CHAPTER 5

"Have a nice day, Jodi," the salesclerk said with a fond smile as he handed her the two grocery bags. She smiled and hoisted the brown paper sacks higher in her arms. As she got to the door, she paused. Both of her hands were full and the doors only opened toward her.

She was about to turn and ask for help when Free stepped around her and opened the door. He held it for her, a paper bag of groceries in his other arm.

"Thank you!" Jodi laughed and walked out through the door. He followed behind her. "You'd think they could get paper bags with handles."

"Well, then how would us men ever get to flirt with pretty girls like you?" Free teased. Their eyes met and held for a long moment. Butterflies took flight in her belly, making her knees feel weak. "Where's your car?"

Jodi pointed with her chin. "Over there. It's the white Jeep."

He nodded and smiled, his lips pulling back to reveal his straight, white teeth. His smile always did funny things to her. "Right, I knew that."

He followed her to the Jeep, and she was acutely aware that the short jean skirt she wore left little to the imagination. She lifted the hatch and set the grocery bags in the trunk area, reaching forward to tuck them into the corner. She heard a low groan come from Free, and she straightened quickly, turning to look up at him quizzically. His eyes burned hotly as they met hers.

"You okay?" she asked, tilting her head slightly. He nodded and shifted his eyes away from her, allowing her a moment's reprieve. She took a deep, steadying breath and reached up to close the hatch of the Jeep. She dusted her hands and smiled awkwardly up at him.

Glancing around, she noticed several people were watching them as they passed in the parking lot of the market. She licked her lips, suddenly nervous. She used to love the close-knit feel of the community, like an extended family. Now, she hated that everyone in town knew everything about her, and her personal business. Small town folks tend to do a lot of talking, and recently she had become a popular topic of discussion.

Wanting to break the awkward moment and distract herself from idle minds, Jodi murmured, "You're up and out awfully early on a Sunday morning."

"I needed to grab a few things that I forgot to pack," Free shrugged, holding up the single paper bag in his hand. "What are you doing out so early?"

"Just picking up a few things for the shop for tomorrow morning," Jodi said, tucking a wayward curl behind her ear.

"Oh? What shop?" Free asked curiously.

"My bookshop. I opened a bookstore a little over a year ago," she said and smiled proudly. "Actually, a friend of mine and I did it together. We offer baked goods and coffee as well, so that's what I was shopping for. When I'm not busy there, I try to find time to write. After my first novel was a success, I was given a three-book publication deal that I'm currently working on."

Free's face split into a wide grin, his eyes crinkling at the corners. "That's awesome, Jodi. I'm proud of you. I always knew you would do it."

Jodi couldn't stop the beaming smile that came across her face at hearing Free say those words. They meant more to her than he could possibly understand.

"Thank you, Free." Still smiling like a fool, Jodi said softly, "How is Shane doing with the big day just around the corner? These last several days are going to fly by."

"As good as any expectant groom can be," he chuckled, and their eyes locked. Jodi loved the sound of his laugh. The corners of his eyes crinkled when he smiled, a testament to how long he'd been gone. He wasn't the same young man that she'd met and fallen for all those years ago. "I guess I'm going to stick around and house sit for him and Cassie while they're on their honeymoon."

Again, Jodi couldn't stop the beaming smile that spread across her face as she looked up at him. He was wearing the same black felt cowboy hat that he had been wearing last night, and his face was shadowed from the early morning sun. She hated how happy this news made her. She had sworn off men. Damn him for coming home now! "How long will you be here for?"

"At least three weeks or so," he said quietly, his eyes searching her face.

She was so conflicted. Her heart was guarded for a reason, and he flustered her in ways she hadn't thought were possible anymore.

"That's really great, Free," she said and smiled again, trying not to let herself be too excited that he would be home for nearly a month. She motioned toward the driver's door and murmured, "I should probably get going though. It was nice running into you this morning."

"Right," Free said, his smile fading slowly. "I'll see ya later, Jodi."

"Bye," she said as she stepped into the Jeep. She started the motor, but didn't drive off right away. She watched out of the corner of her eye as he walked toward the same truck he'd been driving the day before. Jodi closed her eyes briefly and took a restorative breath. She opened her eyes just as he turned around and came toward the driver's door. She rolled down the window as he got close. Setting his bag of groceries on the hood of her Jeep, he then rested his forearms on her windowsill and pushed his Stetson up over his forehead with his thumb.

"This might sound ridiculous, but would you like to get some ice cream with me tonight? I haven't had Kilwins ice cream since I left, and I am dying for a double scoop of Butter Pecan."

Jodi's eyebrows shot up and she smiled over at him. His face was so close to hers she could see the flecks of darker teal in his eyes. Nodding, she said, "I would love to get ice cream."

He smiled, his straight white teeth showing brilliantly against the dark tan of his face, his eyes crinkling at the corners again. "Great. Meet me downtown at let's say, seven?"

"Sounds perfect," Jodi murmured.

He touched the brim of his Stetson, lowering it back over his brow, shadowing the upper part of his face once more. "I'll see you at seven, then. Bye."

"See you," she agreed, smiling once more.

Jodi was giddy the whole drive home. She was floating high on cloud nine. Putting some music on, she was in the process of putting her groceries away when there was a knock on her door.

Jodi turned down the volume of the music before crossing to the front door and swinging it open, her good mood fading instantly, replaced with trepidation.

"What are you doing here?" Jodi asked, her heart thundering in her throat.

"Come on, now. Is that any way to talk to your husband?"

CHAPTER 6

Jodi crossed her arms over her chest, blocking the doorway as best she could. "You mean ex-husband, Joshua."

Leaning his shoulder against the door jamb nonchalantly, he shrugged arrogantly. "Schematics."

Refusing to let him bait her, Jodi stared stonily ahead. "It's not schematics, Josh. The divorce was finalized three months ago."

Straightening to his full height of six-foot, Josh's hazel eyes narrowed on her face, making fear tighten her throat. His dark blonde hair was cut short, and several days of growth shadowed the lower portion of his face. Jodi had once found Joshua Murphy incredibly handsome, but dread and loathing had taken its place long ago.

"You look nice," Josh muttered, ignoring her statement. Making a point to rake his gaze from her bare feet to the top of her head, Jodi shivered with revulsion. "Apparently I'm not the only one who noticed this morning."

Jodi shifted her weight nervously, wishing she wasn't still wearing the short jean skirt and white tank top she'd worn to the market earlier. She should have known Josh would have heard about Free and her talking this morning. He had a network of people who were loyal to him and kept him abreast of her comings and goings.

"Don't your friends have anything better to do than to report to you what I'm doing? Would they like to see my grocery receipt so they can tell you what I bought?" Jodi asked acerbically.

Josh smiled, though it didn't reach his eyes, which Jodi knew meant his temper was simmering just below the surface. She swallowed hard. She despised how much he could still intimidate her with such little effort.

"I could care less what bullshit you bought for your stupid bookstore this week, Jodi," he murmured quietly.

"If you don't care about my *stupid bookstore*, how about you let me buy you out of it?" Jodi asked sweetly, though the false sweetness didn't reach her eyes.

Josh smirked and tilted his head to one side slightly. "Nah, I like to be able to come and go as I please." He stretched his arms out to brace his hands on either side of the door frame and leaned forward ever so slightly, knowing full well it would cause her to take an instinctive step back. "What I don't like, is finding out my wife—"

"*Ex-wife*," Jodi reminded again, but he shushed her quickly, making her bristle with anger.

"—*finding out my wife* is entertaining another man, while in a public parking lot," Josh finished, his voice lowering menacingly. He brought one hand down from the door jamb and Jodi flinched unconsciously. Seeing her reaction, one corner of his mouth tilted up in a twisted smirk. Oh, how she hated him! "You can imagine what people are saying, Jodi."

"You have a girlfriend, Josh, you've *had* a girlfriend, for almost a year. And seeing as we are no longer married, I don't really give a damn what people are saying about it," Jodi snapped, bracing one hand on the edge of the storm door. "I wasn't *entertaining* anyone. I was talking to an old friend… not that it's any of your business who I talk to, anyway. Especially since you didn't give a shit about being unfaithful *during* our marriage. You have no room to talk to me about discretion."

Before Josh could make a rebuttal, they both heard a car coming down the driveway, and a moment later Jodi recognized her sister's Chevy Silverado as she parked beside Jodi's Jeep. Josh coughed a snide laugh as he straightened, stepping away from the door as Shauntelle Kendall climbed out of her truck.

"The fu—"

"I'm leaving," Josh snapped loudly in annoyance, cutting Shauntelle off before she could finish the expletive. Quietly, for only her ears, he muttered, "We're not finished with this conversation, Jodi."

"Yes, we are," Jodi hissed as Shaun crossed the driveway. "Please leave my home."

Josh narrowed his eyes on Jodi before turning and walking toward the steps, passing Shauntelle as she bounded up them. Smiling sweetly at Josh as she passed him, Shaun flipped him off with both middle fingers for good measure. Jodi grinned with perverse pleasure as Josh's lips tightened in anger at Shaun as he headed down the steps. As Shaun reached the front door, she put an arm around Jodi's shoulders, and they both turned to watch as Josh climbed into the sleek black Lincoln and drove back down the driveway.

Jodi breathed a sigh of relief when Josh's car disappeared around the corner of her driveway. Shaun squeezed Jodi's shoulders and said candidly, "I hate that douche bag."

Jodi laughed gustily at her sister's frankness. "I know."

The two retreated into the house, walking together into the kitchen. Jodi and Shaun were almost identical in likeness. Both had long, curly brunette hair and sapphire blue eyes. The main difference was their height; Jodi was petite, and had been five foot two since she was twelve, whereas Shaun had kept growing; now standing just shy of six feet tall and had an hourglass figure that Jodi envied. Their personalities were polar opposites, though. Where Jodi was soft, quiet, and reserved, Shaun was loud, brash, and stubborn as a mule.

Today, she wore a pair of cutoff camouflage shorts that showed off her long, tanned legs, and a simple black t-shirt that hugged her curves. Slip on Chuck Taylor All-stars that had seen better days adorned her feet. Shaun's curls fell in haphazard riots down to the lower part of her back.

"Do I dare ask what *La Douche* was doing here before noon? I'm surprised he's not home hung-over as hell," Shaun mumbled, her tone unapologetically snarky.

Jodi shook her head and chuckled. Her sister had her ex-husband pegged to a T. One of the many reasons she had requested the divorce after only ten months of marriage was his alcoholism. The domestic violence charges were another. The infidelity had just made the whole thing humiliating. "Just being his usual dickhead self."

Shaun made a noise in the back of her throat and crossed to the cupboard, picking up a coffee mug. Jodi held out the coffee pot and filled the mug to the brim. Shaun liked her coffee bitter and black. Jodi made a face and Shaun smiled as she took a long drink. Hopping up onto the counter, Shaun tucked her legs under her crisscross and watched Jodi as she moved around the kitchen. She sat studying her cuticles intently, and with feigned disinterest, "So... did you hear that Free is back in town?"

Jodi rolled her eyes. "Is that why you came over so early?"

Shaun shrugged and one corner of her mouth tilted with a telling smirk. "Maybe. So? Did you know he's home or not?"

Jodi poured herself a cup of coffee, lightening it with some French vanilla creamer. She could sense Shaun's giddiness as she stirred the coffee, intentionally making her sister wait.

"Well!" Shaun insisted, her impatience taking over. She set her coffee down on the counter beside her, leaning forward excitedly.

Jodi turned and leaned her hips back against the counter where she stood directly across from where Shaun was sitting. Jodi smiled and shrugged coyly. "He may or may not have stopped by here last night."

Shaun's blue eyes that were so similar to her own widened. "No way! He already came to see you?"

Jodi nodded and she could feel a grin splitting her face.

The younger woman's mouth fell open. "And you failed to tell me this? What kind of sister are you? Spill, woman!"

Jodi laughed and raised her hands in the air helplessly. "It just happened last night. He came over and we talked. That was it."

The look Shaun sent Jodi was withering. "*Puh-lease.* The last time you guys 'just talked' you ended up kissing and he left for reasons unknown."

"Not so unknown anymore," Jodi whispered and shrugged awkwardly. "He said he left because he couldn't be near me."

"How rude!" Shaun sputtered, outraged.

Jodi rolled her eyes again. "Shaun, he said he couldn't be near me because he wanted to kiss me again."

Shaun's mouth opened in a silent, *O*. "Well… That certainly changes things a bit."

"Tell me about it," Jodi muttered and fiddled with the handle of her coffee cup before setting it down. "He actually asked me to go get ice cream with him tonight."

"Ice cream?" Shaun asked, her eyebrows shooting up. "So, like a date?"

Jodi lifted and dropped her shoulders in a quick shrug. "I don't know. Maybe? Is an ice cream date even a thing after the age of thirteen?"

Shaun chuckled softly, rolling her eyes. "I think any time spent between people who are crushing on each other counts as a date."

"I didn't say he is crushing on me," Jodi interjected quickly, picking up a dish towel sitting on the counter beside her. Shaun rolled her eyes again, but didn't say anything. Jodi knotted her fingers in the dishtowel nervously, whispering, "I feel like I'm seventeen again, all jittery and awkward. I haven't felt like this in a long time."

"Isn't that a good thing?" Shaun asked quietly.

Jodi took a deep breath, letting it out slowly. "I don't know. I'm finally getting back to myself. What is the point of doing all this inner work, healing all this hurt, if I'm going to just throw it all away on a guy *I know* would break my heart if I gave him even the slightest chance? I don't want to do this again. I can't."

Shaun pursed her lips and then slid off the counter and landed on her feet. Lost in thought, Jodi watched her sister. She was voluptuous and unintentionally sexy, had one hell of a temper, and a mouth like a sailor. Now, she paced to the sliding patio door and looked out, then back to where she'd been sitting. Perhaps that coffee had been a bad idea. Jodi observed her in silence for several minutes before Shaun spoke again.

"So…what are you going to do?" her sister asked.

"I don't know that either," Jodi said honestly. "I told myself I was swearing off men entirely after the divorce was final."

Shaun stopped pacing and looked at her sister. "And that includes a specific cowboy? Even now?"

Jodi shrugged. She honestly didn't know how to answer that question. "I would never in a million years have guessed that I would ever see Freeman again. And this is just a ridiculous crush that I've had on him since I was a kid. He's only home long enough for Shane's wedding, and then he'll leave again. I…" she sighed heavily, shaking her head sadly. "I'm elated that he's home, of course. I'm glad he's here for Shane, as he should be. I'm not the only one that missed him. We all did. He was always special to this family. He *was* family."

She crossed her arms over her middle and uncrossed them again, fidgeting mindlessly. She heaved a heavy sigh, "I won't lie and say that there isn't this teeny tiny part of me that would love for something to happen with him, just to see if it's real or if I've been holding on to a pipe dream for years. But… I don't think I'm ready for anything new, and I know my heart couldn't handle some temporary fling. Not with Free. To me, it would mean too much, and my heart would break all over again when he leaves in three weeks."

"So… why did you say yes to going out with him tonight?" Shaun asked, her eyebrows knitting together.

Jodi laughed self-deprecatingly. "Because I'm a glutton for punishment, I suppose." She shook her head and chuckled again. "I mean, have you seen him since he got home? How the hell was I supposed to say no when he looks so damn good. And I am not going out with him— it's just ice cream."

"*Yeah, okay*," Shaun snorted scathingly. "But yeah, I did see. Pretty sure Fallon had to pick my jaw up off the floor when he walked in with Dad."

Jodi laughed gustily, nodding in agreement. "I think mine hit the floor when I saw him standing in my doorway last night. I felt like one of those old cartoons with the heart eyes that boggle out of their eye sockets."

Apparently the word picture she painted was hilarious to Shaun, who cackled heartily, which made Jodi laugh all the harder. The two sisters fell into a laughing fit that lasted minutes. By the time their mirth had subsided, Jodi was wiping tears from her face and Shaun was clutching the stitch in her side.

Shaun blew out a deep breath to steady herself, which made Jodi start giggling again, to which her sister pointed a finger at her and said sternly, "No! I can't breathe!" Taking deep, restorative breaths, Shaun finally said, "Okay. I actually have to go. Tommy and I are going to lunch later. But I want to hear all about your ice cream date tonight!"

"It's not a date," Jodi insisted. Shaun rolled her eyes and Jodi shook her head with a laugh. "Okay, fine! I will tell you all about it Thursday night. I'll have all the makings for margaritas; you're doing the snacks, right?"

Two thumbs up was Shaun's response as she headed toward the front door. "Yes, taskmaster. I'm bringing chips and salsa. I still think we need strippers though."

Jodi rolled her eyes. "Cassie specifically said she wanted something casual. I don't think strippers count as casual."

"Killjoy," Shaun groaned dramatically from the door. Then, as she was about to close the door, she called back, laughing, "Have fun on your not-a-date!"

CHAPTER 7

Jodi parked along one side of the city's downtown district at quarter to seven, about a block away from Kilwins, their town's claim to fame of all things sweets. The downtown district was several blocks of tall, brownstone shops and locally owned restaurants that doubled as apartment rentals above the majority of the storefronts.

As she stepped out of the Jeep, she let her eyes wander up and down the street, taking in all the different shops. It was the middle of August, just a couple weeks before the end of summer vacation, and the downtown sidewalks were filled with locals and tourists alike milling about.

Stepping onto the sidewalk, Jodi headed up the slight hill toward the treat shop just around the corner. She had changed outfits so many times her bedroom now looked like a disaster zone. She had finally settled on a simple, royal blue t-shirt dress. It fit close to her body, but floated around her legs, hitting mid-thigh, leaving the lower half of her thighs and calves bare to the evening summer air. Strappy white sandals adorned her feet, and she had a small leather cross body purse hanging from one shoulder. She had left her hair to curl naturally after her shower, letting it part off to one side dramatically, the other side she pinned back away from her face with a decorative comb.

Rounding the corner, she couldn't help the smile that tugged at her lips when she saw Free climbing out of the truck across the street. She waved and a thousand butterflies took flight in her belly when he did a double take. A wide grin split his face as he trotted across the street to join her.

"Hi," Free said when they were close enough to hear each other. He smiled broadly at her and she reciprocated the smile with a brilliant one of her own, butterflies still on a chaotic spiral in her midriff.

"Hi," she repeated as she stopped a few feet in front of him.

"You look… amazing," Free breathed appreciatively, letting his eyes travel up and down. When they landed back on hers, the heat in them made the butterflies flutter faster.

"Thank you," she murmured and gave a small curtsy. "You look nice, too."

He had on his usual well fitted jeans, and had paired it today with a dark gray t-shirt that made her mouth water. Whatever he did to stay in shape, it was working, she thought as her eyes drank in all of him. The dark facial hair was something she had never imagined on him, but he pulled it off well. His black cowboy hat was replaced tonight with a plain black baseball cap that he had on backward, which was doing nothing to shield his eyes from the setting sun, but Jodi admitted to herself that a new kink had been unlocked; backwards ball caps made her knees weak.

He smiled and offered her his hand. She blushed and hesitated only a heartbeat before placing her hand in his. "Your hands are soft," he murmured, looking down at her as they walked the last stretch toward the sweet shop.

"Thank you," Jodi whispered hoarsely, her vocal cords not working correctly with his skin touching hers.

"After you," he said huskily when they stopped in front of the busy confection store. Delicious aromas lingered in the air as Free held the door open for her to enter, and she felt his stare on her backside as she walked in front of him. The small shop was crowded. Jodi and Free joined the queue, chuckling slightly at being jostled around. When Free stepped toward her to let another customer pass, his front made contact with her back ever so briefly, and the laughter stalled in her throat. She stopped breathing altogether for several heartbeats, those damn butterflies wreaking havoc on her insides.

When he retreated a step, she peeked up at him through her lashes, and heat spread over her cheeks when she caught him watching her intently. The moment was interrupted when the teenage boy behind the counter called them forward to take their order.

"What would you like?" Free asked, smiling down at her.

Jodi stepped forward and said, "I'll take a Strawberry Chunk in a waffle cone, please."

The teenager nodded and reached for one of the freshly made waffle cones behind him, then came back and reached into the wide coolers and delved in, coming back with a large scoop of the fruit riddled ice cream. Wrapping it in a paper napkin, he handed it across the tall counter and Jodi thanked him. The teen then turned to Free, asking for his choice.

"Double scoop of Butter Pecan in a waffle cone, thank you," Free said loudly over the bustle of the crowd around them. Just a few seconds later, Free was handed a tall cone and both he and Jodi said another thank you to the busy teen. Jodi reached for her wallet, but Free gave her a withering look before fishing his wallet out of his back pocket, handing the sales clerk the cash. They waited for Free's change, and he slipped several dollars into the tip jar, making the harried teenage girl smile appreciatively.

"Thank you!" they both called as they wound their way back toward the door. Free held the door open for Jodi and she exited the crowded shop quickly. Free got stopped at the door, holding it for a large group that was trying to enter. When he caught up with her, she smiled up at him broadly.

"Where to now?" Jodi asked, taking a lick of the delicious ice cream. She swallowed hard when Free's eyes followed the route her tongue took on the frozen treat, and once again heat spread over her cheeks. "Thank you for the treat, by the way."

Free nodded his head, taking a taste of his own ice cream. Jodi lowered her gaze and they fell into step side-by-side.

Free gestured to the garden park across the way and they headed toward it. The spring and summer florals that usually adorned the walkways were long gone, but had been replaced with early autumn blooms of roses, hydrangeas, and daylilies. Lush green lawns spread on all sides of them, and towering maple trees dotted the landscape, offering welcome shade from the late summer sun.

As they walked, Jodi pointed out her storefront shyly. Free grinned broadly and stepped close to the window, peering inside. Jodi could see Tessa, her friend and business partner, behind the desk speaking with a customer.

"Turn the Page," Free read aloud the gold decal across the front window. He turned and smiled at her. "That's clever!"

"We have comfy lounge chairs, a small selection of coffee and tea, and Tessa makes homemade baked treats that we offer, too. We aren't as well-known as McLean & Eakins on the main street of town, but we have a loyal following," she laughed. "Tess and I split shifts evenly, and we actually just hired another employee. It's not grand by any stretch of the imagination, but I'm pretty proud of what we built."

"You should be. It looks great, Jodi."

Free's praise meant more to her than he could possibly know. Tessa looked up and waved, Jodi waved back with a smile. Tessa's eyebrows went up in a silent question, her eyes pinging between Jodi and Free quickly. Thankful that Free had turned to look out over the park, Jodi grinned broadly and shrugged her shoulders in answer. She mouthed "tomorrow" and Tess nodded excitedly.

Free turned back to Jodi and with a smile, they continued down the busy side streets. They finished their ice cream and each threw their paper napkins in a nearby garbage receptacle. The sun was getting low on the horizon over the bay that extended out into Lake Michigan. Harbor Springs on one side of the bay, Bay Harbor on the other, with Petoskey nestled neatly between them both. Jodi had always loved her hometown and the beauty of it. The resort town was well known across the world for the jaw-dropping, traffic stopping sunsets on the bay.

About three blocks away, they could hear a commentator over a loudspeaker announcing the score of a local softball game being played at the Bay Front Park, right at the water's edge of the bay. "Do you want to walk down and watch the game?" Free asked.

"Absolutely," Jodi laughed. They headed down the sloped sidewalk, passing other busy storefronts and restaurants. A concrete walkway tunneled beneath the highway above them leading to what the locals referred to as the Waterfront. To their left, the water's edge was home to a large marina, rows of docks filled to the brim with all kinds of boats, ranging from small speedboats to sailboats with towering masts, and even several impressive yachts. To their right, a baseball diamond that butted right up to the boulder strengthened shoreline was lit up with tall flood lights. The announcer's voice carried over the vast area.

A concession stand stood just below the announcer's box, and Free stepped toward it. "I think some salty popcorn after that ice cream sounds just about right," he said and winked down at her.

Free bought a small white bag of popcorn and they meandered along the wide path that ran alongside the first base line. Metal stands were filled with game watchers, and along the grass were blankets and folding chairs where other spectators lounged.

"I haven't been down here in so long," Free laughed heartily, looking around at everything. "I remember driving down here at night and parking way back in the loop as a teenager. That was where we did our drinking and smoking, until the police figured it out and busted us. Your dad was furious when Officer Easton showed up with me in the back of the squad car in the middle of the night. I hadn't gotten a talking to like that, ever."

"I remember that night," Jodi laughed, nodding her head. "I had woken up to the lights flashing through my window. I snuck down the stairs and hid around the corner and listened to Mom and Dad talking to you. I think I was eight or nine, you and Shane had only been here for a few months."

Free nodded, wrinkling his brow. "I was seventeen and not used to having to answer to anyone. It had been just me and Shane for almost two years after my mom died, and my dad had never been in the picture.

My mom's little sister had taken myself and Shane in, but I was a hellion, hurting and not mature enough to process it yet. I caused a lot of trouble and made my aunt's and uncle's lives hell. I told Shane I was leaving, and he chose to come with me." He shrugged, chuckling with contrition. "We bounced around Texas for a little while before migrating North. I had heard that some of Dad's family was up here, but I didn't know where to start looking. We had gotten to Petoskey from me working odd cash jobs here and there to make gas and food money. We hadn't eaten in days, and we found the old shack on the far side of your folk's property. Shane and I snuck in and had started a fire, it was cold as the dickens."

"It had snowed for the first time that year, I remember because I was mad that Mom was going to make me wear my snow suit under my Halloween costume the next day to go Trick-or-Treating," Jodi laughed. "I had told Dad I had seen a car go down the two-track in the back. He didn't believe me until he heard you breaking branches for the fire."

"He scared the shit out of me and Shane when he showed up, shot gun in hand," Free chuckled, turning his head to look down at her as they walked. "He wanted to call the police for trespassing, but you convinced him not to."

Jodi smiled, remembering the night she'd first met Freeman and Shane Thorp. "I just reminded Dad that once upon a time, Gram and Papa Storm had taken in two young men and a toddler when their world was falling apart."

"That's right," Free breathed, tossing a handful of popcorn into his mouth. He swallowed before continuing, "Your dad told me that he and your uncle had lost both of their parents young, too. I think that's why we always got along. Your dad was one of the few people that understood."

"Grandpa and Grandma Kendall were killed in a car accident when I was almost two. I don't remember them. I had only seen them a couple times, I guess. They had moved North and met Gram and Papa on a couples bowling league after Uncle Micah graduated from high school, and since Dad had moved to New Mexico after graduation to go to college, he hadn't made it up North to visit. He had met my birth mom while in college. I don't remember her either, she gave me up to Dad when I was born. We have a very convoluted story."

"I was in my twenties before I found out that Serenity wasn't your biological mom," Free said gently. "I had always just assumed."

Jodi smiled. "Even though I'm not hers biologically, it never felt like I wasn't one hundred percent her daughter. She's been the only mom I've ever known. She's been in my life since I was two. I'm sure it helped that I look just like her, too. Shaun, Fallon, and myself all inherited the Kendall blue eyes and brown hair from Dad's side, but hers is just similar enough to not make many people question anything. She was the best thing to happen to me and Dad."

"Your folks were the best thing to happen to me and Shane, too. After that night with the police, your parents told me I needed to straighten my shit out. I remember feeling disappointed in myself for letting them down. That was when I knew I had found home finally," he said quietly with a small smile. "The rest was history."

"Dad wouldn't ever tell you this, and if you repeat it to him, I will deny I said anything," Jodi warned, shaking a finger at him and laughing, "but he was… crushed when you left. He felt like he had lost a son and best friend."

Free nodded sullenly. "I know. I left a lot behind."

Jodi bit her tongue until it was painful. She had promised herself not to bring up his leaving again, but of course they had come full circle and it hung in the silence between them as they continued to walk.

"He missed you," Jodi murmured. Then, garnering all of her courage, she whispered, "I missed you."

Free turned his head to look at her as he took a deep breath. "I missed you, too."

"You did?"

"Of course," she heard him say, though she was entranced by his aquamarine eyes in the setting sun beyond the horizon. "I thought about everyone all the time."

"Why didn't you come back before now?"

They had walked far enough to come up on a large pond with a wooden bridge that crossed over it. They started across but stopped halfway down, and Free leaned his forearms against the wooden rail. Jodi leaned with her back against it directly beside him. She watched as he squinted against the setting sun, those impossibly dark lashes spiking away from those eyes she loved to look at.

"I've already explained this," he breathed finally, keeping his eyes trained forward and away from her.

"I didn't want you to go," she whispered, her throat dry from nerves.

"Please, let's not talk about this," he implored gently, bowing his head. "I told you why I had to leave, why I didn't come back."

"What did you think was going to happen when you came back?" she asked quietly, both praying for and dreading his answer.

"I don't know," he murmured honestly, still staring out over the horizon. They stood shoulder to shoulder, mere inches separating them. She shifted her weight from one foot to the other anxiously, waiting for him to expound, but he remained quiet.

Dragonflies skimmed over the surface of the water below them, racing after insects her eyes couldn't detect. Jodi turned her head to watch him in profile. His lips were thinner than would be considered classically attractive, but she knew those lips were softer than they appeared and damn did he know how to use them. His nose was sharp and slightly crooked, broken in his twenties when he was head butted by a grouchy mare. The dark facial hair covering the lower portion of his face was trimmed short and still called to her fingers to touch. The baseball hat that he had on backwards was doing things to her midsection. As if reading her thoughts, he reached up and took it off his head, working the brim with tense fingers before raking his dark hair back with those same fingers and replacing the hat on his head.

Breaking the silence other than the commentator's voice in the distance and the sounds of bullfrogs beginning to sing, she breathed, "Do you ever think about it? About me?"

Whipping his head around toward her, aquamarine eyes speared into her sapphire blue ones, burning with intensity. His voice was low as he husked, "I never stopped thinking about it, Jodi."

Fireworks went off in her belly when his words registered. She didn't know where the bold words had come from and was even more stunned by his admission. Her lips parted in surprise, and she watched as his eyes dropped to her mouth, staring intensely. She licked her lips unconsciously and watched as his eyes darkened. He remained leaning against the wooden rail, statue still other than his eyes as they moved over her face.

The setting sun was beautiful, but Jodi hardly noticed. Never taking her eyes off his and whispering huskily, she taunted, "So do it."

CHAPTER 8

Jodi closed the lid of her laptop in frustration. She had been up since four in the morning, unable to sleep. She had stared at her laptop for hours, praying, begging, for her inspiration to return. All she had managed to put down were two words... *Chapter Eleven.*

Sighing in aggravation and giving up for the moment, she stood and crossed the kitchen to the coffee maker, pouring herself another cup of coffee, desperate for the pick-me-up after the night she'd had. The sun was just coming up, the sky out her dining room window turning brilliant shades of fuchsia, violet, and orange. Taking a tentative sip of the hot beverage, she padded to the sliding doors off her kitchen and peered out over the field behind her house. Stifling a yawn, she shook her head to wake herself up.

Had it only been two days since Free had shown up on her front porch?

Had it only been twelve hours since their disastrous ice cream date? Not-a-date?

Rolling her shoulders to alleviate the tension in them, she exited the kitchen, walking down the hallway to her bedroom and into the connecting master bathroom. Reaching into the shower, she turned the taps on, then turned and took another sip of coffee before stripping, allowing the old, faded flannel shorts to drop to the tile floor. Pulling the burgundy CMU t-shirt over her head, she let that fall to the floor to join the shorts, and her panties were next.

Jodi cringed when she thought back to her brazen taunt the night before. She could have kicked herself as soon as the words had left her mouth. He had immediately closed himself off, making some lame excuse about needing to get back to Shane's and that she had an early day to prepare for. He had walked her back to her Jeep, barely speaking to her the whole way back. He'd mumbled a terse good-bye and had disappeared down the street and around the corner to his truck.

Jodi had driven home, embarrassed and angry with herself. Why did she continue to throw herself at him when he made it so very clear he isn't interested?

Taking another sip of coffee before stepping into the hot water of the shower, she sighed heavily in frustration. It's obvious he *is* interested; he had said as much, so *why* was he still fighting against it so vehemently?

Why do you care so much? her mind taunted. You swore off men anyway, remember?

Scrubbing the shampoo into her hair with more vitriol than normal, Jodi hushed the voice in her head. Instead, she let her mind wander…

The glass door of the shower slid open almost silently. The only reason she knew he was there was the draft of cool air that hit her. She didn't turn around, instead keeping her back to him. The door closed with a quiet thud, and she waited with bated breath for him to touch her.

She didn't have to wait long, sighing softly as his fingers trailed feather light over the curve of her shoulder and down her arm. His other hand swept the wet strands of her hair to one side, her knees going weak when she felt his lips touch the meaty part of her shoulder. The fingers trailing down her arm slid around her waist, flattening against her stomach and guiding her back a half step until her backside met his front. She gasped, her head tilting back when she felt his steely length press into the fleshy part of her bottom. His other hand knotted into her hair, pulling her head back slightly, granting himself better access to her neck, where his mouth settled hotly, stealing her breath.

Her hand reached behind her to touch his hip, but he was quick, slapping her bottom smartly and grasping her wrist in his work roughened fingers. Reaching forward, he placed first one hand, then the other on the cool tile wall in front of her. Taking a love bite out of her shoulder then soothing it with a kiss, he husked harshly, "Don't move. Close your eyes."

She did as she was told, painfully aware of the thundering of her heart in the chest and just how aroused she was. Wet heat pooled between her thighs at his rough command, and as if reading her mind, he slid one palm down the side of her ribs and over her hip, then squeezed a handful of her bottom in his hand before sliding his fingers between her thighs.

She spread her legs to allow him better access, and heard his growl of approval when he felt her eagerness for him. "Good girl," she heard him whisper near her ear, and white hot heat spread through her body, zinging along every nerve ending.

Letting out a mew of disappointment when he removed his hand, she gasped when his palm swatted her bottom sharply again. "Shhh. Keep your eyes closed."

Doing as she was told, she felt him reach around her and then heard him open a bottle of body wash, then snapped the lid closed again. She moaned when his hands came back to her body, the loofa that had been hanging on the wall soaped up and gliding across her skin. He dragged it across every inch of skin, paying close attention to her breasts, the rough material abrading her nipples deliciously. "Oh my god," she moaned without thought, then smiled involuntarily when another slap landed on her backside, this one harder than the others.

The fingers of one hand fisted in her hair again, pulling her head back sharply as he whispered gruffly, "I think you like that too much. Bend over and hold on, baby."

Bending at the waist and gripping the small bar she usually hung her washcloth on, she waited only a half a heartbeat before he grasped handfuls of her hips in his large hands and sank into her in one long thrust, impaling her fully. Risking a glance up at him over her shoulder, his eyes burned with aquamarine fire as they met hers even as he began to move inside her, stealing her breath...

Jodi gasped and opened her eyes, her whole body on fire. Why was it always Free's face she saw in these daydreams? Couldn't he leave her to her fantasies?

Rinsing and shutting off the taps, she stepped out of the shower and wrapped herself in a towel before padding to the bedroom to dress for work. She chose a flouncy, tiered skirt with a navy-blue floral print and paired it with an oversized white blouse, one side slipping to leave a sun kissed shoulder bare. Tucking it into the waistband of the skirt, she added a simple belt that accentuated her waist. The skirt hit a few inches above her knees, floating gracefully. A long silver necklace bounced over her breasts as she moved, and she put on the same strappy white sandals from the night before.

Towel drying her hair, she added her hair cream to shape her curls, leaving it to finish drying in ringlets down her back and over her shoulders. Simple make up of blush, mascara, and a sheer pink lip gloss finished the look. She was out the door moments later, the sun rising over the trees at the far side of her property, casting gold sunlight across the yard.

Jodi parked in the designated parking spot behind her store, walking around the block to the front door to unlock it, a beverage carrier in one hand holding two iced coffees and a chai tea, along with the bag of muffins and ground coffee from the store the morning before. It felt like a lifetime ago that she had been there talking with Free yesterday morning.

Letting herself into the store, Jodi stopped briefly in her tracks, unsure whether she had unlocked the door or if it had been unlocked before turning the key. She shook her head to herself; she certainly was preoccupied with thoughts of Free if she was doubting the door being locked. Stepping inside, she turned on the lights as she went, checking through all the book aisles as she cleared the building. Setting the bag of goodies and the tray of coffees on the front desk, Jodi turned on the computer that was used to ring up sales, place orders, and track all inventory.

Still, her mind wouldn't let go of the fantasy she had had that morning, and again her body flushed hotly. She nearly jumped out of her skin when Tess came around the corner and startled her with an excited squeal and swung her purse up onto the top of the desk with a crash. In her other hand was a large white baker's box of homemade cookies and brownies that she slid onto the desk a little more gently than her purse.

"I neeeeeed to know who that hunk was you were with last night!"

Jodi laughed and handed Tessa the chai tea, who took it with a thank you. Tall, blonde, and a year younger than Jodi, Tessa Milne had quickly become one of Jodi's closest friends. They had met at a writing convention they had both attended the spring before. After learning that they had grown up a town away from each other and realizing they had many of the same interests, they had exchanged phone numbers and had been friends ever since, one of the many things that had upset Josh during their short marriage.

Jodi was grateful for Tessa's friendship. She had been a much-needed ally during the failing of Jodi's marriage and the beginning of her divorce.

Tossing her wavy blonde locks away from her face, she pushed the red frames of her glasses back into place on her nose, then took a drink of her tea. A simple black maxi skirt with a surprisingly high slit up to the middle of one thigh was paired with a rolling stones logo band tee and strappy red flats. She also had her signature red lipstick on, which always made Jodi smile. "Well? Who is he?"

"Who is who?"

Tess and Jodi both turned at the new voice and greeted their friend and part time employee, Kit, as she made her way toward them. Pleasantly round in all the right places, she was always impeccably put together. A white and purple striped blouse with cuffed sleeves was tucked into eggplant purple wide legged trousers, and a large leather purse was draped over one arm. Her caramel brown hair was pulled back into a stylish topknot, several strands left out to frame her face. Kit worked full time at a real estate office across the street and was taking classes to get her real estate license, but had been friends with Tessa since grade school and had volunteered to help out at the store when needed.

The three women had made a habit of having coffee together on Monday mornings to start their work week off. Jodi handed the remaining iced coffee to Kit and opened her mouth to speak, but Tess beat her to it.

"Umm, just this *insanely* hot guy I saw Jodi on

a date with last night!" Tess exclaimed excitedly, her blue-green eyes wide.

Kit's honey brown eyes swung from Tessa to Jodi, who blushed to the roots of her dark hair and laughed shyly. "Ohhh-kay. Well, now I'm invested. Who is he?" she asked, repeating Tessa's question from earlier.

Jodi took a deep breath and took a drink of her own iced coffee and stepped behind the cashier desk. "It wasn't a date."

"Yeah, that's why you had that stupid grin on your face," Tessa muttered but was smiling to herself. "Come on! Who is he?"

Opening the baker's box Tessa had brought in, Jodi began unloading the individually packaged treats, setting them in the display case neatly. "He was my dad's foreman, before he moved."

Kit narrowed her gaze, her lips pursing, "There's more to the story than that."

Jodi rolled her eyes before saying, "I may or may not have had a massive crush on him when I was younger."

Tessa's mouth opened in a silent 'O' of exclamation. She slapped the countertop and squeaked, "*Wait, that's Freeman?*"

Jodi nodded and wrinkled her nose.

"But what's he doing here? I thought you said he was gone, never to return?"

Jodi gave Tessa a baleful look. "I don't think I used those exact words. It sounds way more dramatic than it is."

"What am I missing?" Kit asked, setting her purse down on the counter.

"It's nothing," Jodi protested lamely, but was cut off by Tessa's excited explanation.

"Freeman worked for Jodi's dad, a long time ago. He's older, but fine as hell. If my memory serves me right, then I recall the catalyst of this story being that he kissed young Jodi," Tessa made a theatrical gasp of horror before continuing. "He left, hasn't been back since. And our dear heroine here has been carrying a torch for this cowboy ever since." Tessa looked over at Jodi, straightening her glasses again. "Did I miss anything?"

Jodi laughed gustily, shaking her head. "I think that's the gist of it, yes," she said, still laughing. "It's not that exciting though, I swear."

"Whatever," Tessa sing-songed.

"I want to hear more about this mysterious cowboy later, Jodi," Kit said and pointed a finger at her chest. "I have to run, but I want more info!"

"There's nothing to tell!" Jodi called on a chuckle as Kit turned and headed back toward the front door. She waved as she stepped out onto the sunlit sidewalk, turning and vanishing from view. Jodi turned to Tessa and rolled her eyes again, saying with false sternness, "Come on, let's get this place open for the day. Your brownies smell divine, by the way."

"Thank you, but don't change the subject. I want to know how your date went!" she said as she flipped the hand painted open sign so that it faced out the window.

"We got ice cream, we walked around down at the Waterfront. That was it!"

"That's all that happened? You swear?" Tessa quizzed, narrowing her eyes on Jodi.

"Nothing happened. I told you I am going to be a single pringle," Jodi insisted emphatically. "Free just happened to come home at a very emotional time. And he's not staying. He will be gone, back to Texas in a month. I'm not starting anything temporary. It was just nice to see him after so long."

The bell over the front door jingled softly and they both looked over at the door to greet the customer that had just walked in. The welcome froze on her lips, and Tessa whispered out of the corner of her mouth for only Jodi to hear, "Just ice cream my ass."

CHAPTER 9

"Hi," Free said huskily.

He watched as a blush stained her cheeks. "Hi," she whispered.

Free stepped forward slowly, then smiled at the blonde standing next to Jodi, extending his hand toward her to shake. The blonde took it enthusiastically, and he had the feeling they had just been talking about him.

"I'm Freeman," he said, "a friend of Jodi's."

"I'm Tess, also a friend of Jodi's," the blonde said, continuing to shake his hand. When she released it, she slapped her hands on the outside of her thighs and turned to Jodi, saying, "I'm uhh, gonna go to the back to get some of the, uh, some of the things."

Jodi blushed again, staring at her friend like she'd sprouted wings.

Yep, they had definitely been talking about him, he was sure of it. The thought of Jodi talking about him made him smile involuntarily.

As the blonde retreated to what he assumed was their stock room, Free watched Jodi. She was wearing a short, flowy skirt and a white top that hung off one of her shoulders, leaving the skin bare down half of her arm. He swallowed hard when he realized he could see just a hint of the curve of the side of her breast. Her skin looked soft and sun kissed, and he wished he could touch to see if it was as soft as it looked.

He'd kicked himself all the way home for running scared from her last night. She had all but begged him to kiss those lips, and he'd chickened out like a damn teenager.

"I actually—"

"Free, I—"

They both stopped at the same time, laughing together. "Go ahead, Jodi."

Jodi lowered her gaze to the floor and he watched as she fidgeted nervously. "I just wanted to apologize. What I said last night was inappropriate. You were more than fair being honest with me about everything, and I have this terrible habit of not taking hints. So, I just wanted to say that I am sorry."

Free tilted his head to one side, surprised at the one-eighty she'd taken from last night. "You have no reason to apologize, Jodi," he said slowly, softly. They stood mere feet from each other. She raised those blue eyes he loved so much to meet his. "Just because I didn't... doesn't mean I don't want to."

He watched her swallow hard, and she dropped her gaze from his at the same time reaching up to tuck a wayward curl behind her ear nervously. She licked her lips and Free swore silently.

"What brings you out so early again?" Jodi asked, stepping around the corner of the counter. She straightened a display of bookmarks that was already perfectly aligned, and one corner of his mouth tilted up in a quick smirk. He flustered her just as much as she flustered him.

Leaning one elbow on the counter, he shrugged casually with the opposite shoulder. "I was instructed by the bride to come downtown to get fitted for my suit. I just finished up over there and saw that you were open. I thought I'd come see what you've built for yourself."

Jodi's mouth tightened in suspicion, her eyes narrowing, but the corners of her lips tugged up with a grin. "You can't see my store from the suit shop."

Free grinned slyly, enjoying the banter back and forth. "Guilty. But I did want to come see what you've done here."

Jodi laughed and shook her head. "Your flattery is outrageous… but I appreciate it."

"Flattery," he scoffed, but winked. "I mean it. I'm proud of you. You always said you wanted to own a bookstore. I always knew you could do it. I think you and—" he squinted, trying to remember the name of the girl he'd met just moments ago, "—Tessa will be very successful here."

"Thank you," Jodi said earnestly, her blue eyes shining from his praise. "Do you want a tour?"

"Of course he does!"

Jodi and Free laughed at Tessa's outburst from the back of the store, where she was obviously eavesdropping. Jodi showed him around the small store. She offered him a cup of coffee, which he accepted gratefully. When the short tour ended, they had made their way back to the front door. He lifted the cup of coffee to his lips, taking a drink before saying quietly, eyeing the back room furtively, "I actually had an ulterior motive coming here this morning."

"Oh?"

"I was wondering if you have plans tonight?" he asked, holding his breath, waiting for her to let him down gently.

Jodi shook her head slowly, a blush tingeing her cheeks again. "No, I'm free after work tonight."

Lifting one corner of his lips in a quick smile, he murmured, "Can I talk you into having a drink with me?"

"I could be persuaded," Jodi murmured back coyly.

Another grin split his face. "Awesome. Pick you up around say, eight?"

"She'll be ready!" they heard from the back. Jodi laughed and he loved the sound of it.

"See you then," Jodi said around her laughter. She was blushing again.

"See you then," he parroted with a smile, and without a thought ducked his head to press a quick kiss to her cheek, his lips brushing the corner of hers. His breath stilled, as did hers. Lingering for a heartbeat longer, he slowly raised his head, his eyes searching hers. Her lips were parted slightly, and he could feel the soft puffs of her breath hitting him. Barely breathing, he whispered, "Bye, Jodi."

She nodded, and he stepped away, reaching for the door handle. Letting himself out onto the sunlit sidewalk, he took a deep, steadying breath as he walked toward his truck.

As he opened the truck door and slid in behind the wheel, his cell phone started to buzz. Fishing it out of his pocket, he glanced at the name on the screen before answering.

"Hi."

"Did you ask her yet?" was the first thing he heard.

Free chuckled as he started the truck and pulled away from the curb. "No, not yet."

Colorful expletives blessed his ear and he laughed again.

Roxsanna Roberts was the closest thing he had to a best friend in Texas. They had met his first week back seven years ago, when he'd stumbled into the young woman in a heavily drunken stupor. He and his cousin Kasey had gone out for a wild night of drinking and debauchery, which ended with Kasey thrown in jail for pissing on the corner of the sheriff's building, and Free in Roxy's bed. That night had been a strange start to an even stranger relationship between him and the fiery redhead. Best-friends-with-benefits, or so Kasey had dubbed them. Free often occupied Roxy's bed and vice versa, but it was purely physical. She had known from the start that his heart was closed off, and she was okay with that. He had not been in a serious relationship since he'd left Michigan. He had dated superficially and was notoriously known for having commitment issues. Roxy was the only woman he'd spent more than a few weeks with, but there was an understanding between them. When it came to the bedroom, it was just sex. Their friendship had nothing to do with what happened between them, and they both liked it that way.

Whenever Roxy started dating someone new, their physical relationship halted, but their friendship always stayed the same. She had met and began dating a guy named Neal about a year ago, but when he had turned physically abusive several months ago, she had ended the relationship. With nowhere to go, she had moved in with Free as his roommate. Roxy had needed time after the end of her relationship, and the two of them had a mutual understanding that for the time being, that aspect of their friendship was on an indefinite hiatus.

She had been there the morning Shawn had called to ask him to come home for the wedding, and he knew she had sensed the shift in him immediately. His thoughts had gone straight to Jodi, and he ached from missing her, even after so many years away. He had never come out and told her about Jodi, but somehow, the damn redhead knew. It had been Roxy that had convinced him to come home, telling him to 'Stop being a pussy and just tell her you love her already'.

Still muttering a string of curses at him, she finally sighed heavily and snapped, "Have you even seen her yet?"

Free sighed, turning the truck with one hand on the wheel in the direction of Shane's house. "Yes, Red."

"Well? What happened?" she snapped impatiently. Chuckling, he could just imagine her fiery hair bristling with frustration at him.

"We've just talked," he said quietly.

He could practically hear her roll her eyes. "Have you kissed her yet?"

"No," Free said and grimaced, because he knew the tirade that would be coming.

"Quit being a gentleman and just kiss the crap out of her already," Roxy snapped.

Free sighed in frustration, running his other hand through his hair before placing it back on the wheel. "It's not that easy, Red."

"I never said it was going to be easy. But you need to shit or get off the pot. Either do something about it, or let her move on," Roxy muttered stonily. "She's not going to wait forever, Free."

One of the things Free both loved and hated about his best friend was that she was not a bull shitter. Free was instantly and irrefutably uncomfortable with the idea of Jodi being with someone else, and jealousy ripped through him like an un-caged monster.

"I'll get back to you on that," Free muttered. "I'll talk to you later."

"Bye!" he heard her call as he hung up the phone and tossed it into the passenger seat beside him. Raking his hair back with tense fingers, he cursed the hours that stood between him and seeing Jodi again.

CHAPTER 10

Jodi looked at the clock on the wall in the bathroom when she heard a hard knock on her front door. Free was early! It was only quarter after seven!

Frantically slipping the earrings she had chosen to wear into the holes in her ears, she hurried out to the door and took a deep breath before opening it.

Dread iced her like a bucket of cold water over her head, her body tensing with apprehension.

"I really hope you don't plan on going out wearing that."

Jodi bit her tongue until it hurt to keep the sharp retort from escaping her lips. Instead, she smiled sweetly and said, "Last I checked my life was none of your business anymore. I thought I asked you not to come here again."

"Knock your shit off, Jodi, I'm not in the mood to deal with your attitude today," Josh snapped from the doorway.

Jodi's eyebrows raised in astonishment, and she snorted a laugh. "Excuse me? I don't recall asking you to come here to begin with."

"I heard you have a date tonight."

How? Jodi thought. *How* did he know already?

But she rolled her eyes in frustration, snapping, "Like it or not, I am a grown adult and I'm allowed to go out with friends to have a drink if I'd like. Even if it was a date, I don't need your permission to do so. Not that it's any of your business. *We are divorced,* Josh. Now, if you'll excuse me—"

Josh caught the edge of the door in his hand before she could close it. Forcing herself to remain calm, she squared her shoulders and steeled her nerves. She knew he reveled in the knowledge that he could still illicit fear in her, and she didn't want to give him the pleasure of seeing her rattled.

"Leave my home," she grated out through clenched teeth. "Don't make me call the police. You know I'm not afraid to."

Jodi could see the indecision and fury battling for supremacy in his hazel eyes. She could tell he'd been drinking; his eyes were glassy, his cheeks were flushed, and his breath reeked of cinnamon whisky and cheap beer. She had no qualms calling the police. She'd done it before, and he knew she could and would do it again if necessary.

Backing away and releasing his hold on the door, he smirked. Holding his arms out away from his body in a defenseless gesture, he patted the air and snickered, "Calm down, geez. All I wanted to do was talk, and you're acting all crazy for nothing."

Jodi was shaking her head before he finished talking. Her breathing was elevated, and she snapped, "No. You don't get to do that. You don't get to talk to me like that anymore, Josh. Leave. Now."

Josh turned and headed back down the porch stairs, crossing the short way to his Lincoln. He climbed in and flipped her off out the window as he spun his tires, pulling out of the driveway with a spray of gravel behind him.

Jodi closed the door and leaned her back against it, taking several deep, restorative breaths.

How did he always know everything, almost as it was happening? She wondered again. It was unnerving how close of a watch he kept on her.

Padding back to the bathroom, she glanced at her reflection in the mirror. Her face was pale, her hair was only half done, and she now second guessed her outfit of choice. Then, she shook her head and muttered darkly to herself, "He doesn't get to do this to you anymore, remember?"

Taking another deep breath, she continued getting ready. At five minutes to eight, she was just dabbing perfume on her wrists and at the base of her throat when another knock sounded on the door. Checking her reflection one last time, she tried to reign in the butterflies that took flight in her stomach again. Walking out to the door, she opened it, sighing in relief at the sight of Free standing on the doorstep.

Free stood on her front porch, hands shoved into the back pockets of his indecently tight jeans, his head bowed slightly. The black shirt he wore was stretched tight over his upper body. He had on the same black baseball hat, but tonight the brim was turned forward, and with his head lowered slightly, she couldn't see his face beneath the brim of the hat.

His eyes traveled from the simple black sandals she wore, up her bare, tanned legs, over the cutoff jean skirt that hit mid-thigh, and continued up over the black halter style tank top that left her shoulders and arms bare. Her hair had been left curly, and it cascaded down her back and over her shoulders in soft, touchable ringlets. She had kept her make-up simple and chic, with just a hint of a smokey eye. A mauve tinted lip gloss gave her lips just a hint of color.

"Hi," she breathed. "I'm almost ready. Come inside while I grab my purse."

Free's aquamarine eyes met hers and she sucked in her breath at the power of his stare. He stepped inside.

"Free?" she whispered breathlessly.

He stepped closer to her, pulling his hands from his pockets. One of those hands came up and flipped the hat around on his head, so that the brim was backward, the way Jodi liked it best. When she took an instinctive step back, he reached out and threaded his fingers into the hair at the nape of her neck and drew her closer to him. He angled his body against hers, nothing but their clothing whispering against each other, all the while lowering his head to hers. He rubbed his lips against hers, softly, sweetly, again and again. She sighed, and her eyes slid closed in exultation as his lips pressed and stayed. Tilting his head to one side, his mouth opened, and hers reciprocated. His tongue was inquisitive and hungry, and it spiraled into the sweet cavern of her mouth to taste all of her.

Jodi's fingers splayed wide against the rippling muscles of his abdomen. She could feel his thumb stroking her neck and his heart beating thunderously under her hands. She could taste the spearmint toothpaste he'd used. He sipped at her lips before sliding his tongue between them again to taste her more thoroughly. She met his kiss fervently, her tongue tangling with his in an effort to taste more of him. She could feel his kiss in her belly, sending signals to her cleft, making her wet and wanting.

When he finally drew his lips from hers, he rolled his forehead across hers briefly, their lips barely touching. Free opened his mesmerizing eyes and pecked another light kiss to her mouth.

Speaking directly against her well-kissed lips, he whispered huskily, "I think I've waited long enough to do that."

CHAPTER 11

Jodi peeked at Free out of the corner of her eye as he drove. He drove with one hand draped over the wheel loosely, the other kept her hand captive. He hummed and mouthed the words to the country songs playing softly from the radio.

When he caught her staring at him, he gave her a lopsided grin. "I don't think I've told you how great you look," he said and squeezed her hand gently.

"Thank you," Jodi said and blushed, returning her gaze to the front windshield. She wanted to tell him that his jeans made her mouth water, or that the feel of his hard chest beneath her hands made them tingle. Instead, she took the coward's way out and said, "You look nice, too."

"Do you play pool?" he asked.

"Dad has a table in his den, but I never got the hang of it. Tristan is a shark, though," she laughed, recalling how her youngest brother could win no matter how hard his opposition tried.

"Right, I remember when your dad built that man-cave. Getting that table in was a bitch," he chuckled.

Free pulled the truck into a local dive bar and parked. Jodi knew this had always been his favorite bar. She had been in a few times, but it had been years. Josh wouldn't have been caught dead in such a place, and had essentially forbidden her from going, worried that his reputation as a real estate broker would be tarnished. Jodi had learned shortly into her marriage Josh had only married her for the clout her last name held. Levi Kendall had built a name for himself and his family, and Josh had tried to capitalize on it, which she had figured out too late.

In an effort to get Josh off her mind, Jodi chuckled and said, "I should have known you'd bring me here. It's the only country bar in town."

"Feels like home," he said and smiled wryly. "Texas and Michigan all rolled into one. Ready?"

She nodded and he leaned across the console to press a quick kiss to her unsuspecting mouth. Then he was gone, sliding out of the driver's side and coming around the hood of the truck. He opened the passenger door and offered her his hand to assist her out.

He shut the door and they crossed the parking lot, her hand still entrapped in his. She smiled up at him and he grinned, winking. Those darn butterflies were back in full force.

Free held the heavy wooden door open for her then followed, placing his hand at the small of her back. "Bar or table?" he asked her, leaning close. The soft puffs of air against her ear made goosebumps break out over her skin, and she shivered.

"This is your spot, where would you like to sit?" she asked, looking up at him.

"Let's grab drinks from the bar, then we'll go find a table," he suggested. She nodded, and he placed his hand at the small of her back again, leading her through the crowd. For a Monday night, they were surprisingly busy. Loud country music resounded through the saloon, and the crowd was noisy, trying to speak and be heard over the music.

They stopped at an open spot along the wooden bar, and Free offered her the only open seat. Jodi smiled and sat down, Free standing close beside her, his jean clad thighs brushing against the bare skin of hers. Electricity arched between them, making her heart pound.

The bartender glanced at them and then did a double take, a grin splitting the man's face. "Holy shit, Freeman Thorp!" Wiping his hands on a towel weaved through one of the belt loops on his pants, the man walked toward them, a wide smile still on his face. He extended his hand over the bar to Free. "How the hell are you, man? Shit, I haven't seen you in ages!"

Free smiled broadly and reached forward to shake the bartender's hand heartily. Jodi smiled as she watched the two. "Hiya, Kyle. I've been good. It's been a while. Home for Shane's wedding this weekend."

"No shit," Kyle the bartender chuckled. "I hadn't heard if you were going to make it or not. Mandy and I will be there! We're bartending the reception."

"We'll see you there, then," Free said with a smile. Then, turning to Jodi, he said, "Jodi, what would you like to drink?"

Put on the spot and still dazzled by the brilliant smile he had just turned on her, Jodi fumbled for a moment, glancing along the bar to see what her options were, at the same time pulling her ID out of her purse, a force of habit. "Umm, can I get an Oberon, please?"

"Sure thing," Kyle said and reached out to accept the ID, then handed it back to her with a thank you. He reached into a cooler for a frosted pint glass. "Orange slice?"

"Yes, please," Jodi responded with a smile of her own. He set it down on a beverage napkin and she said, "Thank you."

"Free, the usual?" Kyle asked, leaning with his hands on the bar.

"Absolutely," he laughed.

While Kyle grabbed a PBR can from the cooler behind him, Free chuckled as Jodi put her license back in her purse. She took a sip of her beer as Kyle set Free's beer down in front of him on the polished wood counter.

"I haven't been on a date with a woman that's had to show an ID in a long time," he chuckled, taking a drink from the ice cold can.

Jodi hated the reminder of their age difference, which seemed to be the moral dilemma that Free struggled with the most. She also hated the twinge of jealousy that reared up in her at the thought of him dating other women. She had still been legally married to another man until three months ago, after all. She wasn't sure if Free even knew about Josh. She wasn't looking forward to that conversation.

He must have read the expression on her face, because he grimaced. "I'm sorry. That was insensitive."

Jodi shrugged, taking another sip of her beer. "Everyone has a past, right?"

Free nodded, but reached out his hand to take hers, rubbing his thumb across the back of her hand. "Should we go find a seat by the billiard tables?"

Jodi nodded and stood, taking her beer with her in one hand, her other hand still entwined within Free's strong fingers. He led them through the crowd toward an empty table near the green felt covered billiard tables. There was one open, and as Jodi sat down at their small table, she watched as Free moved around the room. Kneeling, he inserted the quarters necessary into the slotted tongue, then pushed it in to release the billiard balls. His eyes met hers as he rounded the table and he crooked his finger at her, one side of his mouth tilting up in a grin.

She stood and walked toward him, meeting him at the edge of the table. "Would you like to rack or break?" he asked over the noise in the room.

"I'll rack," Jodi responded, reaching down to retrieve the triangle rack, then knelt the best she could in her skirt to place the colorful balls on the table. Free skirted the table again, walking to the wall to choose two pool sticks. The slow, rolling walk was inherently sexual and made Jodi drop one of the balls loudly. She blushed hotly as he turned to look at her quizzically.

She racked them quickly, rolling them along the brushed felt until they were all aligned, then lifted the triangle, leaving the balls in their correct spots on the table. Free chalked both cue tips, and Jodi flushed hotly again. Why was everything this man did so damn sexy?

Retreating to their table, she picked up her beer with a shaky hand and took a long drink as Free bent at the waist, leaning forward on one forearm to align his shot. The muscles of his arms rippled and bunched, stretching the arms of his black shirt deliciously as he catapulted the cue stick forward, making a clean, loud break and sending the balls ricocheting around the table. Jodi's mouth watered and she took another drink of her beer, dropping her gaze guiltily as he glanced at her.

Jodi had told herself this wasn't a date, but it sure felt like one. She hadn't been on a date in years, and she admitted to herself that she was enjoying it very much. As much as Free had fought against whatever this was between them, the way he looked at her and the way he kissed her made her suspect he was losing his inner war. Jodi reminded herself she wasn't looking for a fling with Free, but when he did stuff like brushing his fingertips along the backside of her upper arm ever so lightly, she grudgingly admitted that her resolve was rapidly melting.

When it was her turn, he sidled over to her, reaching around her to pick up the can of beer, bringing it to his lips. It was maddening! He was doing all of this on purpose! She smiled and stepped around him, walking to the pool table to take her turn. Painfully aware of her short skirt—had she known they were going to be playing billiards she would have worn jeans—she cautiously bent at the waist to line up her shot. When she turned around, she blushed again when she realized his gaze was on the backs of her bare thighs.

They took turns, razzing each other until only two balls remained. A waitress came by, asking if they'd like another round just as Free swallowed the last of his beer. They both nodded, and gave the waitress their order.

At regular intervals, they were stopped by people they both knew; friends of Free's, old coworkers, and family acquaintances happy to see Free back home. A petite blonde walked up to them and hugged Free, staying to talk for only a few seconds before continuing on her way to the other side of the room, but had whispered an invitation into his ear for later that made Jodi bristle with jealousy.

The waitress returned a few minutes later with their fresh beers, just as Jodi leaned down to take her shot at the black eight ball. Free razzed her again, telling her not to miss, when a buxom woman with box dyed black hair sidled up to Free, placing her hand on his forearm and leaning up to place a kiss on his mouth, which he dodged. Jodi's hackles went up. The gall of these women made Jodi want to scratch their eyes out!

Free removed the heavily tattooed hand on his arm and stepped away, just as Jodi straightened.

"Mal," Free said, a bit stiffly.

"Freeman," the woman purred seductively, replacing her hand on his arm possessively. "You failed to mention you were back in town."

"Obviously, I failed to mention it for a reason," he grunted rudely to the woman. He shrugged the hand off his arm again, reaching for and taking a drink of the fresh beer.

Mal eyed Jodi up and down shrewdly from where she stood on the other side of the pool table, before muttering, "Robbing the cradle with this one, aren't you? Don't you think you'd have more fun with someone a little more... experienced?"

Free laughed darkly as Jodi came around the table toward them. "I think I'm good, thanks for the offer though. I'd rather keep my shit STD free if you don't mind."

Jodi's eyes widened at the brazen comment. She watched as Mal's mouth dropped open and she snapped, "You asshole."

Free shrugged and quipped, "Not a lie, though. Excuse us."

He took Jodi's hand and led her back to their table, sitting down kitty corner from each other. He held her hand fast as the dark-haired woman stomped away angrily.

"I'm sorry this is so awkward for you," he murmured.

Jodi laughed self-deprecatingly. "You're a very popular person," she said simply. Staring at their clasped hands, she took a deep, steadying breath and continued, "I'm neither naïve nor stupid, Free. I knew a long time ago about your reputation. From my bedroom window I could see the barn and your apartment..." she trailed off quietly.

She glanced up at him to find him watching her closely.

"I can't change my past," he whispered, his thumb stroking the top of her hand.

"I know that," she whispered in return. "I can't change mine, either."

Free dropped his gaze to their hands and she heard him say, "I'm sure you've dated since I've been gone."

Jodi smiled ruefully. "Define dating."

Free raised his eyes to hers and opened his mouth to speak but was interrupted when a couple staggered over to their table, sitting down unsteadily. "Freeman! Let's do shots!" the inebriated woman slurred, while the man slapped Free on the back roughly in hello.

Free smiled at Jodi before introducing her to the two. "Jodi, this is Brad and his wife Sheila. I've known these two for ages."

"Did he ever tell you how I found a morel mushroom the size of my pinky nail?" Sheila mumbled incoherently, holding up one unsteady hand and pointing to her fingernail. "I found it, and he didn't!"

Free leaned over to Jodi and whispered, "I've never been morel hunting in my life. But for some reason, she thinks I have with her. She tells this story every single time I see her."

Jodi laughed heartily. Brad reached out a hand and Jodi shook it. "Nice to meet you."

Sheila was having none of the hand-shaking though, leaning forward in her seat to clasp Jodi in a tight hug. "You're beautiful," she said earnestly to Jodi, then turned to Free and said, "Free, she's beautiful."

"I would have to agree with you," Free said with a smile, which made Jodi blush again. She hadn't blushed this much since high school!

"How have you been?" Brad asked, and he and Free fell into conversation. Sheila whistled loudly, then yelled, "Hey, Kyle, can we get shots over here?"

Jodi saw Kyle give the thumbs up over the heads of the crowd between them, and moments later the waitress was headed over with a tray laden with drinks for the four of them, and four shot glasses filled to the brim with a golden liquor, fresh lime wedges on the rim of each one.

Free groaned, laughing. "Tequila? Really, Sheila?"

"Welcome back, bud!" she crowed, raising her shot glass. Brad, Free, and Jodi followed suit, clinking their glasses before downing the tequila and chasing it with the lime.

The four of them sat talking and laughing for a long time. Jodi smiled over at Free, who smiled back at her warmly. Free checked the time on his cell phone and made a face of chagrin. "Jodi, I should probably get you home before you turn into a pumpkin."

"Tessa opens the store tomorrow, no pumpkin here," Jodi teased. She was pleasantly buzzed, feeling relaxed and enjoying her time with Free.

Free leaned close and whispered, "I've been fantasizing about kissing you for the last hour. I'm afraid if I don't soon, I may be the one turning into a pumpkin."

Jodi turned her head slightly, so that their mouths were mere inches apart. "We can't have that," she breathed.

Free stood and clapped Brad on the back and hugged Sheila, saying goodbye and promising to see them again soon. Free took Jodi by the hand and led her to the bar, where he paid their bill and left cash for a tip for the waitress and Kyle both. They waved goodbye, and he led her through the thinning crowd and out the door to the dark parking lot.

Rounding the bed of the truck, he opened the passenger door for her. However, before she could climb in, he growled low in his throat and pressed her back against the side of the vehicle. Instinctively knowing what he needed and needing it herself, Jodi wrapped her arms around his neck as he pressed his body into hers. Their mouths met fiercely, and the alcohol in her system made her brave. She tilted her hips against his and sighed when his strong hands gripped them and pulled them more firmly against his. Her fingers curled into the soft hair at the back of his neck where it peaked out beneath the ballcap he still had on backwards.

A car pulled into the parking lot and Free released her, cursing under his breath. He stepped away, his breathing harsh. "We need to go before I take you against my truck," he said raggedly and grinned that lopsided grin she loved so much. She nodded mutely and took the hand he extended, stepping up into the truck.

They drove to her house in silence, words superfluous. His hand rode high on her thigh, fingers trailing brazenly close to the apex of her thighs, his fingers leaving fire where they touched her bare skin. He parked in her driveway and cut the motor.

"Do you want to come inside?" Jodi whispered throatily, her voice sounding strange to her own ears.

"Very much," Free whispered back, his own voice strained with want.

They climbed out of his truck and walked side by side up the porch steps to the front door. She let them inside and turned. Free was staring at her, his gaze hot.

Feeling bold, Jodi took his hand in hers and began walking backward toward the kitchen, pulling him with her. Free's breathing was ragged. When she dared a glance down his body, she could see him straining against the fly of his tight jeans.

Jodi didn't turn on any lights, the moonlight filtering through the windows their only source of illumination. Stopping at the refrigerator, she opened it, taking out a cold beer. She was probably going to hate herself for the hangover she was going to have in the morning, but she didn't care. Opening it, she took a long drink and then extended it to him. He took it, tilting it to his lips and taking a long pull of his own. His aquamarine gaze was hot, drinking in all of her the same way he was drinking the cold beer.

He set the bottle down on the counter next to her and reached for her, pulling her forward until her body was pressed closely against his. His arms wrapped around her as his lips found hers with ardor. Tunneling his fingers through her curls at the nape of her neck, he wound his fingers into a fist and held her snugly against him, and she moaned throatily at the sharp sting on the back of her scalp. His other hand skimmed down her spine, past the small of her back, to the flare of her bottom. He cupped one round, firm cheek in his hand, hauling her high and hard against him.

Jodi's hands came up and knocked the ball cap off his head, sending it with a soft thud to the kitchen floor. Her mouth met his fiercely, hungry for all of him. It had been so long since she'd craved a man's touch, and she reveled in the feel of him against her. Finally able to run her fingers through his hair, she found it to be as soft as she'd always imagined.

Releasing her, Jodi gasped in surprise when he grasped her hips in both hands and picked her up to set her on the counter behind her. Spreading her thighs instinctively, Free moved so that he was standing between them. His mouth never left hers, but his breathing was harsh against her lips.

With one hand he pressed her hips closer to his, the other tangling in her hair once more, holding her still as his kisses deepened. When she felt his hardness at the junction of her thighs, she moaned, "Oh my god, Free."

Her body was humming with need. She had never wanted something more.

Free's deft fingers found the bottom edge of her tank top and lifted it, and she raised her arms to assist him. The flimsy piece of material floated to the floor. Her breasts spilled over the edge of her sheer, lace bra and she blushed as she watched him admire her. Free bent his head and kissed each swell and Jodi's hands grasped handfuls of his hair once more, holding him to her.

Her nipple was peaked and just begging to be kissed. He obliged, taking it in his mouth, laving her with his tongue through the sheer lace material.

Her back arched and she moaned again, the feel of his tongue on her driving her crazy with want. Jodi's hands slid over his muscled shoulders and tugged at his shirt. His mouth left her breast long enough to allow her to pull the shirt over his head, dropping it to the floor with hers.

He didn't give her time to look at his magnificent chest, though. He moved between her thighs, his hands running around her middle to flatten against her back, pulling her closer against him. Their mouths met again, passion and unfulfilled need driving them a little insane. Jodi's hands clutched at the smooth, hard expanse of his back.

Feeling more daring than she had in years, Jodi reached between them and fumbled with the top button of his jeans until she managed to wiggle it loose. "Take these off, please."

Free buried his face in her shoulder, inhaling deeply against the skin of her neck. He sucked air into his starved lungs. After a long moment, he raised his head and pressed a tender kiss to her forehead before taking several shaky steps away from her.

"Free...?" she whispered through kiss-roughened lips and watched in confusion as he rebuttoned his jeans and bent down to retrieve his discarded shirt and hat. He pulled the shirt over his head, refusing to meet her gaze. "Why...?"

"Good night, Jodi," he said roughly, then turned on his booted heels, heading back to the door through the darkened room. She heard the front door close with a soft click, and then the tears started to fall.

CHAPTER 12

Jodi washed her face in cool water, then looked up into the bathroom mirror at her reflection. It was a dismal sight.

She looked like hell.

She *felt* like hell.

Her eyes were red, puffy, and gritty from crying all night long. Her head was pounding, a mixture of the alcohol she had consumed and the night of tears. She looked pale and much older than her twenty-five years. She was grateful that it was Tessa's morning to open the store. It gave her several hours to recover before going in for the afternoon to close. Fishing for a Tylenol out of the bottle in her medicine cabinet, she swallowed it with water, praying it gave her some much-needed relief from her headache.

Fresh tears started in her eyes as Free's rejection the night before played through her mind again. He had rejected her more times than she could count, and her pride had taken a debilitating blow last night.

At what point was she going to learn her lesson? At what point was she going to remember she wasn't interested in dating, period? Especially Free, who had admitted to only being here for a short period of time.

She sighed and forced her tears back. Starting the shower, she climbed in and washed away Free's smell on her skin, scrubbing until her skin was pink. She stayed in the shower until the water began to cool, then climbed out and wrapped a towel around herself. She dressed in a comfortable pair of lounge shorts and a white tee shirt, then put in her earbuds, choosing a playlist off Spotify as background noise. Wrapping a fluffy blanket around her legs, she sat down at her desk to write, quickly losing herself in the work.

She was so engrossed in the scene she was writing that she didn't hear Shaun pull into the driveway or knock on the front door. She didn't hear anything until Shaun walked into Jodi's office and tapped her on the shoulder, making her jump.

Minimizing the screen and taking out the earbuds, Jodi turned and smiled feebly at her sister. Tears started anew, much to her dismay, and she tried to swipe them away without Shaun seeing them. Shaun gripped Jodi's shoulders in her hands, holding her so she couldn't hide away.

"Whose ass do I need to kick?"

Jodi laughed through her tears, reaching up to swipe at the fresh tracks down her cheeks. "Nobody's, Shaun."

"Bullshit. Is this because of Josh or Free?"

Jodi sighed heavily, her shoulders drooping. "Free. We went out for drinks last night."

"So… What happened?" Shaun asked when Jodi didn't elaborate.

"We came back here. Made out. Then in the middle of it, he just stopped and left. I don't even know what happened," Jodi whispered. Scrubbing her hands over her face, she blew her breath out. "I know I can't keep doing this back-and-forth thing. It's exhausting. I think I was naïve to imagine anything would actually happen if he ever came back. It hurts too much."

"Well, in my personal opinion, most men are dumb. And they smell bad."

Jodi laughed gustily, and it felt good to smile. Though she wouldn't tell Shaun how wonderful Free smelled. "I love you."

"Love you, too," Shaun said and squeezed Jodi's shoulders tightly with her hands. "Have you gotten a head count for Thursday yet?"

"Yes. Myself, you, Cassie, her three bridesmaids, Zoey, and I invited Kit and Tessa, too," Jodi said, ticking them off on her fingers as she named them.

"Awesome," Shaun sing-songed, then stood in one fluid motion. "I have the strippers scheduled for eight thirty. I need to get back to work, lunch break is over. You should probably get a job, slacker."

Jodi didn't miss the not-so-subtle mention of male entertainment and threw a highlighter pen at her sister as she sashayed toward the open door, missing by a mile. "No strippers, Shaun!"

"I can't hear you!" Shaun sing-songed back, laughing. "Later, sis!"

Jodi rolled her eyes. Checking the time, she sighed. It was a good thing Shaun had stopped over; she had been writing for so long she'd lost track of time. Standing, she hurried to the bathroom and washed her face once more. Quickly applying her make-up, she raced out to the bedroom to get dressed. Today she chose something simple and comfortable, a pair of black leggings and an oversized, off the shoulder top in a rich olive-green color. Securing her curls on the top of her head in a messy topknot, she slid her feet into black low-top converse. Racing out the door, she made it to the bookstore just in time.

Flying through the door, Tessa eyed her up and down, her brow furrowed. "Spidey sense is telling me last night didn't go well."

Jodi sighed and begged out. "Please, I really don't want to talk about it. I don't want to cry anymore today."

"Eww, that bad, huh? Bummer," Tessa said and made a face. Reaching behind her, she grabbed a coffee cup and poured Jodi a hefty serving, sliding it toward her. "You look like you could use this."

"Thank you," Jodi murmured, taking a generous swallow. "I was up all night, and then got caught up writing this morning. I'm sorry I was late."

Tessa laughed and gave her another side eyed glance. "Late? You're still ten minutes early. And progress is progress. Take it any way you can!"

Jodi nodded in agreement. "You're right, of course. It felt good to finally get over that block."

"Oh, I did want to ask you, did you lock the front door last night before you left? It was open when I got here this morning," Tessa said, coming around the counter. "Everything looked fine when I got here, but it was strange."

Jodi stilled, her coffee halfway to her lips. She set it back down slowly. "It was unlocked again? I thought I was going crazy; it was unlocked on Monday morning when I got here, too. Maybe the lock is faulty? I'll have my dad come by this evening before closing to look at it."

"That's scary that it's been unlocked two nights in a row," Tess said and shivered. "Ugh, that gives me the creeps. What if someone was here?"

"Yeah, that is scary," Jodi agreed softly. She had brushed it off as being distracted the other morning by thoughts of Free, but her gut had been right after all.

CHAPTER 13

"I don't know what to tell you, sweetheart. The lock is fine," Levi Kendall rumbled apologetically. He pulled himself up from the kneeling position in front of the door, dusting off his knees. "Are you positive you girls locked it correctly?"

"Of course we did. We've been here for over a year, we've never had problems with it before," Jodi murmured. Anxiety was running rampant through her, making her skin crawl. "I'm just glad no one was here when Tessa and myself got here in the morning."

"Have you checked your cameras?" Levi asked, closing the door and striding to the back room. Jodi followed.

"I was going to, I just hadn't had time. We were surprisingly busy today. It was a really good day," Jodi said and smiled.

Levi winked at her, his cobalt blue eyes twinkling. His dark hair and beard were sprinkled with silver strands throughout, but it only made him more handsome. Jodi had always thought her father was one of the most handsome men she'd ever seen. He and Serenity were both gorgeous inside and out. Levi Kendall had made a name for himself in their small town. He owned and operated one of the largest and most successful contracting companies in the tri-county area. Serenity Kendall was an elementary teacher with a heart of gold. Married for nearly twenty-three years, Levi and Seren were still madly in love. Jodi and her siblings had grown up with the luxury of a healthy and happy home, with two parents that loved each other and their children with their whole hearts. Jodi had always wanted a love like her parents had. It had been a hard pill to swallow when she'd told her family after less than a year of marriage that she was filing for a divorce from Josh.

"Let's take a look at the video," Levi rumbled. He reached for the eject button on the recorder, but nothing happened. His brow wrinkled. "Uh, Jodi, there's no tape in here."

"What?" Jodi asked, shocked. "That's impossible."

Levi shook his dark head. "There's nothing here. Did either of you take it out to replace it and forgot to put it back?"

"No, of course not," Jodi mumbled, her mind reeling. What was going on! "I just checked it a week ago. It was there, I swear."

"I believe you, sweetheart," Levi soothed. "Do you have extras to put in?"

"Yeah, in the bin below," Jodi said, distracted. She reached for the small cardboard bin and pulled it out, lifting the lid. She gasped. It was empty. "What the hell is going on?"

"I'll call Warren and get him here to install a new system. I don't like this," Levi muttered darkly, fishing out his cell phone. Moments later, Jodi could hear her brother Warren's voice on the other line. "Hey, it's Dad. I need a new security system down here for Jodi's store. Something isn't right."

Wrapping her arms across her middle tightly, Jodi shivered again. Something was definitely not right. The front door being unlocked was one thing, but missing security tapes, too? That was no coincidence, she was sure of it. She had a deep suspicion that it was Josh's doing. But why?

Jodi went through the motions of closing the store. Seren sent down a delivery for dinner while they waited for Warren to arrive with the new system. When he arrived, it was nearly dark out, and the old fashioned, wrought iron streetlamps that the downtown district was known for had all come on, illuminating the sidewalks and streets like a runway.

They were there until nearly midnight, Levi and Warren working to install all new cameras, motion sensors, and a wireless backup system that would send footage to Jodi's computer at home.

Yawning broadly, Jodi thanked her father and brother again. Warren Kendall was the third child of Seren and Levi, twenty years old, a giant at six foot four inches, and a tech genius. He was headed to Michigan State University at the end of the month for his sophomore year of college.

"This should cover everything you need it to. And I set up a camera for the back lot, that way your cars are under surveillance while you're parked here, too," Warren said, showing Jodi on the brand new, large monitor that he had installed. There were six cameras altogether covering nearly every inch of the store.

"I feel better already, thank you, Warren. Sorry we kept you up so late," Jodi said and yawned again.

Warren laughed, his green eyes crinkling at the corners. "I'm a college student, Jode. I don't usually go to bed until two am, back up for classes at eight. Usually hung over as fuck, to boot," he mumbled out of the corner of his mouth so only she could hear. Jodi laughed.

"I heard that," Levi muttered darkly around a broad yawn of his own. "If we're done here, I think it's time to head home. Your mom is probably waiting for me."

Jodi laughed heartily. "Yeah, right. She's sound asleep, loving that she gets the bed all to herself."

Levi chuckled. "You might be right."

Jodi went through and checked everything before they all made their way to the front door. Closing and locking it securely behind her as they left, she checked it three times to make sure it was locked properly. Levi insisted on walking Jodi around to the back of the building to make sure she got to her Jeep safely. They waved Warren good-bye as he climbed into his Subaru and pulled away from the curb.

Jodi hugged Levi tight, burying her face in the vastness of his hard chest. He always smelled of cedar, pine, and horse leather. He squeezed her back, then pecked a kiss to the crown of her head. "Good night, sweetheart. Get home safe, okay?"

Jodi nodded and stepped back. "Good night, Dad. Thank you." She slid into the driver's seat in the Jeep as Levi ambled over to his pickup truck and climbed in. They waved to each other as they both pulled out of the parking lot, driving in opposite directions.

Falling into bed without even washing her face, Jodi was asleep minutes after her head hit the pillow.

CHAPTER 14

"You did *what*?"

Free grimaced. "Don't make me repeat it, Red."

"You're an idiot!" Roxy exclaimed heatedly from the other end of the phone. "Why would you do that? She probably thinks you hate her now!"

"Of course I don't hate her," Free snapped, scrubbing one hand down his face before raking those same fingers through his hair, pulling it away from his eyes. "I don't know what happened. I panicked."

"You panicked."

"Yeah," Free sighed heavily. "I panicked."

Roxy was silent on the other end of the line for long moments, and her silence made him sweat bullets. "Ummm… *dude*. I know you're not like, real good with relationships and all, but *daaaamn*. You've got some serious damage control to do. A really good apology and a *really* big bouquet of flowers is going to be your best bet."

Free groaned and flopped backward onto the bed. "I've wanted Jodi for so long, I didn't want it to just be over."

"So… rejecting her yet again seemed like a good life choice?" Roxy quipped dryly.

"I didn't reject her, I just…didn't want that to be it. She deserves better than getting drunk fucked on the kitchen counter," Free mumbled sullenly.

"You might not see it as a rejection, but I guarantee she does," Roxy said quietly. "Free, you are my best friend. And I'm telling you, you're going to lose your chance with her if you don't quit being a jackass. It's great that you're trying to be a gentleman, really. It's one of the things I love most about you. But it sounds to me like she's a grown woman who knows what she wants; she wants you, and she maybe kinda likes you, too."

"What would I do without your wise words and expertise, Red?" Free chuckled.

"You'd probably die a lonely ol' cowboy," Roxy muttered dryly.

"Any word on Neal?" he asked.

Roxy sighed through the phone. "No, they served him with the restraining order papers, I haven't seen or heard from him. Hopefully it stays that way."

"Keep me posted if anything changes, okay? I mean it. I'm worried about you. Bobby knows to check in every few days while I'm gone."

Roxy scoffed. "I'll be fine, worry about your own damn self. I don't need Bobby checking in on me. I'm a big girl."

Free rolled his eyes. "Yeah, well, humor me, please."

"Yeah, yeah," the redhead mumbled stonily. "I'll talk to you later, Free. Do me a favor and quit being a dumbass?"

"Yeah, yeah," Free parroted with a chuckle. "Later, Red."

"Bye, you big dummy."

Tossing the phone beside him on the bed, Free stacked his hands beneath his head and gazed up at the ceiling. He hadn't talked to Jodi since Monday night when he'd left her alone in the dark. He was being a coward and he knew it. He'd heard her crying before the door had closed completely, and it had hurt him more than he'd expected it to. Climbing into his truck that night, he'd slammed his hands into the steering wheel, calling himself all the worst names he could think of. He had wanted her so bad; he'd ached with it. He hated himself for leaving her hurting.

Checking the time, he rolled to a sitting position on the edge of the bed. Standing and crossing the room, he pulled his boots on, grabbed his wallet, stuffed the baseball cap on his head, and was out the door minutes later. He drove into town, stopping at a local flower shop on his way in.

"What's the occasion?" Short and plump, the florist ambled around the tiny floral shop, Free right behind her.

"Uhh… I made an ass of myself, and I need to apologize," Free mumbled honestly, dropping his gaze guiltily.

"Ahh," the middle-aged woman said kindly, her eyes knowing. "I've got just what you need, dear boy."

CHAPTER 15

The bell jingled over the door as it opened, and Jodi looked up from the counter where she was ringing up a customer. The welcome froze on her lips, and she dropped her eyes from his quickly. Wrapping the book her customer had chosen in brown paper, she sealed it with a sticker, and then slid it into a brown paper bag stamped with *Turn the Page*'s logo on it. Handing the bag across the counter to the young woman, Jodi said, "Thank you so much for coming in today. We look forward to seeing you again."

As the young woman made her way toward the door, Jodi stepped out from behind the counter and busied herself with straightening a shelf of children's books, keeping her back to him. Jodi could hear his boot heels on the polished wood floor, and knew when he was right behind her. Still, she ignored him, hurt and anger warring for supremacy.

"Jodi, please look at me," he whispered earnestly.

"I'm busy working," she said stiffly, moving on to another shelf. "You can take those back with you when you leave."

She heard the plastic wrapping crinkle noisily as he set the bundle of flowers down on the countertop beside him, then felt his warm hand on her shoulder. She shrugged it off, rounding on him, blue fire spitting from her eyes.

"Don't," she snapped, her voice brittle. "Please go away, Free."

His aquamarine eyes were full of remorse as he stared down into her own. "Jodi," he whispered forlornly, "I'm sorry. I was an ass the other night. You have every right to be upset with me."

Jodi scoffed, crossing her arms over her chest. "I'm not upset."

She knew he knew she was lying. One corner of his mouth tilted up slightly, but the baleful glare she gave him made him straighten his face. "I'm sorry I hurt your feelings."

"You didn't," she muttered, turning again to the bookshelf that didn't really need straightening.

"Mmmhmm."

Waving her hand in his general direction, she snapped, "I'm not interested in whatever roller coaster this is, Free. You're giving me whiplash."

"I know, and I'm sorry," he murmured solemnly, following her as she moved around the store. "Look, I know I messed up. Jodi—" he grated, sidestepping her quickly and forcing her to stop and look at him, his gaze intense, "—I like you. A lot. And that still scares the shit out of me. I have spent the last decade trying everything in my power to get rid of these feelings I have for you. Allowing myself to act on this is strange to me still. Please be patient with me while I learn."

He was good, she admitted sullenly. She dropped her eyes to stare at the floor, studying the pattern of the wood grain in the flooring beneath their feet. She saw his hand reach out toward her, his fingers gripping her chin lightly, tilting her head up until she was staring at him again.

"Will you go with me to Shane's wedding? As my date, I mean?" he asked quietly, his eyes searching hers gently.

"I don't know, Free," Jodi whispered forlornly, her gaze dropping from his. "This back-and-forth thing is too confusing for me. Maybe you were right to leave the other night before anything happened."

"I know it's confusing, and I'm sorry," he murmured earnestly. He sighed. "It's confusing for me, too, I won't lie to you. Like I said, I have spent a decade wrestling with these feelings I have for you." Tipping her chin back up with his fingers, she was forced to look at him. "Because of our age difference. Because I have known you since you were in grade school. Because you are the daughter of one of the best friends I've ever had. You asked me why I didn't come home before now. It's because I knew the second I saw you again I was going to be a goner, and in spite of all those reasons I gave myself to not want you, I still do."

"I can't just be a fling for you while you're here," Jodi whispered, her heart thundering in her chest at his profession.

Free's thumb stroked along the edge of her jawline, making her skin tingle where he touched. "I'm not interested in a fling. How about we take it one day at a time? Be my date for my brother's wedding?"

"Can I think about it?" Jodi breathed. She couldn't focus with him so near.

Free smiled gently. "Of course." He stepped back just as the door of the shop opened, the bell jingling softly. Jodi stepped out from between the shelves they were hidden behind, welcoming the newcomer.

While Jodi showed the guest where to find a set of novels they were looking for as a gift, she was keenly aware of where Free was at all times. He wandered the shelves, picking up random books to peruse before replacing it. When Jodi came back to the counter, Free sauntered over.

"May I get a cup of coffee?" he asked huskily, pulling out his wallet. The muscles of his arms and shoulders bunched and shifted as he moved, the sleeves of his t-shirt barely containing them. Jodi wished she could run her hand along that arm, to feel the muscles and soft, tanned skin of his bicep.

"O-of course," Jodi stuttered, turning quickly to pour a cup of freshly brewed coffee into a cardboard to-go cup for him. Lidding it, she handed it over the counter to him, and as he took it their fingers brushed, sending sparks through her.

He extended cash out to her, but she shook her head. He gave her a baleful look and set it on the counter instead, grumbling, "You'll never make a dime if you keep giving coffee away."

"Consider it a trade," she said, glancing at the elaborate bouquet of flowers still lying on the countertop beside her. "I should probably get those in some water."

Raising the steaming cup of coffee in thanks, Free eyeballed the cash still on the counter, then raised his eyes to hers once more. "Put that in the till, Jodi. I look forward to your answer."

CHAPTER 16

"Well look what the cat dragged in."

Free's mouth lifted in a grin, a chuckle escaping him as he climbed out of the truck, closing the door and lifting his shoulders in a shrug. Gravel crunched beneath his boots as he ambled over to the covered porch that extended the full length of the Big House, where Levi sat in an old wooden rocking chair. A glass tumbler of whisky was in his hand, balanced on one knee that was crossed at the ankle over the other knee.

The sun was beginning to set on the horizon, painting the sky brilliant shades of vermillion and blood orange, extending into the opposite direction where it darkened into violet and indigo. Crossing the wide wooden porch, Free motioned to an empty chair beside his friend. "This seat taken?"

"Doesn't look like it," Levi drawled, though he grinned as he took a sip of the whisky.

Free lowered himself into the chair and sighed, rocking back and forth a few times, running his hands over the soft, worn wooden arms. Taking off the cowboy hat that sat on his head, he crossed one ankle over the other knee, at the same time dropping the hat to the floor beside him. His visit several days before had been brief, only stopping in long enough to say hello. The two old friends sat in silence for a few moments, each staring out over the open field that extended a quarter mile from the front of the house to the road that passed by. Every few minutes, a vehicle would pass in the distance.

The front door opened and Serenity stepped out, the screened door slapping shut behind her. A thin dish towel was tucked into one of the belt loops of her jeans, and she was drying her hands as she walked toward the two men, a smile on her face. "I thought I heard someone drive up," she said and extended a hand, squeezing Free's shoulder in hello before stepping around him to lean down and peck a kiss to Levi's bewhiskered cheek. "Free, would you like a drink?"

"I would love one, but I can get it," Free said and made to stand, but Serenity shushed him gently.

"Nonsense, I'll be right back. What would you like?" she asked, heading back toward the door.

"Whatever Levi is sipping on looks fantastic," Free chuckled, resettling back into the chair. "Thank you."

"You know she's going to come back out with a plate of food for you," Levi rumbled beneath his breath as Serenity walked back into the house. "She's always thought you were too skinny."

Free chuckled again and shook his head, patting his stomach. "I'd love to say I agree, getting old has put on some pounds though."

Levi guffawed, throwing his head back and laughing heartily. Patting his own stomach, he chuckled, "I'd love to say this is old age, but it's all Seren's cooking that's made this old man soft."

Free laughed, eyeing the older man's impressive physique with a sidelong glance. "You look like you're in the same shape as when I left, old man."

Silver hairs threaded through the older man's dark hair and beard, a testament to how much time had passed since Free had been home last. At almost fifty, Levi Kendall was still a handsome man, and built like a brick house. Laugh lines crinkled the corners of Levi's cobalt blue eyes, his smile broad, revealing straight white teeth. Free watched his friend in profile as he took another sip of the whisky.

Serenity came back out, bringing Free a glass highball of whisky and a plate full of beef roast, potatoes, and carrots slathered in a brown gravy, a giant slice of buttered bread on the side. Levi winked at Free as he took the plate with a hearty thank you.

Seren smiled, her baby blue eyes sparkling. Her dark hair was pulled into a high topknot, soft tendrils framing her face. Stepping to Levi's side, Levi shifted his weight, moving his leg and allowing Seren to sit on his knee. She wrapped one arm around Levi's broad shoulders and leaned back into the corner of the chair, her fingers finding the hair at the nape of her husband's neck.

Free's mouth tilted up into a small smile as he watched the two. Free had once had a crush on Serenity Kendall, when he first came to Blue Haven as a teen. He'd envied his friend and mentor the love that his wife gave him. Now, Free loved Seren as a friend, sister, and mother all rolled into one.

As Free finished the plate of food, he said, "That was delicious, Seren, thank you."

Seren smiled and leaned down to press a kiss to Levi's mouth before standing and reaching for Free's empty plate. Grasping one of his hands with her empty one, she squeezed it tightly. "You're welcome, Free. I'm just glad that you're back. We missed you around here. You weren't here long enough the other night when you stopped by."

"I know," Free said softly, squeezing her hand back gently. "I missed you all, too. I wish I could stay."

Levi harrumphed in his seat, grumbling, "You always have a job here or with the company, if you ever decide to come back."

Free nodded, but fell quiet as Seren went back into the house. He still wasn't sure what he was going to do. He'd made a life in Texas in the last seven years, but the thought of leaving Michigan again now that he was back was painful. He didn't want to think of leaving Jodi again, either.

Free motioned to Levi's almost empty glass with his own. "Want another?"

Levi nodded. "Bottle is in the den, thank you."

Free stood and stretched, walking to the front door and letting himself inside the familiar house. He made his way to the wet-bar in Levi's den, picking up the bottle of whisky before heading back through the hallway toward the kitchen. Seren met him there.

"It's good to see you here," she said again, her soft voice like a soothing balm on his tired soul. He'd missed them more than they knew. "It hasn't been the same without you."

Free set the bottle of whisky on the kitchen counter, then leaned his hips back against it, crossing his arms over his chest. He watched Seren as she moved around the kitchen, putting away the roast she'd gotten out to make his plate. She wore a pair of faded, light wash blue jeans, and a white v neck blouse that had a row of buttons down the front, the edges tied together at her waist. Free smiled, thinking how much Jodi looked like her.

Turning and wiping her hands on the towel still tucked into the belt loop of her jeans, she tilted her head to the side slightly. "So, how long are you actually here for?"

Free shrugged again. "Not sure. Originally, I just came home for Shane's wedding."

"And now?" Seren asked, perceptive as ever. He could never keep secrets from Serenity Kendall.

Free swallowed hard, dropping his eyes to the floor, studying the pattern in the tile. "I think you know."

Seren walked over and leaned her hips against the counter next to Free, crossing her arms over her middle and bumping her shoulder into his gently.

"Are you going to tell Levi?" he asked, his voice low.

Seren laughed, shaking her head. "And take that honor from you? I don't think so." Leaning into his shoulder, she whispered, "Levi may be my husband, but there are some things he needs to hear from his best friend, not his wife."

"When did you figure it out?" Free asked quietly.

Serenity breathed in deeply, letting it out slowly. "I think I always knew. Little things, glances between you and Jodi when the other wasn't looking. Then when you left so suddenly and Jodi's reaction to it, I figured something had happened. I just wasn't sure what."

"I left before anything did happen, I swear it," Free whispered hoarsely, looking over at her, his face serious. "I didn't trust myself to stay. I never wanted to betray you and Levi the way I did."

Serenity laughed, ducking her head and he watched as she peered at him sideways. "I knew Jodi had a crush on you for years. When Jodi decides on something, she doesn't usually stop until she gets it. I know my daughter." Again, she bumped her shoulder against his. "And I know you."

"I still have feelings for her," Free admitted quietly, the words sticking in his throat.

"I know," Seren stated simply. Then, "Just… be careful with her, Free. Her heart is tender right now, she's going to guard it fiercely. As will myself, and Levi."

Free nodded solemnly, dropping his gaze to the floor again before sighing heavily and pushing himself away from the counter, picking up the glass bottle. "Here goes nothing."

Seren patted him on the arm gently. "Good luck."

Retreating back out onto the porch, the skyline had darkened, and in the distance, he spotted fireflies. He extended his hand, pouring several fingers worth of whisky into Levi's glass, before sitting and doing the same for his own.

"I thought maybe you got lost," Levi chuckled. "I know it's been a while, but I thought you'd still know your way around the house."

Free's lips tilted up at the corner as he took a sip. "I ran into Seren. We talked for a minute. Actually," Free murmured, "I need to talk to you about something. Promise me you won't hit me though."

"Never a good way to start a conversation," Levi rumbled. He tipped his drink toward Free. "Go ahead."

Free swirled the contents of his glass, his elbows braced on his widespread knees. "It's about Jodi, Levi."

"How drunk do I need to be for this conversation, Freeman?"

Free laughed out loud. "Finish that." Levi did, draining the glass, then held it out for Free to refill. The older man's eyes never left his face, and Free could feel his collar getting hot. He took a deep breath and let it slowly before saying, "I've asked Jodi to go to Shane's wedding with me."

"We were all invited… we'll be there anyway," Levi murmured gruffly, taking another sip of the whisky.

Free nodded. "I've asked her to go with me as my date, Levi. I wanted to tell you myself."

"As your date?" Levi chuckled, but then his eyebrows lowered into a deep V. "You're damn near ten years older than she is, Freeman."

Sitting forward in his seat and leaning his elbows on his spread knees, Free picked up his hat from where he'd set it beside him on the porch earlier. He worried the brim between his fingers, nervousness making him fidgety. Staring out over the field, he nodded again. "I know."

Taking another long drink, Levi held out his glass for Free to fill again. His foot tapped on the wooden slats of the porch, and Free could see the wheels turning in Levi's head. "Is that why you left? Because of Jodi?"

Free swallowed hard, dropping his gaze to the space between his booted feet, and nodded. "Yes," he whispered hoarsely.

"Ooookay," Levi said on a long breath, rocking back and forth in his chair. He muttered a vile curse into the dark. "Do I dare ask why?"

"I swear to you nothing happened back then. But I had to go before something did," Free said honestly, looking his friend in the eyes. "I respect you too much to be dishonest with you. I have feelings for Jodi; I have for a long time."

Levi scowled darkly. He nodded brusquely. "I respect you for telling me. Doesn't mean I like it," Levi grumbled. He tipped his drink toward Free and said fiercely, "You better not hurt her. We may be friends, but that's my baby girl."

"I understand, Levi," Free said quietly.

Levi set his glass down, leaning forward.

"Then you'll understand this," Levi muttered a second before his fist shot out and landed squarely on Free's cheekbone, snapping his head back sharply. Levi leaned back in his chair, shaking his hand out. "And before you start bitchin', I never promised not to hit you."

"*Goddamn*," Free hissed between clenched teeth, touching the tender spot on his cheekbone. He glared over at the older man, though he knew he deserved much worse. "Asshole."

"She cried for days after you left," Levi snapped gruffly. "I suggest you think twice before you do this, Freeman, because I won't stop at one next time." Leaning back in his chair, he tilted one corner of his bewhiskered mouth up in a grin, his blue eyes twinkling. "Now that that's settled, how about we get drunk?"

CHAPTER 17

"Okay, so, run this by me one more time," Tessa said, twisting her face in confusion as she unloaded a box of new releases while Jodi scanned them in and placed them on the shelf. "Our door has been unlocked every single morning, our security tapes are all missing, but nothing has been taken? Why would someone break in and then not even take anything but the video surveillance tapes?"

"I don't know," Jodi murmured, straightening and tucking a stray curl behind her ear. "Until we figure it out, just be careful in the morning when you open. We should probably tell Kit for the weekend, too."

Tessa stood, dusting off the knees of her tight black jeans. A faded Jack Daniels t-shirt was tied at her waist, leaving several inches of her abdomen bare between the knot and the top of her high-rise jeans. Her blonde hair was left down in loose waves, and as she straightened, she pushed her red rimmed glasses back into place on her nose. She bit her bottom lip, her trademark red lipstick unmarred. That lip stain deserved an award for longevity, Jodi thought with a smile.

Tess reached for a bottle of water and chugged half of it in one swallow. "That reminds me, since you're off this weekend for the wedding. What is your answer going to be? Have you decided yet?"

Jodi shook her head, walking over to the counter and taking a bite of the breakfast sandwich on the counter. She and Tessa had come in before opening to get started on new stock that had been delivered the night before. Tessa had brought breakfast for the two of them, which Jodi had been grateful for. That's when Tessa had seen the flowers Jodi had left on the counter overnight and had started in on questioning Jodi.

"I don't know what I'm going to say," Jodi said after swallowing the bite of the breakfast sandwich. "I want to say yes."

"So, say yes."

Jodi rolled her head over her shoulders, stretching the muscles out. The boxes of books they'd carried up from the back were heavy. "I don't know if it's a good idea."

"Seriously, what is so wrong with a fling? How long has it been since you got laid?" Tessa asked candidly, reaching for and taking a bite of her own breakfast. After swallowing, she continued, "What's the saying? Save a horse, ride a cowboy?"

Jodi laughed, choking on a swallow of coffee. "Oh my god! Tess!"

"What?" Tessa exclaimed, laughing to herself. "If you don't, dammit I want a go! He's fine as hell!"

Jodi laughed, shaking her head in disbelief. "I can't believe you just said that."

Tessa threw a wadded-up napkin at her, and it bounced off her shoulder to the floor. "I know you don't want a fling, but I think a good roll in the sack with that man would do you a lot of good. And he's obviously into you. No one sends flowers like that—" she motioned to the bouquet, "—unless they really like someone."

"They were apology flowers," Jodi said.

"Who cares what kind of flowers they were? They're gorgeous. I think you should say yes. Just see where it goes, please! I have no love life. I'm living vicariously through yours," Tessa whined.

"Oh, good lord," Jodi laughed, rolling her eyes. "You might be waiting a lifetime for me to get back into the dating scene."

"I think had your Freeman not shown up when he did, that would be a true statement," Tessa said, clearing the remnants of their breakfast off the counter and throwing it into the trash behind her. She leaned on her forearms across the counter toward Jodi, whispering conspiratorially, "Call me crazy, but I think he showed back up right when he was supposed to."

Picking up her purse, Tessa slipped it on over her head before heading toward the door. "I'll see you later for margaritas, bish."

CHAPTER 18

"Shots! Shots! Shots!"

Kyle the bartender obliged, lining up a row of shot glasses, fluidly pouring out the clear liquor in a line without spilling a drop.

"Shane, you poor bastard, get over here!" Kasey Corcoran, Free and Shane's cousin, shouted over the noise in the crowded dive bar. Kasey, along with Free's aunt and uncle and younger cousin, had traveled north from Texas for the wedding. Kasey had joined them for Shane's bachelor party, and was making sure the poor groom was getting properly hammered. When the small group of guys had downed their shots, Kasey yelled, "Another!"

Free groaned, waving his hand across his throat in a slicing motion, pleading for a respite. He hadn't recovered from the hangover from the night of drinking he'd done with Levi the night before, and was sporting a helluva shiner beneath his left eye. Shane was happy and hammered, having a blast playing billiards and losing brilliantly. Kasey, who was several years younger

134

than Free, was one of the best friends he had in Texas, aside from Roxy. He was glad his extended family had made the trip for his brother's wedding.

Kasey slumped into the empty chair beside Free, wrapping one arm around Free's neck and pulling him in for a tight hug. "Tell me, will there be any hot girls at this wedding this weekend?"

Free wriggled out of the choke hold and chuckled, patting Kasey on the back. "Hell if I know, man. I'm sure you'll seek out one of the bridesmaids. I'll tell you right now, the Kendall women are off-limits. I mean it."

Kasey's dark blonde head bobbed in an enthusiastic and drunk nod. Free hadn't seen his cousin this hammered since the night his girlfriend had broken up with him, and that was three years ago. Kasey was a hellion, but typically was the broody, silent type. This Kasey was in rare form, and Free didn't envy him the hangover he was sure to have in the morning.

"Who gave you the black eye, man?" Kasey asked, gesturing to his bruised face.

Free chuckled again, taking a sip of his PBR bottle. "The Kendall women's dad."

Kasey snickered, "Back not even a week and you're already in trouble." Taking a deep, steadying breath, Kasey asked, "Is that the girl you're hung up on? The Kendall woman?"

Free rolled his eyes and slapped Kasey on the back, laughing, "Guess you'll have to wait and see."

Kasey bobbed his dark blonde eyebrows comically. "Damn straight, I can't wait to meet the chick that stole Freeman Thorp's heart."

Free took another drink of his beer, falling silent. Had Jodi stolen his heart?

Glancing down the bar, Free noticed that Kale, Kasey's younger brother, was starting to look a little green around the gills, so Free excused himself from Kasey and helped the younger man out the back so he could empty his stomach in private. The bushes behind the bar were a haven for drunk patrons, and Free admittedly had used them a handful of times.

Chuckling, Free patted his younger cousin on the back and said, "First time?"

Kale groaned miserably and Free chuckled again. Jordan, Shane's best friend and one of the groomsmen, found them in the back. "Want me to have your uncle take him home?"

Free nodded, still smiling. "Probably should," Free murmured, then helped Kale to his feet and headed to the dark parking lot while Jordan found Adam Corcoran, Kale and Kasey's dad. He had volunteered to be their designated driver for the evening, wanting to make sure everyone got home safely, which they all appreciated greatly. Free was certain this wouldn't be the first trip home Uncle Adam would make.

Waving goodbye as Adam drove away with a miserable Kale in the passenger seat, Free turned to head back into the bar, but was brought up short when a man with dark blonde hair stepped out of a black Lincoln parked several vehicles away.

"You Freeman?" the man asked, walking toward him slowly. He seemed out of place, his nice jeans and button-down shirt not the normal attire you'd find at the dive bar. Free stayed where he was, raising his chin slightly. The man was a couple inches shorter than him, but the glint in the stranger's eyes made Free wary.

"Depends. Who's asking?" Free muttered, eyeing the stranger up and down, as the other man was doing the same to him.

The stranger finished looking him up and down and snorted a derisive laugh. "Of course she didn't tell you."

Free rolled his eyes then, not in the mood to play games in a dark parking lot with a complete stranger, one who obviously knew who he was. "I'm not interested in riddles, man. What are you talking about?"

Stepping forward until only a few feet separated them, the stranger raised his eyes to Free's, and said coolly, "I'm Josh, Jodi's husband. Or didn't she mention that she's married?"

CHAPTER 19

Stretching languidly, Jodi yawned broadly, rubbing the sleep from her eyes. Her foot bumped another, and she turned her head and a smile tugged at her lips. Shaun was sound asleep, her curly hair spread out across the pillow next to Jodi. Rolling out of the queen-sized bed, she was careful not to wake her sister. Pulling on a light robe, she left the bedroom and padded down the hallway quietly. Entering the kitchen, she prepped a large pot of coffee to brew.

The margarita night-bachelorette party had gone off wonderfully. It had turned into a slumber party, something Jodi hadn't done since she was in college. It had been a night full of stiffly poured margaritas, hordes of chips and salsa, and an abundance of laughter. Shaun had fashioned a bridal sash for Cassie to wear for the evening in honor of her upcoming nuptials. They'd played *Cards Against Humanity*, and Jodi had laughed until her sides and cheeks ached. It had been a houseful of giggling women. To Jodi's relief, Shaun had not scheduled any strippers, though she had insisted they watch *Magic Mike* while munching on buckets filled with buttery popcorn.

Jodi had enjoyed having all of them over, she hadn't had that much fun or laughed that hard in years, Josh would have never allowed a gathering such as that to occur while they'd been married.

The large, U-shaped couch in the living room had the pull out drawn, and somehow Cassie and her three bridesmaids had all slept on it together. All she could see was a pile of blankets and heads from where she stood in the kitchen, and she smiled. Tessa and Kit had taken the guest room, and Jodi had made up an extra bed in her writing office for Zoey, who had brought her two month old daughter with her. The baby had been passed from woman to woman the night before, each woman's ovaries exploding at the precious, golden-haired newborn.

Zoey Chandler had been Shaun's best friend since kindergarten, which Jodi attributed to the reason Shaun started dating Tommy, who was Zoey's older brother. Tommy adored Shaun, but Jodi couldn't help but wonder if maybe Shaun needed someone who would challenge her a little more than Tommy did. Her sister was pure fire; she needed someone that was going to nurture the flame without letting it turn into a wildfire, or smothering it completely.

Pouring herself a cup of coffee, she took it with her into the bathroom, starting a hot shower. She showered quickly, an idea forming. Stepping out, she towel dried, walking to the closet to pull on clothes hastily. It was one of the last hot days of autumn, the humidity stifling. She chose a pair of old, comfortably soft cutoff jean shorts that left her legs bare to high thigh, and then pulled on a racerback style tank top. Loathing to leave her heavy hair down in the heat, she piled it high on her head and secured it with a twist, though with the humidity in the air, tendrils curled around her face almost immediately. Sliding her feet into comfortable sandals, she exited the bedroom.

Calling ahead, she placed an order from a local bagel and donut shop nearby, then climbed into the Jeep. Within minutes she was at the small cafe, picking up several large bags laden with assorted bagels, cream cheeses, and donuts. Pulling back into the driveway, she carried two of the bags into the house, saying a quiet good morning to Cassie and the other two bridesmaids, who had awoken and were sipping coffee on the couch. The others were not out of bed yet.

"I brought breakfast," Jodi said softly, setting the bags on the counter. "Cassie, did the guys say where they were staying last night?"

Cassie stretched and yawned broadly, nodding around her yawn. "Shane messaged me last night that they were all back home safe."

"Good," Jodi said and smiled widely. "I'm going to run food over to the guys, I'm sure they're all much more hungover than they expected, and I doubt any of them will be in any shape to make breakfast."

"You're so sweet," Cassie said and smiled. She took another sip of coffee. "And thank you for breakfast and coffee. It smells delicious."

"You're welcome, take your time. I'm just going to run this over and then I'll be back!" Jodi called softly as she headed back out the door. Driving the short way to Shane and Cassie's home, Jodi pulled in and parked, glad to see a plethora of cars were still parked in the driveway. Picking the remaining bags up by the handles, Jodi slid out of the Jeep and climbed the few steps up to the front door.

Before she could knock, the door opened and Shane stepped halfway out, scratching his bare chest and yawning loudly.

"Hi," she said cheerily.

He groaned and clapped one hand to his head, massaging his temples dramatically. "Hiya, JoJo."

"I brought you all breakfast," Jodi said merrily and smiled, holding up the two bags. "I'll just put them on the table, there should be plenty. And I wanted to see Free for just a quick second."

She made to move past him, but he sidestepped quickly, blocking her path into the house. Jodi raised quizzical eyes to his, tilting her head slightly in confusion.

"Uhh… Jodi, honey, that's really nice of you, but you don't want to go in there right now," Shane said and cast an anxious glance backward. "We all had a lot to drink, and Free's not feelin' too good."

"Bachelor parties tend to do that to everyone. You don't look that bad," Jodi teased, winking, though her heart had started racing. "As long as everyone is fully clothed, I think I'll be okay. I'll just be quick—"

"*Jodi*," Shane said a bit more forcefully and stepped backward into the house, using the door as a shield.

"As your friend, I'm telling you, you don't want to see Free right now."

"What's going on?" Jodi whispered, her breath coming in quick, shallow puffs now. Anxiety had begun to claw at her chest. "Is something wrong? Is he okay?"

"Just— just trust me, Jodi. Please," he begged quietly, and when he looked into her eyes again, she saw what looked like pity in his soft brown eyes.

Jodi shook her head slowly, her eyes never leaving Shane's. Understanding dawned, and she was sure her stomach was going to climb its way out of her throat. Her heart thundered in her ribcage, making her feel lightheaded. "He didn't... He wouldn't have..."

"I'm sorry," Shane whispered miserably.

"No," Jodi whispered gruffly and pushed past Shane, dropping the bags of food by the door. She strode down the hall to the bedroom that she knew was their guest room. Shane followed close behind her, doing his best to get in front of her to stop her. She dodged him and shrugged off his hands, flinging the bedroom door open, not caring that it crashed into the wall noisily. Jodi came to an abrupt halt, and Shane ran into her from behind.

Free moaned at the commotion and turned over in bed, opening his eyes. When they lit on Jodi, his head fell back against the pillow before he rolled into a sitting position. When he did, the other occupant in the bed stirred. The blonde-haired woman mumbled something that sounded like "Go back to sleep, baby" and Jodi couldn't move.

His eyes were full of agony as he stared at her, holding the sheet to his lower body. "Fuck."

CHAPTER 20

All the air in Jodi's lungs rushed out and she felt like she was going to faint. Without a word, she turned and walked out of the bedroom.

"Jodi!" she heard Free shout, then the linens rustling, followed by a loud thud and muffled cursing. The commotion must have woken the other guys up, because several men she didn't recognize stood awkwardly by, peering out of other doors and around corners. Moving past Shane and shrugging off his consoling hand, she kept her eyes down, too humiliated to look anyone in the eye.

Breaking into a run when she hit the porch steps, Jodi almost made it to the Jeep before Free caught up to her. "Jodi, stop!"

At the touch of his hand on her shoulder, she came out of her misery induced fog. She spun and faced him angrily. His left cheekbone beneath his eye was bruised, which surprised her momentarily, not having noticed it until now. She realized that his jeans had been hastily pulled on, as they were still unbuttoned, and he was bare-chested. She could see the band of his black boxer briefs above his jeans. His feet were bare, and he was out of breath from sprinting to catch up to her.

"You. Complete. *Ass!*" she railed, punctuating every word with a hard shove into his chest, pushing him back and making him lose his balance in the gravel. "For someone pretending to give a shit about me, not wanting to hurt my feelings by sleeping with me, you sure do get around a lot with other women! You're a fucking asshole, Freeman! Ugh!" she shouted, clenching her fists at her sides.

"Jodi," Free growled, taking a step closer.

She backed away and pointed a finger at his bare chest. "Get away from me," Jodi whispered fiercely, blue fire shooting from her eyes. Spinning on her heel, she made it two full strides toward the Jeep before he caught up with her. She made to open the door, but his hand shot out, holding the door closed. "Let me go, Freeman!"

"No, not until we talk," Free snapped, bending his face close to hers, the blue-green of his eyes luminous.

"I have nothing to say to you anymore," she snarled, yanking on the door handle, but it didn't budge with his strength holding it closed. "Let go!"

"Not until we talk," he repeated in a growl, wrapping the fingers of his other hand around her upper arm and hauling her away from the car door, placing himself between her and the Jeep.

"*Damn you*, Freeman Thorp!" she shouted when he released her several feet away. "You could have had me the other night! I wanted you to stay, I wanted *you*! You walked out on me! Then you came *begging* me for forgiveness, with that load of crap about how you feel about me. Just to turn around and fuck some other woman *the next day!*" she cried, mortified when tears stung her eyes. Unable to stem the tears, they fell down her cheeks. "Dammit, why *her*? Why not *me*?"

"Number one, I wasn't pretending, and my feelings for you aren't a load of crap. Number two, I didn't fuck anybody last night. And number three—" he snarled, cutting her off when she went to open her mouth to argue, "—I had just found out you're *married*, Jodi!" Free shouted, throwing his bare arms out wide. Her heart stopped, then thundered back to life painfully. Pointing one accusing finger at her chest, he bellowed, "You love to crucify me for all of my wrongdoings, but yet you never mentioned that you're married! I had to find out from *your husband!*"

"I am not married," Jodi seethed, swiping at the tears sliding down her cheeks. "My divorce to that narcissistic bastard was finalized three months ago, though I'm sure he failed to mention that. We've been separated for over a year. This is what Josh does, Free. He *thrives* on causing drama and making my life hell."

"Why did I have to find out from him, huh? Cornered me at the bar last night," Free snarled, sweeping his arm out to point in the general direction of town. He laughed bitterly, his aquamarine eyes fierce, his chest heaving with fury. "Here I was, spilling my guts out to you about how I feel about you like some big dumb idiot, and the whole time you're hiding that fucking bombshell! So, yeah. I was angry as hell, and got really fucking drunk last night, Jodi."

Staring up into his face, twisted with anger and pain, Jodi couldn't stop the tears that continued to track down her cheeks. Her shoulders started to tremble from trying to hold back her tears, and she sobbed once, one hand flying up to cover her mouth before more could follow. Taking a half step away from him, she turned so that she could hide her face. Her shoulders began to shake in earnest, and another broken sob escaped her. Wrapping her arms around herself tightly, she cried mournfully.

"Jodi," he whispered after long moments, his voice thick with emotion. "Jodi, please don't cry. Yell at me, scream at me. I can handle anything but your tears."

She heard when he took several steps toward her, felt when he placed his warm hands on her shaking shoulders. Shrugging away from his touch, she took a shuddering breath. He wouldn't let her go easily, though, as he replaced his hands on her shoulders gently, putting light pressure on her arms until she turned so that she was facing him. Embarrassed, she refused to lift her eyes to his.

"I didn't sleep with her," he whispered despondently, his thumbs rubbing circles on her skin where they rested. His fingers tightened marginally when she tried to pull away at his words. "Not in the way that you think I did, anyway. I was drunk and angry. I know that doesn't excuse what I did, but I swear to you, I didn't sleep with her."

"Don't," Jodi whimpered wretchedly, trying to pull away from the hold his hands had on her shoulders. "Please, just… don't."

The front door opened, and the blonde woman stepped out, walking quickly to her car without glancing in their direction. The car started, and she pulled out of the driveway without a backward glance. Dust hung in the air after she pulled away, their silence stretching out interminably.

She sniffled once and finally braved a look up into his face. She avoided looking at his naked chest, or lower to his abdomen where the open V of his jeans revealed the elastic waistband of his boxer briefs. He was deeply tanned by the Texas sun. He was beautiful and even now she ached to touch him.

She reached up and swiped again at the tracks her tears had left. Gathering her into his arms, he pulled her close, and she struggled for only a fraction of a heartbeat before settling into his embrace, wrapping her own arms around his bare middle, her fingers trailing along the muscles of his back briefly. His chin rested on the top of her head, where she buried her face into the curve of his chest.

"I'm sorry," she heard him whisper morosely.

Jodi nodded into his chest, whispering back, "Me, too."

Taking a deep, shuddering breath, she pulled away, doing her best to straighten her clothes, running one hand over her hair, fidgeting nervously.

"I need to go," she whispered, unable to meet his gaze. She knew she had to look like a wreck.

Embarrassment swept through her again, making her cheeks flame.

Free nodded, though she saw it more out of her peripheral vision, still unable to look at him. "Jodi…"

She stepped around him, reaching for the door handle of the Jeep and pulling it open. She climbed in, closing the door behind her before starting it.

Finally daring to look him in the eyes, she raised her tear-stained face to his. His aquamarine eyes filled with anguish as he looked at her. Tucking one strand of curls behind her ear, she whispered, "Bye, Free," before putting the Jeep in reverse and backing out of the driveway.

When Jodi looked in the rearview mirror, Free remained standing where he'd been, staring after her as she drove away. A fresh round of tears started anew, and Jodi was powerless to stop them as they fell.

CHAPTER 21

"Don't," Free snarled when he walked back into the house. Shane shrugged his shoulders where he leaned against the doorframe leading into the kitchen, one hand wrapped around a cup of coffee.

"I didn't say a word," Shane muttered, raising his eyebrows and taking a sip of his coffee.

Free strode past his brother into the kitchen, going to the cupboard and grabbing a coffee cup. Kasey sat at the kitchen table, and Free could sense the two younger men's eyes on him as he poured himself a cup of coffee. Putting the coffee pot back, Free braced himself against the counter with his hands, dropping his head between his shoulders.

"You knew she was married," Free stated from where he stood, not moving.

Shifting his weight where he stood, Shane looked down guiltily. "Yes, I knew she had gotten married. I also knew she had gotten a divorce. I had no idea you didn't know. It's not like it was a secret."

Bringing his head up, he looked over at his brother. "How was I supposed to know from two thousand miles away? Why did no one ever tell me she had gotten married to begin with? No one could have mentioned it in passing on a phone call for christ sake?"

"I didn't tell you because I knew it was going to hurt. You would have been a wreck, and I didn't want to be responsible for that. I also knew it wasn't going to last," Shane snapped, pushing himself away from the doorframe. "Josh Murphy is a fucking tool. No one wanted her to marry him."

"How long?" Free asked.

Shane shrugged his shoulders. "I don't know, Free. It wasn't long. Maybe a year? Less? They've been separated for longer than they were even married, man. Jodi doesn't like to talk about it, I think she's embarrassed. From what I've heard—and this is all second hand, mind you—he was abusive, I guess he put his hands on her a couple times. He's an alcoholic, and had multiple affairs throughout the majority of the time they dated and into their marriage. That's all I've heard. I don't know anything more than that."

"That jackass put his hands on her?" Free snarled, standing up straight. Shane gave him a look, and Free took a deep breath.

"Like I said, I don't know all the details. It's just what I've heard from people like Shaun and Levi," Shane muttered, pouring himself another cup of coffee. Kasey stood and crossed the kitchen to the coffee pot, pouring himself a cup as well. "I guarantee he knew what he was doing last night when he talked to you. He's crazy as hell."

Free blew out his breath and hung his head again, muttering a string of self-deprecating curses. "I don't blame Jodi for thinking what she did. It took me by surprise, and the more I thought about it the angrier I got."

"I didn't even know what the hell happened last night," Shane said, shaking his head. "One second you were fine, the next you came inside angrier than a pissed off hornet. You started slamming shots, and then you were making out with that blonde. Did you…?"

"No," Free muttered, shaking his head. "I didn't."

Free walked over to the kitchen table and slumped into one of the chairs. His head ached abominably. He'd done some stupid shit in his life, but this took the cake. Last night he'd let his pride take over, and instead of talking to anyone about it and getting the truth, he'd jumped to the conclusion that Jodi was lying to him, and had done the only thing he knew how to do to get Jodi Kendall— Jodi Murphy— off his mind. He cringed at the name, hating it with a deep passion.

CHAPTER 22

"How dare you?"

Josh straightened from where he was standing, loading a cooler with ice and a pack of beer cans. Two golf bags leaned against the back of his Lincoln, ready to be loaded into the trunk along with the cooler. His eyes traveled up and down Jodi from toes to the top of her head.

Angrier than she'd been in a long time, she'd driven to Josh's apartment, slamming the Jeep door with more force than necessary. He was wearing shorts and a short-sleeved polo shirt, flip flops on his feet. He leaned his shoulder against the side of the car, crossing his ankles casually, crossing his arms over his chest. His hazel eyes were bright; she knew he was enjoying seeing her flustered, but she was too angry to care.

"You look like hell, Jodi. What happened?"

"You stay away from me, stay away from Freeman, stay away from my home, and stay away from my store!" Jodi snarled, pointing her finger at his chest angrily. She was shaking with fury. The door of his condo opened and a woman with light brown hair stepped out, wearing a golf skirt and polo'd tank top. Jodi laughed derisively. "How dare you seek him out and tell lies! We are not married anymore, Josh! I am allowed to move on, just like you have! At least I waited until the divorce was final, because you sure didn't!"

"I don't know what you're talking about," Josh murmured innocently, pushing away from the side of the vehicle. "Are you sure you're okay? Maybe you need some help?"

Barely controlled rage trembled through her, making her entire body shake. "You know what you did, and I know you're the one breaking into my store. Leave me alone, Josh."

Josh looked over at the brunette, who was watching them closely. He blew out his breath and shook his dirty blonde head, "Yeah… you're acting crazy. You need to leave."

"Go to hell," Jodi seethed. Walking back to the Jeep, she opened the door and climbed in. "Stay away from me."

"You came here," Josh chuckled, holding up his hands in feigned innocence, walking several steps forward to stand next to her window. Leaning forward and whispering quietly, "You have no proof that I was at your store, Jodi."

"Not yet, but I will."

He laughed then, his eyes narrowing on her face. "If you want to go down this road, that's your choice. Have a good day."

Jodi backed out of the driveway of his condo, driving away, still shaking. Pulling over onto the side of the road when she'd gotten far enough away, she screamed in the private confines of the car, then buried her face in her hands, crying until she was hyperventilating.

She knew his game, knew the way he worked to threaten her, using manipulation and gaslighting her into questioning her own sanity. She hated him. She'd hated herself for a long time, hated how weak she'd been, how weak he still made her.

Pulling herself together, she scrubbed at her face, snorting a laugh when she looked at herself in the rearview mirror. One thing she knew for sure, she would catch him in the act of breaking into her shop. If she knew Josh, he wasn't going to give up anytime soon.

CHAPTER 23

Slipping the simple gold hoops into her ears, Jodi looked around in surprise when a knock sounded on the door. She had showered and pampered herself all morning in preparation for the wedding celebration later in the afternoon. Her makeup had been deftly applied and she was pleased with the results, grateful that the puffiness from crying the day before had subsided and was easy to conceal.

The temperature had cooled slightly from the day before, the humidity lower, to which Jodi was thankful. She had left her hair unrestrained, and her curls cascaded down her back in ringlets, her hair parted drastically to one side, the other side clipped back with a decorative comb.

The dress she had chosen was navy blue and fit snuggly, showing off her curves. It hit just above her knee, with a slit up one side, leaving one thigh tantalizingly bare. The sleeves were long, flowy, and cuffed at her wrists. The rounded neckline cut across her chest below her collarbone, but the back dipped into a deep V to the middle of her spine, just above the small of her back.

Another knock sounded, and she padded on bare, freshly manicured feet to the door. Opening it, her heart climbed into her throat, and she swallowed hard.

"Wow," he whispered hoarsely, his aquamarine eyes traveling over her, and she was just vain enough to enjoy his appreciation.

"What are you doing here?" she asked, her throat tight.

"Uhh," he stuttered, bringing his gaze back to hers. The discoloration under his left eye was darker today, his eye swollen just the slightest. It looked painful to Jodi. He shook his head slightly and one corner of his bewhiskered mouth tilted up. "I'm sorry, I—" he blew his breath out. "You look stunning."

Jodi gave him a baleful look, but said, "Thank you." She waited several seconds before repeating, "What are you doing here, Free?"

"You never gave me an answer."

"I'm pretty sure going to bed with another woman two nights ago was enough of an answer," Jodi muttered.

"I didn't sleep with her, Jodi, I told you that," Free said earnestly. "I swear to you, nothing happened. I was just angry and really drunk. Which I know—" he said and raised his hands in front of him placatingly "—isn't an excuse. I never meant to hurt you. My pride was hurt and I reacted abominably, and I'm so sorry."

Chewing on the inside of her cheek, she nodded and then sighed, still staring at the bruise on his cheekbone. Opening the door wider, she moved aside. "Come in. Let me do something with that bruise."

Free's mouth tilted up again slightly, stepping through the door. Jodi closed it and walked down the hall to the bathroom, coming back a few seconds later with her makeup bag. She motioned for him to follow her to the kitchen, sitting him in one of the barstools that she moved in front of the sliding glass door, which offered the best light.

Opening the makeup bag, she rifled through, looking for a shade dark enough to match his tanned skin.

The way he sat perched on the stool, one booted foot on the floor, the other bent at the knee with his boot heel hitched on the bottom rung, made Jodi vitally aware of his body. She kept her eyes away from him, though she had noticed how incredible he looked in his suit. Slim fitted, it detailed every inch of his body, much to Jodi's consternation. Light gray suit pants hugged his lower body in a way that made Jodi blush. A matching, slim cut vest was buttoned closed over a black dress shirt that he had left unbuttoned at his throat, a forest green neck tie fashioned loosely around his neck. He wasn't wearing a hat today, and his dark hair that was slightly too long looked soft and fell over his brow.

Turning back to him, she held up two different colors of concealer next to his face, matching the closest one to his complexion before beginning to apply it with a makeup sponge. Dabbing it gently over the bruise, careful not to cause him undue discomfort, she was distinctly aware of how close they were. His thighs had parted, allowing her to stand between them, granting her closer access. The cologne he had on was intoxicating to her senses. That tantalizing mix of cedarwood and citrus that she had begun to associate with him. He was silent as he watched her work.

"I never meant for you to find out the way you did," she murmured quietly after a while, never taking her eyes away from what her fingers were doing. "It wasn't fair of me to keep it from you. My marriage to Josh was brief. I'm not proud of it. It's a time in my life that I want so badly to forget."

"He cheated on you?" Free asked gently, and her eyes finally met his.

She nodded, and then shrugged one shoulder in dismissal. "Among other things." His mouth tightened and she smiled wanly, reaching for a setting powder to make sure the concealer stayed in place all day. Jodi sighed heavily, zipping the makeup bag closed and setting it back on the counter next to them. "I'm sure you have questions, and I will answer all of them, but not today, please."

Jodi stopped breathing when one of his hands reached out and slid around her waist, putting the lightest of pressure on her back until she inched forward closer to him. Their faces were at the same level where he remained seated on the barstool, her standing between his thighs. His other hand came up and cupped her cheek in his palm, turning her face toward his. She let out a shuddering breath, her gaze captured in his like a vice.

"Free…"

He lifted his head slightly, brushing his lips across hers once, twice, before they pressed and stayed. The fingers of the hand cupping her cheek slid until they were tangled in the hair at the back of her head, using them to pull her lips closer to his own. His mouth settled firmly over hers, his short, trimmed beard tickling her slightly, his tongue delving deeply into hers, kissing her slowly, sweetly.

Jodi's hands slid around to his sides, her fingers gripping lightly the fabric of his vest. Breaking away to catch her breath, Jodi pressed her forehead against his. The hand at her back slid down and around until his fingers touched the bare skin of her thigh that peeked out of the high slit in her dress. His breath was harsh against her lips, matching her own. His palm slid flat around to the back of her thigh, beneath the fabric of her dress.

Jodi was on fire.

Their mouths met again fiercely, kissing hungrily. She felt more than heard his growl of approval when she let her body settle against his front, and she gasped when she felt his hardness at her belly. The hand on the back of her thigh squeezed tightly, then soothed gently. His fingers were dangerously close to the cleft of her thighs, and she was already wet and achy.

Free tore his mouth from hers, dropping his forehead to her shoulder, where he panted heavily. "Fuck, Jodi." When he had caught his breath, he raised his head to look at her, sweeping stray tendrils of hair away from her face with his fingers. "Shane's going to have my hide if I'm late. Will you come with me? Please?"

Jodi blushed, thinking of another way she'd like to come with him. He must have read her mind, because his eyes darkened lasciviously and he grinned slyly, slapping one of her ass cheeks with the palm of his hand sharply. "That's for later, Jodi."

She backed away and he stood, running his hand down over his distended fly, making her blush again.

Backing her up against the counter, Free ducked his head and kissed her again soundly before growling, "Yeah, that's what you do to me. Ready to go?"

"Uhh, almost," Jodi stuttered, flustered. "I just need to grab my purse and slip on my shoes."

Free walked with her into the living room, waiting at the door for her. She padded down the hallway to the bedroom, picking up a gold beaded clutch and slipping her feet into nude heels. She stopped in the bathroom to check her makeup, reapplying lipstick after being thoroughly kissed. Meeting him back at the door, he extended his hand out to her, and she placed her hand in his as he opened the door and escorted her out. He assisted her down the porch steps, then held the door open for her and helped her climb into the passenger seat of his truck. He rounded the hood of the truck and climbed in beside her, starting the engine.

Free looked over at her as he fastened his seatbelt, grinning broadly. "I can't stop staring at you."

Jodi blushed and said a quiet, "Thank you." He took her hand in his, squeezing lightly. "You look very handsome, too."

"Thank you," he said and raised her hand to his lips, kissing the backs of her fingers tenderly. "And thank you for covering up that bruise."

"What happened?" Jodi asked, laughing. She still couldn't believe the last hour had transpired. So much for sticking to her guns. She was powerless where Free was concerned.

"Uhh," Free hedged, looking over at her nervously. He made a face. "Your dad, actually."

"What?" Jodi exclaimed. "Why would he hit you?"

Free chuckled darkly, squeezing her hand again. He drove leisurely, his other hand draped over the steering wheel loosely. He looked over at her. "I may or may not have told your dad I had asked you out."

"You told him?" Jodi asked, shocked.

Free shrugged. He slowed for a red light, stopping. "I knew he was going to be here today. I thought I owed him the courtesy of finding out about us from me beforehand, that way he wouldn't do this—" he gestured to his face, "—at the wedding when I lean in to do this—"

He leaned over the console and pressed a kiss to her surprised mouth, dipping his tongue into her mouth languidly. When he pulled away, he grinned, his straight white teeth making her melt all over again.

"Because I plan on doing that a lot," he murmured huskily before turning his attention back to the light, which had just turned green.

Pulling in and parking, Free hopped out of the truck and came around to her door, opening it and assisting her out. The ceremony location was a secluded park shaded by towering maple trees. The site was used frequently for weddings and the landscapers had paved a walkway from the parking lot to the ceremony location.

Taking her hand in his, they walked hand in hand down the walkway. Autumn florals bloomed along either side of the path. In the distance, Jodi could see white chairs lined up in front of an immense willow tree. Several men in suits that matched Free's were mingling along the walk. Beyond the ceremony site, string lights made a path toward a large white tent, where the reception would take place.

"I'm sorry you had to be so early," Free said, looking down at her while they walked.

"I don't mind," she said and smiled. Shane found them moments later, walking up and hugging Jodi tightly. "Congratulations, Shane. You look so handsome!"

Shane chuckled nervously, rolling his shoulders. "Thank you, sweetheart. I was starting to worry that Free wasn't going to make it back in time."

"I touched up his face," Jodi said, motioning to the side of Free's face that had previously sported the dark bruise. "I thought Cassie might appreciate it for the pictures."

"Nice work," Shane said and laughed, checking out his brother's face. "Can't even tell it was there."

A tall, dark blonde-haired stranger sidled up to the three of them, wearing the same light gray suit and vest, black shirt, and green tie as Free and Shane. Free turned to Jodi, saying, "Jodi, this is my cousin, Kasey. Kasey, this is Jodi Kendall."

The blonde's gray-blue eyes widened, and he extended his hand to her. "Ahh, so *you're* the famous Kendall woman."

Jodi smiled nervously, glancing at Free, who rolled his eyes comically. "Nice to meet you, Kasey," Jodi said with a smile.

Kasey dug a flask out of his back pocket, offering it first to Shane, who took it with a thank you, taking a swig. Shane handed it to Free, who took a shot, before offering it to Jodi. She laughed, then said, "Shit, why not?"

She took a tentative sip, the cinnamon whisky burning all the way down.

"I like her," Kasey whispered loudly, jabbing Free in the ribs.

"I do, too," Free murmured, winking down at her.

More guests had begun to arrive, and the wedding coordinator came walking smartly over to them, clipboard in hand. "Shane, dear, it's time to get lined up. I'm gathering all the groomsmen now, if you three want to head over."

Shane nodded, and Jodi could see the nerves come back full force. She reached up and hugged him tightly, whispering, "I'm so happy for you, Shane."

He squeezed her tightly back, breathing in deeply. "I'm happy for you, too, sweetheart. I'll see you afterward!"

Shane released her and Kasey winked, offering her another shot. She shook her head, no, laughing. The two walked away, following the lady with the clipboard. Free turned to her, clasping her face in both hands and kissing her thoroughly again. "I could do that all day," he husked against her lips. "I'll find you after the ceremony?"

"Of course," Jodi breathed. She was never going to get used to how easy being with Free was. Butterflies still erupted in her belly whenever he touched her, but she felt at home in his arms, which terrified her more than she wanted to admit.

"Free, come on," Shane called back, and Free grinned at her once more before following his brother toward the altar.

CHAPTER 24

Jodi remained at the entrance of the ceremony site, waiting for others she knew would be arriving. At the sound of her sister's voice, she turned, smiling broadly before her mouth dropped open at the sight of her.

Shaun's black dress had a corseted top that delineated her breasts and narrow waist, thin straps that went over her tanned shoulders, and a tightly fitted, ruched skirt that hit mid-thigh, leaving her long legs bare. As if she wasn't tall enough, black sky-high heels adorned her feet. Her long, dark hair had been straightened and looked soft to the touch.

"Damn, Shaun," Jodi said and whistled appreciatively as Shaun stopped beside her. "You look hot!"

Shaun grinned. "Thank you. What about you, Miss Thing. You look incredible yourself!" Leaning down, she whispered, "So, are you here with Free?"

Jodi nodded. "I agreed to be his date."

Shaun wiggled her eyebrows and Jodi laughed. "And...?"

Jodi shrugged. "Guess we'll see how the night goes."

"Mom and Dad were right behind me," Shaun said and turned, waving. Serenity and Levi were walking down the pathway, hand in hand, followed by Jodi's other siblings, Warren, Tristan, and Fallon. They made a handsome group, Jodi admitted fondly.

Serenity's royal blue sheath dress was the same color as the late summer sky, her dark hair pulled into a sleek French knot. Levi, ruggedly handsome as ever, had traded his usual faded blue jeans for a pair of black slacks. A white button-down shirt was tucked into the waistband of his slacks, though his shirt had been left unbuttoned at his throat and he did not have a tie. A black blazer that made his shoulders look impossibly broad completed his ensemble.

Jodi's brothers, Warren and Tristan, were dressed more casually. Warren had on gray slacks and a white button-down shirt, foregoing a tie as well. Tristan wore a pair of khakis and a light blue polo shirt, and Jodi smiled; it was the best they could hope for from the seventeen-year-old that rarely changed out of mechanic coveralls. Fallon, the baby of the family, was fourteen and a mini version of Jodi and Shaun. She had on a simple, dusty blue sundress, and her dark, wavy hair had been left down around her shoulders.

When the Kendall clan met up with Shaun and Jodi, they exchanged hellos and hugs, before being seated by the ushers. Jodi was surprised when they were escorted to the first row, Seren and Levi given the seats typically reserved for the parents of the groom. Seren immediately got teary eyed, grabbing the small packet of tissues awaiting her on the seat of her chair. Shaun rolled her eyes and Jodi patted her mother's shoulder. Out of the corner of her eye, she saw Tristan hand Shaun a five-dollar bill, muttering sourly, "She cried before we even sat down!"

Jodi sat between Levi and Shaun, the rest of the Kendall's filling the seats along the first row. Shaun turned and smiled when Zoey arrived, baby Verity in her arms. She sat in the row of seats directly behind them, along with others Jodi assumed were part of Shane and Free's extended family.

When nearly all the seats were filled, the officiant walked out to stand at the center of the altar, followed by Shane and his groomsmen. They lined up on the side closest to Jodi and her family, and she blushed when Free winked at her from where he stood next to Shane.

Soft music began to play from around them and Jodi turned in her seat just as the bridesmaids began to walk down the aisle one at a time. Each woman wore a different style dress that complimented her body perfectly. Jodi looked up into the majestic, sweeping branches of the maple tree they sat beneath, the sun filtering through the leaves high above them, the exact same color as the dresses of the women that walked toward the altar now.

Jodi looked back when the officiant said softly, "Please stand for the bride."

The music changed as they all stood, and Jodi recognized it as an acoustic instrumental version of Elvis Presley's "Can't Help Falling In Love", and tears instantly filled her eyes.

While everyone turned to watch Cassie as she came into view, Jodi instead turned to look at Shane, wanting to catch his first glimpse of his bride. She wasn't disappointed.

The beaming smile on his face was brilliant to look at as he watched the stunningly beautiful woman walking toward him. The tears in Jodi's eyes spilled over and she smiled broadly. This moment was her favorite part of weddings.

Jodi's eyes flit to Free and she blushed when she realized he was watching her. The officiant asked them to sit, and as they all took their seats, he began, "Cassandra and Shane would like to take a moment to thank you all for being here with them today…"

Cassie was trembling slightly where she stood, and Jodi's heart melted when Shane captured her hands in his, squeezing them gently, and the nervous energy seemed to disappear from the bride at his touch. The love that fairly radiated from the two was palpable and more tears stung Jodi's nose as she witnessed the commitment they promised to each other.

Jodi's eyes sought Free again, and she smiled at the loving grin that tugged at his mouth and crinkled his eyes at the corners as he stood beside his brother.

When his eyes slid to hers and held, her breath stalled in her throat. What could have only been seconds felt like an eternity as they stayed just like that, lost in each other.

Jodi was pulled from her reverie as the officiant called out, "You may now kiss your bride, Shane," and Shane didn't waste a heartbeat before pulling his glowing bride to him for a scorching kiss.

Next to her, Shauntelle put her fingers to her lips and whistled loudly as the guests stood, applause ringing out.

As Shane and Cassie ended their first kiss as husband and wife, Jodi beamed when the officiant called out proudly, "It is my pleasure to introduce to you for the first time, *Mr. and Mrs. Shane Thorp!*"

The newlyweds walked back up the aisle hand-in-hand to rounds of cheers, whistles, and applause. Free stepped forward, extending his elbow to Cassie's sister and Matron of Honor, escorting her back down the aisle. After the bridal party, the Kendall family made their way to the receiving line, hugging Cassie and Shane hard. Seren was still dabbing at tears as she hugged Shane tightly. "I'm so proud of you, honey," Jodi heard her mom say.

"Thank you for being here," Shane murmured, emotion clogging his throat. "It means a lot to me to have you all here."

Levi clapped the young man on the back, shaking his hand, before saying gruffly, "You're family, son. We wouldn't have missed it for anything. Cassie, my dear, you make a beautiful bride!"

Jodi hugged Cassie first, welcoming her to the family and said reverently, "This dress is absolutely stunning on you!" The young woman thanked her and squeezed her hand. Jodi squeezed it back and smiled once more before turning to Shane, who bear hugged her hard, lifting her off the ground and making her laugh. He kissed her cheek as he set her down, and she whispered, "I'm so happy for you. You two were meant for each other."

Shane grinned and looked over at his new bride and nodded. "I don't know how I got so lucky. Thank you for being here, Jodi. I love you, sis."

Jodi wrinkled her nose as tears threatened again, slapping his arm lightly. "Don't make me cry again. Love you, too."

Jodi stepped toward Free where he stood next to his brother, and he surprised her by leaning down to press his lips to the corner of her mouth fleetingly, making butterflies take flight in her middle. His lips moved against her skin as he whispered, "I'll find you inside," and she nodded, too breathless to speak.

A short time later, Free found Jodi at the bar in the reception tent, waiting for a glass of champagne from Kyle the bartender. He slid one hand, palm flat, around her waist and her body tingled deliciously at the contact.

"Ready for a party?" he breathed in her ear, then grinned when she shivered slightly. She nodded, looking up at him. "My aunt and uncle are here, I'd like you to meet them, if that's okay."

"Free, do you want a drink while you're here?" Kyle asked before Jodi could respond.

Free nodded, then said, "I'll take a whisky on the rocks, please." Kyle had it made in seconds, handing it over to Free, who took a generous sip. "Thank you," he said, placing cash in the tip jar. "We'll be back."

Free took Jodi's hand in his, leading her around the gorgeously decorated tent. Guests were milling around, getting refreshments from the bartenders, and handsomely dressed caterers were busy setting out hors d'oeuvres. The tables were covered in crisp white tablecloths and tasteful centerpieces.

"Freeman!"

Jodi turned to see a woman with light brown hair making her way toward them, followed by a tall, black haired man with broad shoulders and an impressive black mustache. He reminded Jodi of the actor Tom Selleck.

Free smiled and reached out to hug the woman, then shook hands with the man.

"Jodi," he said and turned to her, "this is my mother's sister, my Aunt Leah, and her husband, my Uncle Adam. This is Jodi Kendall."

Jodi smiled warmly and shook both of their hands. "It's nice to meet you."

"How is Kale feeling?" Free asked his uncle, who chuckled.

"I don't think he's going to be doing any drinking like that for a long time," Adam laughed, raising his glass to his lips. "He's still a little queasy."

"Kasey mentioned Sara wasn't able to make it," Free said to his aunt, who nodded.

"She actually just had her baby a couple days ago," Leah said and beamed proudly, pulling out her cell phone to show them both pictures of the newborn. "We figured Shane and Cassie wouldn't mind her and Mason missing out."

Free smiled as he looked at the photo of the newborn. "He's perfect!"

They were joined by Kasey, who was bringing his mother a glass of wine. Leah accepted it with a quiet thank you. Jodi liked Free's family very much.

Kasey was incredibly tall, perhaps six foot five, and was extraordinarily handsome in his suit. Vivid gray-blue eyes didn't seem to miss anything going on around him, but Jodi could see the mischievousness in their depths. He was reserved, but in a mysterious way. He was also extremely quick witted with a razor-sharp tongue.

As they stood talking, Jodi saw Kasey's eyes widen and his mouth fell open the slightest bit, his drink stalled halfway to his lips. Jodi followed his gaze to find what had captured his attention so ardently and nudged Free when she realized it was her sister, Shauntelle.

Shaun, glass of champagne in hand, along with Tristan and Zoey, who was still holding the wiggling infant, were making their way around the outskirts of the tent, looking for their seats.

Free leaned over to Kasey and muttered into his cousin's ear, "Remember when I said stay away from the Kendall women? That's one of them." Then, handing him a napkin, he teased, "Here, you're drooling."

"Fuck you, man," Kasey snapped, though he did finally close his mouth, averting his gaze, but it quickly found its way back to the tall bombshell.

As Jodi watched, Shaun's eyes came up as if sensing the ardent stare, locking with Kasey's. Kasey didn't lower his gaze however, instead, raising his glass to her in a subtle salutation from across the room. Shaun, not one to back down herself, stared back until Kasey looked away. Jodi smiled, confident her sister had just met her match.

Free drained his glass, then motioned to hers. "Would you like another drink?"

"Yes, please," Jodi said appreciatively. He trailed his fingers along the exposed line of her spine, and she shivered, her breath hitching. He winked down at her as he took her glass from her hand, and then he was gone, disappearing into the crowd.

Jodi made her way over to her sister, sitting down next to her. Shaun motioned with her head over to where she'd just been standing. "Who is that?"

Jodi smiled, then hid it before her sister could see it. "That—" she whispered, "is Free's cousin, Kasey."

Shaun made a disgruntled sound in her throat. "He seems like an ass."

Jodi laughed and turned to look at her, admonishing gently, "Shauntelle Kendall! You haven't even met him! Just because he's ruffled your feathers doesn't make him an ass."

"He's cocky and it's damned irritating, the way he keeps looking at me," she muttered sourly.

"Then maybe you shouldn't have worn that outfit," Jodi whispered conspiratorially, winking. "He actually seems really nice."

Shaun rolled her eyes and brushed her hair over her shoulder, away from her face, taking another sip of her champagne. "Tommy should be here soon; he wasn't able to get out of work early enough to make the ceremony."

Jodi rolled her eyes but smiled.

Free found her, handing her a full glass of champagne, a fresh whisky in his hand. He leaned down and asked, "Are you okay for a few? The bridal party is being summoned for photos."

Jodi turned and smiled, "Of course."

He pressed a kiss to her lips, then was gone again. Shaun leaned in close, wiggling her eyebrows at her, then whispered, "Yeah, you're getting laid tonight. Bow-chicka-wow-wow."

CHAPTER 25

"If I may, I now introduce you all to Mr. and Mrs. Shane Thorp!" a loud voice came over the speakers strategically placed around the tent. The sun had begun to set, and hundreds of candles had been lit throughout, casting everything in a soft glow. The bride and groom walked in and a cheer rose among the seated guests. Cassie's smile was bright, and Shane grinned broadly.

As best man, Free gave a beautiful, heartfelt toast, as did Cassie's sister as matron of honor. Dinner was delectable. As the servers, dressed in all black, cleared plates, the same man that had introduced Shane and Cassie now said, "Please give your attention to the new Mr. and Mrs. as they take the floor for their first dance."

Shane led Cassie out to the middle of the dance floor and a familiar, romantic country song started to play. The two seemed to glide around the floor fluidly, perfectly in sync with the other. Jodi dabbed at tears, shushing Shaun when the younger woman made fun of her.

Shortly after, upbeat music started to thump from the DJ's booth, and the dance floor was packed, dancing and singing along to Usher's 'Yeah'. Jodi begged out when the song ended, parched and in need of water. She had long forsaken the heels and she padded barefoot to the bar, where Kyle handed her a bottle of water which she took gratefully. Free had followed, taking one as well. Laughing together at an over exuberant uncle on Cassie's side dancing excitedly, Jodi sighed, enjoying herself immensely.

Free reached up and loosened the tie knotted as his throat, releasing the top button as well. The sleeves of his black button down had long since been rolled up to his elbows, leaving his tanned forearms bare.

Leaning down, Free spoke into her ear over the music and crowd, "Wanna take a walk outside? Cool down a bit? I'm roasting in this suit."

Jodi nodded, then followed him out of one of the tent's draped entrances. String fairy lights hung in the towering maple trees sprawled everywhere, and solar powered patio lights lit several different paths into the darkness. They wandered out, following one dimly lit pathway.

"Are you having a good time?" Free asked softly. They had traveled a few hundred feet away from the reception tent, and it was much quieter. Crickets chirped and bullfrogs sounded in the distance. Here and there, a firefly would illuminate in front of them.

"Of course," Jodi said and smiled up at him. The lights strung in the trees cast just enough light for them to see each other. "I love weddings. They make me happy."

"Did yours?" he asked quietly.

Jodi shrugged, staring down at her feet as they walked. "I didn't actually have a wedding when I married Josh. He didn't want a wedding, so we just went to the courthouse."

"So, you didn't get to do any of this?" Free asked, gesturing back to the tent and party behind them.

Jodi shook her head, no. "It's okay, though. I'm glad we didn't. It would have seemed like a waste."

Jodi was grateful that Free left it at that. She didn't want to talk about her marriage to Josh, not tonight.

A creek babbled about ten feet ahead of them, where the trail they had taken ended. A wooden bench stood just before it, and Free took Jodi's hand, leading her over to it. He sat down and spread his knees, pulling her toward him so that she stood between them.

Jodi's fingers tunneled through his soft, dark hair, pulling it away from his brow before letting her hands move down to cup his strong jaw in her palms. Her fingers played with the dark, trimmed hair that covered his jawline, chin, and upper lip. He stared up at her from where he sat, letting her explore, his blue-green eyes intense as he watched her. Feeling bold, she ducked her head and pressed her lips to his, her hands cupping either side of his face.

His hands trailed along the bare skin of her calves, moving up, skimming under the fabric of her dress. Palms flat against the backs of her thighs, he squeezed lightly, and with gentle pressure urged her closer. Their mouths melded, tongues tangling, trying to taste all of the other. Pulling slightly, Free collapsed her knees, hauling her closer until she straddled his lap, her knees on either side of his hips. Her dress rode up, leaving the majority of her thighs bare to his ardent touch.

Jodi gasped, the wood of the bench cool against her shins. Free's hands settled on the curve of her hips, at the same time rotating his hips upward. Jodi moaned quietly, biting her lip, when she felt his hardness between her thighs. She settled more firmly onto his lap, and this time it was Free's turn to groan.

"Fuck," he whispered hoarsely, threading his fingers up through her hair and pulling her mouth back down to his, ravishing it with his own. Breaking the kiss to breathe, he chuckled breathlessly against her lips. Shifting his hips again, he breathed, "I've wanted to do this for so long."

Jodi nodded, her lips brushing back and forth against his. "Me too."

"I should probably get you back to the party before I try to fuck you here on this bench," Free growled, nipping her lip with his straight white teeth. "Or before your dad comes looking for us." Jodi giggled, and Free groaned again. "Oh god, don't do that."

Assisting her back to her feet, he stood, too.

"It's a real good thing we've got a bit of a walk, because this isn't acceptable party attire," he jested, motioning to his fly.

Jodi laughed lightly, stepping close to him. Bravely, she ran her hand along his left thigh, letting her fingers flit over his front teasingly. Growling darkly, he captured her hand and pressed it to him, and she gasped again, her eyes flying to his, at the same time her fingers closing around the hard ridge there. His eyes fluttered closed briefly, and he gnashed his teeth around a groan. "This is what you do to me."

Swooping down to press another fiery kiss to her lips, he pulled away, leaving her breathless. "I mean it. We need to go before I take you out here right now."

"I'm not objecting," Jodi whispered throatily.

She watched as he shook his dark head. He tucked a stray curl behind her ear. "I've waited a decade for you, a few more hours won't kill me."

Pressing her front against his enticingly, he groaned and slapped her ass with his palm. "Then again, it just might."

CHAPTER 26

When they rejoined the reception a few minutes later, Jodi excused herself to the ladies' room to freshen up, and make sure she didn't look like she'd just been ravished. Her lips were kiss roughened, the skin around her mouth deliciously abraded by Free's beard. She fixed her makeup best she could, then joined Free by the bar.

There was a slow, romantic ballad playing, and the dance floor was filled with couples swaying slowly together. Free took her hand in his and led her out onto the dance floor, pulling her close. They swayed together on the edge of the dance floor, and Jodi's eyes flit from one couple to the next.

Cassie's head rested on Shane's chest as they swayed back and forth, and Shane pressed a tender kiss to his bride's forehead. Among the couples out on the dance floor were Cassie's parents, Seren and Levi, and Leah and Adam.

Free's younger cousin Kale had asked Shaun to dance, and she laughed softly at something the young man said. As Jodi watched, Kasey walked up to the two of them and tapped his younger brother on the shoulder.

Kale grinned and let Kasey cut in. Shaun stiffened and said something that made Kasey grin widely, even as his hand splayed wide on her back. He murmured something quietly in return and Shaun's blue eyes narrowed ominously. Unperturbed by Shaun's ire, Kasey chuckled and twirled her around the floor effortlessly.

Jodi then noticed a newcomer to the reception. Tommy Chandler searched until he found Shaun and he stared at the man holding his girlfriend much too intimately to be appropriate. Shaun looked up as if sensing his gaze and extracted herself from Kasey's arms. She said something to Kasey and then walked away, hips swaying beguilingly, leaving him in the middle of the dance floor. His eyes stayed on her even after she reached Tommy and slid her arms around the other man's waist, leaning in to kiss him heatedly.

Kasey sauntered off the dance floor and reclaimed his seat. He took a drink from the glass in his hand, though his hooded gaze never strayed far from Shaun, who stayed close to Tommy's side.

Free chuckled into her ear. "I warned him."

"You warned him? About Shaun?" Jodi asked, laughing. "Why?"

"I know my cousin," Free said with a laugh. "And I know Shaun." He trailed his fingers along her bare back, making her shiver, then said, "If they're not a thing in the next six months, call me amazed."

"She has a boyfriend," Jodi admonished, though she was having a hard time concentrating when his fingers were moving against her skin the way they were.

Free leaned down, whispering, "You know your sister better than anyone. I've only seen her with that boyfriend of hers together for ten minutes, and I can tell they have no chemistry. She's forcing it. It's not supposed to be like that." He motioned toward Kasey. "He sees it, too. I think she likes him."

"I think she wants to kill him," Jodi corrected and laughed. "I've never seen her take such a passionate dislike to someone she just met."

"That's because she's going to fight it like hell. You'll see," Free chuckled again.

As the reception began to wind down, the DJ announced that the bride and groom would be making their exit in approximately ten minutes time, and for all of the guests to join them outside along the walkway for a sparkler send off. The wedding guests made their way out of the tent doors, lining up on either side of the lit pathway that led toward the parking lot. The wedding coordinator was back, handing out sparkler wands to all the guests, along with matches so they could all be lit at the same time.

With all of the sparklers lit, Cassie and Shane exited the tent last, passing beneath the tunnel of fireworks and beyond, where their getaway car awaited.

Jodi and Free headed back inside to gather her purse and shoes. Jodi offered to stay and help clean up, but the lady with the clipboard shooed them out with a smile.

She leaned in close to Jodi as she slipped her shoes back on and said quietly, "You know, I've worked a lot of weddings and that man has been looking at you all night in a way that I don't see often. Best not keep him waiting any longer!"

CHAPTER 27

Free and Jodi slipped out of the reception after a few quiet goodbyes to those that remained. They said a brief goodbye to Seren and Levi, and Jodi blushed furiously when Free and her father shook hands, the older man's cobalt blue eyes drilling into the younger man's aquamarine ones. Free held Levi's gaze steadily, before they turned to wave goodbye to Shaun and the rest of her siblings. Free led her out through the draped doorway of the tent, his hand at her back.

Jodi's skin tingled where his fingers rested at the small of her back, against her bare skin. They walked toward the truck side-by-side, through the tunnel of maple trees lit by string lights. She was deliciously buzzed and relaxed, at least until Free swept her curls away from her back and lowered his lips to the curve of her bare shoulder, making her body zing with anticipation.

Free opened the passenger door and Jodi took his hand as he helped her up into the seat. He closed the door and rounded the back, climbing into the driver's seat next to her. He started the truck and turned to look at her. His aquamarine eyes searched hers and he reached for her hand, squeezing it gently before raising it to his lips, pressing a tender kiss to her knuckles.

He drove them to her house and parked the truck beside her Jeep, killing the engine. Exiting the truck, he came around to open her door and helped her out, his hands splaying wide on either side of her ribcage as he lifted her down.

Without speaking, Jodi took his hand in hers and led him up the porch stairs and to the front door, letting them in quietly. Free closed the door behind them, the soft click of the latch loud in the otherwise silent house.

"Don't go shy on me now," Free whispered huskily, reaching for her and pulling her close.

Jodi's lashes fluttered closed briefly, shading her eyes from his. "It's... been a long time for me, Free. I'm afraid I'm out of practice. I don't want to disappoint you."

Lowering his mouth to hers and sipping at her lips softly, he murmured, "You could never disappoint me, Jodi. I've waited so long for this, for you."

She sighed against his lips a heartbeat before his tongue delved between her lips to taste her fully. Their heads tilted, kissing hungrily. Jodi's lower body ached, want and need and desire all rolled into one. Lifting his head, he panted heavily, swearing under his breath.

"Fuck, you make me so hard," Free husked, taking her hand in his and bringing it to his fly, leaving it there, letting her make the decision. Her hand curved around the hardness there, and he groaned a half a second before sliding his hands beneath the curves of her ass, hauling her up and against him.

Jodi gasped against his mouth, wrapping her legs around his hips even as her arms slid across his shoulders to hold on. He carried her through the darkened living room, down the shadowed hallway, and into the bedroom where only the moonlight spilled through the windows. His mouth was ravenous on hers, even as he set her down on her feet beside the bed.

Jodi felt his hands on the bare skin of her lower back and she shivered, gooseflesh breaking out at his touch. His hands skimmed up the bare skin of her back, then slid beneath the fabric at her shoulders, lowering it, pulling the sleeves down her arms. She had not worn a bra with this dress, and as Free's hands lowered her dress, her breasts spilled out. Her breath came in gentle puffs against his face as he peeled the dress down her narrow waist, then let it fall in a puddle of fabric at her feet when he skimmed it over the curve of her bottom.

Free took a half step back to better view her. All that kept him from seeing all of her nakedness was a tiny lace thong. She blushed deeply at his intense perusal of her, and she lifted her hands to cover her breasts, suddenly shy.

His eyes were bright with desire as he looked at her, raising his eyes to hers. "Please don't hide yourself from me," he whispered, his voice thick. Taking a deep, steadying breath, she lowered her hands to her sides, trembling slightly.

He reached out to trace the lacy edge of her panties against her flat stomach with his fingertips, and Jodi sucked in her breath at the contact. "You're beautiful."

Jodi blushed and took another deep breath, which brought his attention to her breasts, and his hands raised to cup them tenderly. His fingers found her peaked nipples, rolling them between his thumb and forefinger, and her head dropped back on a moan.

"You have an unfair advantage," Jodi whispered brokenly between gasps as his fingers continued to manipulate her breasts tormentingly. "You're wearing too many clothes."

Free chuckled in the dark, but released her breasts and stepped back far enough for her to reach for the necktie that was still fastened loosely at his throat. Pulling the knot to loosen it, she raised it over his head, tossing it aside. She reached for the buttons of his vest, and when those were undone, she slid it down his arms and let it join her dress on the floor. Her fingers were trembling slightly when she began to unbutton his shirt, each undone button revealing more of his magnificent chest. She pulled the tail out of his slacks and then flattened her hands against his chest, sliding them up and over his shoulders, taking the shirt with them. It dropped to the floor, and she leaned forward, pressing her lips to his bare chest. Free's eyes closed, and one hand tangled in her hair, holding her there.

Free growled low in his chest. Jodi raised her head and reached for his belt. She teased him, releasing it slowly. She slid her hand down, over the bulge there.

Free gasped and clenched his teeth tight, his hands reaching out and gripping her upper arms. Jodi smiled and lowered the zipper. His erection strained against the fabric and he moaned when her knuckles skimmed over him. When it was completely undone, she slid both hands into his slacks at his hips and pulled them down his long, hard thighs until they dropped around his feet.

The only thing between them now was her flimsy underwear and a tight pair of black boxer briefs that were tented. She looked at him, admiring how incredibly handsome he was.

He skimmed his hands over her shoulders and down her back, cupping her ass in both hands. He hooked his thumbs into the waistband of her panties and shimmied them down her thighs, where they too, joined the rest of their clothes.

As they dropped around her ankles, he moved them backward until the backs of her knees touched the edge of the bed. Threading the fingers of one hand into the hair at the back of her head, his mouth met hers fiercely as he lowered her to the bed. He covered her with his body, pressing into her, moving rhythmically against her. Jodi wrapped her legs around his narrow hips, her hands skimming over his broad shoulders, his muscled arms.

"Jodi, sweetheart, you've gotta let me go so I can take these damned tight underwear off," he hissed through clenched teeth.

Jodi let her legs fall open from around his hips. He stood, and she remained reclined on the pillows, her body completely naked to him. Free hooked his thumbs into his underwear and pulled them down his thighs, letting them fall to his feet. Jodi's mouth fell open at the sight of him.

He knelt on the bed beside her and bridged himself above her with his arms. He lowered his mouth to hers and kissed her fervently. Her hands came up to grip his arms as she met his kiss more fully. And then he was gone, his head moving lower, dropping hot, open-mouthed kisses along her jaw, her ear, her throat. He kissed each shoulder, the hollow at the base of her throat. His mouth loved her neck ardently, and then he grinned wolfishly and touched the light bruise his kiss had left there. His lips moved lower until they encountered her puckered nipple. He nudged it with his tongue, laved her gently. She cried his name, her hands sliding up his tight arms to his shoulders, then into his hair. He took her into his mouth and suckled her.

Jodi's back came off the bed with a sharp, moaning cry. He suckled harder and she felt it deep inside her. His mouth moved to her other breast and paid tribute to that one as well until she was writhing beneath him. She felt his arousal at her hip and she moaned throatily.

"Free," she moaned. "Please."

He shook his head, his lips brushing back and forth over her sensitized nipple. "I'm not even close to done yet, sweetheart."

Her fingers tightened in his hair, holding his mouth to her breast. But he moved lower, pressing kisses to her ribcage. Slipping one hand between her thighs, he coaxed them to open. When they fell apart, he moved so he lay between them. His abdomen pressed against the apex of her thighs and his hands smoothed over her hips.

He pressed his lips to her belly button, then his lips moved lower to the junction of her thighs. Jodi cried out in shocked dismay and released a handhold on his hair to cover herself.

Free looked up at her, smiling quizzically. He kissed the back of her hand and asked softly, "Don't you want me to?"

Jodi's other arm raised so that she covered her eyes with her forearm in embarrassment, while leaving the hand that shielded her sex from him in place.

"Hey," he whispered, moving up her body so that he lay with half his body covering hers. He moved her arm, making her look at him. "I told you not to go shy on me."

Jodi's fingers trailed over his brow, feather light. She shrugged, raising and dropping her shoulders quickly. She swallowed, then licked her lips. "I've never done… that… before."

Free's eyebrows shot up in surprise. "You mean he never…?"

Jodi shook her head vehemently, while continuing to touch his jawline with just the tips of her fingers, playing with his facial hair. "No." She glanced into his eyes shyly. "You mean you want to…?"

Free lowered his lips to hers, kissing her sweetly, before whispering huskily, "Yes, very much so. But only if you want me to."

Reaching for his mouth with her own, she kissed him hungrily. He slid his palm down her body, over her abdomen and between her thighs, which dropped open for him once more. She sighed into his mouth when his fingers slid inside her, finding her already wet for him. He groaned, working his fingers until she writhed against him.

"Let me do this, Jodi, please," he whispered against her mouth. "Let me show you how good it can be."

She nodded, and that was all the encouragement he needed before disappearing down her body.

Laying between her thighs, he bent one of her knees, lifting her thigh and pressing a hot, open mouth kiss to the tender skin on the inside of her thigh. His lips traveled up, and instinctively she raised both knees, granting him better access.

Jodi opened her eyes and watched him as he lay his most intimate of kisses on her. She cried out softly as his tongue and mouth seemed to drink her, devouring her. She threaded her fingers through his hair, desperate for something to hold onto that was tangible. Her eyes slid shut as pleasure she'd never imagined spiraled upward through her. Free continued to lick and suckle her until her body was trembling, her muscles tightening in anticipation. Jodi called his name as she began to convulse, her fingers releasing his hair and gripping handfuls of the sheet beneath her.

Free groaned as she came hard, her thighs shaking where they were draped over his shoulders. He moved up her body as she continued to tremble. His lips captured hers and she was shocked to taste herself. Free positioned himself between her thighs and then Jodi's mouth fell from his, her breathing harsh. He moved against her, rubbing his length along her wetness, and she moaned at how hard he was.

Free took her hands in his, twining their fingers together and pressing them into the bed beside her head on the pillow. He rocked above her ever so slightly, prolonging the pleasure of having him enter her for the first time.

Jodi gripped his fingers and begged, "Free, please."

Releasing her hands, Free moved over her, sliding one arm beneath her back, the other he used to hold himself off her, his fingers fisting in the sheet beside her head. His mouth found hers again, kissing her deeply. Jodi slid her arms around his hard waist, pressing her hands into his back, urging him closer.

"No," Free ground out, his breathing harsh. "Wait, Jodi."

"No, please," she moaned, moving her hips against him. Her hands moved up his back to splay wide on his shoulders. He lowered himself ever so slightly, until his chest rested against her breasts. "I need you."

"Oh, sweetheart, you have me," he breathed against her lips.

Capturing his mouth with her own, she kissed him hungrily. With a low groan, Free slid inside her, burying his rock-hard cock to the hilt in one smooth thrust. He ground his hips into hers, driving deeper, and she cried out against his mouth, "Holy fuck, yes."

"Christ, Jodi," he panted raggedly, and she reveled in the feel of him. She moved her body beneath his, taking him deeper, smiling against his mouth when he shuddered and groaned gutturally. "Oh, god, you feel so good."

Circling her hips against his again, she clutched at his taut shoulders. "Free, please."

Finally beginning to move, Free rolled his hips, retreating and then sinking fully into her again. With each deep, slow thrust of his body into hers, she met him with a lift of her hips. He whispered ragged words of pleasure into her ear as they rocked together. His movements began to quicken, and she met him eagerly, pushing her hips against his hard as he pumped into her. Their lips met in fervent kisses as sweat began to make their bodies slick. Jodi pulled him closer, harder, pressing him with her hands.

Jodi shuddered as spasms began to close her body around his and she tore her mouth from his to cry his name in alarm at the intensity.

"No, don't stop," he growled fiercely, and she gasped when he gripped a handful of her hair in his hand, forcing her to look up into his face. He was darkly handsome, this ferociousness thrilling her. "Don't you dare stop now. Come for me."

Jodi cried out and her head fell back, his fingers still clutching her curls, pulling tight enough to sting. Her body wasn't hers anymore; her thighs and abdomen shaking uncontrollably with the power of her climax. Her hips slammed against his, taking him as deep as she possibly could.

"That's my good girl," she heard him growl darkly, and she was sure if she hadn't already shattered into a million pieces, those words alone would have done it. She clasped him close as her body convulsed around his, driving him to his own orgasm. Free growled gutturally as he came hard, pounding into her again and again, then stilling, buried inside her as deeply as he could go.

Jodi clutched him close even as their bodies continued to tremble. Free collapsed half on top of her and they held onto one another as they panted raggedly. Free pressed tender kisses to her dewy forehead, while her hands smoothed up and down his sweat slicked back, refusing to let him go. Her legs remained locked around his narrow hips, holding him inside her.

Finally, after what felt like forever, Free lifted his head and peered down into her flushed face. She blushed, but smiled radiantly.

"I've waited so long for you, for this…" he whispered ardently, brushing stray tendrils away from her face and kissing her sweetly, lingeringly. Jodi smiled against his lips, his own tilting up into a contented grin.

CHAPTER 28

Free woke early, opening his eyes, letting them adjust to the gray-blue of early dawn filtering through the window across the room. Yawning quietly and turning his head, he was careful not to wake Jodi who lay sleeping beside him. He watched her as she slept for long minutes, her dark curls tousled from sleep and from his fingers, her dark lashes resting against her cheekbones.

He contemplated waking her, aching to slide between her thighs as he'd done several hours before when they'd awoken together in the middle of the night, reaching for each other instinctively. She sighed in her sleep, her lips parting slightly, and he smiled. He'd let her sleep.

Sliding out from beneath the sheet, he padded quietly to the bathroom after picking his discarded boxer briefs, suit pants, and the button-down shirt. Dressing quickly, he slipped out of the bathroom and through the bedroom, grabbing his boots as he went.

He stopped in the kitchen, rifling through cupboards

and drawers until he found the fixings to start a pot of coffee to brew. He located a pen and scrawled a quick note on a napkin, leaving it by the coffee maker before letting himself out the front door just as the sun started to make its ascent above the horizon.

Driving the short way to Shane's, he let himself in the empty house. The newlyweds had stayed in a hotel for the night, before traveling to their destination for their long-awaited honeymoon. Taking off the suit pants and shirt, he folded both pieces over the back of a chair that sat in the corner of the bedroom. Grabbing a fresh pair of underwear, jeans, and a clean shirt from his suitcase, he headed into the bathroom to take a short shower.

Dressing and heading out to the barn out the backdoor, he ducked into the chicken coop, fetching freshly laid eggs from the laying hens, then refilled the water bucket and scratch feeder, before heading to the goat pen. It was easy, mindless work, leaving his mind free to wander to the night he'd just spent with Jodi.

They'd fallen asleep together late, languid and sated, Jodi draped loosely over his chest. He'd woken in the middle of the night to her wrapping her arm around his waist from behind him, and his cock had hardened almost instantly at her touch, ready for her again. Rolling over to face her, she'd pulled him to her in the darkened room, rolling to her back and letting him settle between her thighs easily. He'd protested for the briefest moment, worried she would be tender and sore, but she shushed him with her lips and reached for him, guiding him to enter her. It was all the invitation he'd needed, sliding into her without another moment's hesitation. It had been quick and hard, different than the first time. He'd collapsed after coming hard, panting into her shoulder before raising himself over her, brushing her sweat-dampened hair away from her face.

"What do you do to me?" he'd husked, and she'd smiled triumphantly, drawing circles with her fingertips along the ridges of his ribs. He kissed her quickly, soundly, before tucking her against his front.

As he'd drifted back to sleep, one thought had come to him, one that thrilled him more than he would have liked to admit out loud.

She was his.

CHAPTER 29

Jodi woke by slow degrees, stretching widely, amazed at how her muscles ached deliciously. The sun was coming up through her bedroom window, leaving rays dancing across the floor where they touched the side of the bed. Reaching out one hand, she sat up when her hand touched nothing but the empty bed beside her where Free had been sleeping. Pulling the sheet up to cover her breasts, she glanced over the foot of the bed, her brow furrowing when his clothes and boots were missing. Hurt made her throat tight, and she kicked herself for thinking Free had wanted anything more from her than what he'd finally gotten.

"You big dumb idiot," she muttered to herself before sighing heavily and swinging her legs over the side of the bed and walking to the bathroom. Pulling on a thin robe, she called herself all kinds of names as she moved down the hall to the kitchen.

The smell of fresh coffee perked her senses, and when she came around the corner, she realized he must have made it before sneaking out, which made no sense to her still sleep fogged brain. A scrap of white by the coffee maker caught her eye, and she stepped over to it, relief sweeping through her as she read the scrawl of his handwritten note.

Had to run to Shane's. Be right back.

She had forgotten the reason he was staying longer than planned.

Reaching for a coffee cup in the cupboard, she poured a cup and sat down at the kitchen table, staring out over the field beyond her house. Tapping her fingernails on the tabletop, she pursed her lips and then stood quickly, taking the cup of coffee with her into the office, picking up a fluffy blanket, then sat down and powered on her laptop.

She was still sitting in the same spot when she heard tires on the gravel in the driveway, then a car door close. Jumping to her feet, she checked her reflection in the mirror, mortified at the mess that was her hair, and the fact that she had yet to wash her face of the makeup from the day before. A soft knock sounded, and she raced down the hall, pulling the door open.

"I wasn't sure if I should knock," he said lamely from where he stood, a white pastry bag in one hand. "I didn't want to assume—"

Jodi stepped aside, motioning for him to come in. "I'm glad you came back," she murmured as he stepped inside. She was painfully aware that she still looked like a wreck, and lowered her eyes from his shyly. Rambling nervously and fidgeting with the tie of her robe, she mumbled, "I'm sorry, I started writing and lost track of time, let me go shower and change. Thank you for making coffee this morning."

"You're welcome," he said, and she made her way toward the kitchen. He set the white pastry bag down on the counter. "I was up early and figured I'd head over to Shane's to get chores done for the morning. I hope you didn't think I left for good."

"Oh, yeah, no, of course not," Jodi stuttered, though her face flamed at the lie.

"Mmhmm," Free murmured, though his mouth tilted up in a slight smile. He sauntered over to her, like a predator after his prey, and she was powerless against it. She took a tentative step back, her hips bumping into the edge of the counter, bringing her up short. "I hope you know I'm not finished with you yet."

Her breath came in soft, quick puffs, the edges of her robe fluttering against her breasts. She clutched the edges closed nervously, more for her fingers to have something to do other than reach for him.

"No?" Jodi whispered breathlessly, caught irretrievably in his aquamarine gaze, like a fish in a net.

Free shook his head slowly, reaching out to brace both hands on the edge of the counter on either side of her hips, leaning in close to her, not close enough to touch, but close enough for Jodi to feel his body heat. His mouth was inches away from hers, his head tilted slightly.

"I'm just getting started, sweetheart," he murmured huskily, trailing his lips along her jawline, and she sighed, letting her head fall back to give him better access. His words were mere breaths against her skin, making her shiver. "And I might be a little obsessed with the way your thighs shake when I make you come… it's so sexy."

"Ohmygod," Jodi moaned, her words bleeding together breathlessly.

His lips flit over hers, barely brushing, teasing her. Tugging at the sash at her waist, her thin robe fell open, revealing her naked body to his gaze. The backs of his knuckles skimmed along the curve of her breast, over the softness of her belly, and down over the apex of her thighs. Jodi sucked in her breath when his knuckles grazed over her stomach, tickling slightly. His palm opened and he cupped her sex in his hand, his fingers deftly sliding into her, and he breathed raggedly against her lips, "You're always so ready for me."

She nodded, her eyes sliding shut as his fingers continued to manipulate her, sliding in and out, first one finger, then two. His thumb found her clit and rubbed at the same time that his fingers moved, and her knees almost gave out beneath her.

Capturing her mouth with his finally, he kissed her hungrily, his tongue spiraling into her mouth, and she clutched at his shirt with shaky fingers. Then, he was gone, dropping to his knees and pressing hot, open-mouthed kisses to her stomach, and lower, making her blush furiously.

Curving his hand around the outside of her thigh, he kissed the tender skin on the inside of her leg, before raising it and hooking it over his shoulder. His mouth found her sex, licking, suckling, devouring her. Jodi's hands clutched at the edge of the counter at her hips, holding on for dear life as he devoured her like she was his last meal. As his tongue did glorious things to her clit, his fingers slid deep into her, moving and stroking.

She released one handhold on the counter, sliding her fingers into his hair, holding him to her. She looked down her body at his dark head between her thighs, before her eyes slid closed again and she let her head fall back even as her thighs started to shake, a cry escaping her lips as she came on his fingers and tongue.

He didn't stop there, though. He gave her only a moment to catch her breath before starting again, growling up at her, "That's a good girl. I want you to come again, Jodi. Come for me again."

Holding herself up on one leg, with her other thigh still draped over his shoulder, she had no other choice but to obey his dark command. Flicking his tongue over her clit again and again, her body shook, her thighs trembling violently with the intensity of her repeated orgasms. "Fuuuuuck," Jodi cried, her head tossing across her shoulders. "Free, please!"

Kissing the inner part of her thigh as it rested over his shoulder, he licked his lips and Jodi blushed furiously again, knowing full well she was still on his lips. He stood, his chest heaving, his eyes dark even as he reached for his belt and unfastened it, quickly undoing the buttons and lowering his jeans and boxer briefs until he could release himself. She reached for him, wrapping her fingers around his hardness. His eyes closed, his breath releasing in a soft groan as her fingers stroked along his hard length.

Reaching down to grab her ass cheeks in his palms, he lifted her up until she sat on the counter behind her, her hips at the edge. Her hand guided him to her, and as he slid inside, she wrapped her arms around his neck, her legs bracketing his hips. He braced one hand on the counter beside her hip, the other he laid his palm flat against the cupboard above her head as he began to move. Their mouths met fiercely as he pumped into her hard.

Already on the edge of another orgasm, Jodi cried out, "Don't you dare make me come without you."

Groaning huskily, he grinned against her lips as he continued to move. "That's my girl," he growled, the fingers of one of his hands sinking into her hair and holding her mouth against his. As her body began to tighten and shake, she felt more than heard him whisper, "Fuck yes. Come with me."

Jodi exalted in the hoarseness of his groan when he came inside her, her own climax making her body squeeze his as he pumped into her. They panted together, his forehead pressed against her bare shoulder, his body still nestled inside hers. Aftershocks rippled through her, and he moaned into her shoulder. Their bodies slowed, and Jodi ran her fingers through the dark hair at the back of his neck.

When he finally raised his head enough to look into her face, she couldn't help the smile that spread across her face. He grinned back at her, leaning in to kiss her languidly, softly. When he released her lips, he whispered huskily, still grinning, "I don't know about you, but I'm starving."

CHAPTER 30

"You're a bad influence."

"I am no such thing," Free said from behind her. His arms wrapped around her, his hands cupping the heaviness of her breasts in his palms, rolling her nipples between his forefingers and thumbs. Jodi's head fell back until it rested on his chest, her hands coming up to cover his where they manipulated her breasts. He was naked, as was she. Standing in the bathroom in front of the mirror, she had been in the middle of putting a curl cream into the wet strands when he'd walked up behind her after shaving in the sink next to her.

Unabashed and comfortable with his nakedness, and expressing great appreciation for hers, they had remained naked while getting ready next to each other.

"Mmmm," Jodi murmured, even as his fingers continued to finesse her nipples. "I have to get ready…"

"I'm not stopping you," he teased, his lips brushing her ear.

"Free," Jodi moaned, finally stilling his hands. "If you keep doing that, we're never going to make it to the store."

"I think I like my suggestion better."

"As much as I would love to stay in bed all day, I need to pick up some things for the shop for tomorrow," she laughed, turning and wrapping her arms around his neck, reaching up to peck a kiss to his lips. "We need food. I've worked up an appetite after being thoroughly ravished for the last fifteen hours."

"Thoroughly ravished?" he chuckled, his hands settling on the sloping curve over her bottom. "I'm still not done with you yet."

"I would hope not," Jodi murmured. "A girl could get used to this."

Slapping his ass cheek with the flat of her palm, she winked at him and walked toward the door, exiting into the bedroom.

He came out a couple minutes later, dressed in the jeans and shirt he'd arrived in that morning. She was pulling on a royal blue high-low skirt, the front reaching her knees, the back dipping down to brush the backs of her ankles. She pulled on a flowy white tank top, tucking it into the high waistband before cinching it with a brown fashion belt. White slide-on sandals came next. Her make-up was simple, and as her hair began to dry, her curls rioted over her shoulders and down her back.

"Ready?" he asked, reaching his hand out to her.

Nodding, she smiled as she put her hand in his. Picking up her purse as they walked through the house,

Free continued to hold her hand as they walked down the porch steps, leading her to the passenger side of the truck. Helping her up into the seat, he closed the door and walked around the hood to the driver's side, climbing up next to her and starting the rumbling engine and driving them to the grocer. Having parked the truck, Free exited and came around to open her door, as always.

Jodi's face flushed and her hand felt hot where it was clasped in Free's as they walked through the doors of the grocery store. She was acutely aware of the two women standing just inside the doors, their eyes watching Jodi and Free as they walked in.

A snorted laugh reached her ears and Jodi steeled herself for what she knew was coming. Free looked down at her quizzically, and she shook her head just slightly, squeezing his hand gently.

"Didn't take her long to move on, huh?"

Jodi bit her tongue, staring stonily ahead as they made their way into the store past the two women. She felt Free's body tense as he heard the mutterings himself, and again, Jodi squeezed his hand.

"I heard she was sleeping around the entire time anyway, so I'm not surprised."

Losing her inner battle and whipping her head around toward the two women, Jodi snapped, "Seriously, Beth? That's rich coming from the woman that pretended to be my friend while sleeping with my husband, while you yourself were engaged. Or how about the fact that you invited just my husband to your own wedding, because you had uninvited me, while still sleeping with him? Does Todd know about that yet?"

The woman's lips tightened, and her pale blue eyes narrowed on Jodi's face. She tossed dull, reddish-brown hair away from her face and muttered, "You're a bitch."

Jodi felt Free's body stiffen next to her, and she squeezed his hand tighter in her own, pulling him with her as she continued to walk. Jodi smiled with false sweetness, and said softly, "I'm okay with that. At least I'm not a backstabbing, home wrecking hussy."

The small blonde that stood next to the redhead let her mouth fall open, and then the two of them turned and walked out the doors toward the parking lot, as Jodi and Free continued into the store.

Jodi released Free's hand and scrubbed her shaking hands over her face, pushing her hair back away from her face and blowing out a tense breath. Free walked beside her silently, and she was grateful for him letting her have a moment to collect herself. He stopped to pull a cart from the carousel, and they made their way toward the baked goods.

As they walked, Free bumped his shoulder into hers and whispered, "Remind me not to get on your bad side. You're kinda scary."

Jodi laughed, ducking her head self-consciously. "I hate that woman."

"I can tell," Free chuckled, pushing the cart in front of him. Jodi stopped at a display stand and picked out several bags of croissants, placing them in the basket of the cart. "Your ex-husband sounds like a piece of work."

"You have no idea," Jodi muttered sourly, but shook her head dismissively when he glanced down at her. She smiled, reaching up on tiptoes to kiss his lips, and said, "I don't want to talk about that right now."

"You don't have to hide anything from me, you know that, right?" Free said gently, straightening after kissing her back.

Jodi nodded, choosing a package of assorted muffins and placing them in the basket with the croissants. "I know. I promised I would answer any questions you have. I just want to enjoy your company for now, please."

Free nodded, though Jodi could tell he was curious. She dreaded the conversation that would come.

Completing their shopping and heading back out to the truck, Jodi glanced over at him when his phone rang. He fished the cellphone out of his pocket, and she saw the name 'Red' come across the screen before he declined the call and put it back in his pocket. He smiled over at her. "I'll call back later."

"Who's Red?" Jodi asked.

"Just a friend," he murmured, leaning over the console to press a kiss to her lips. "I'll introduce you sometime."

CHAPTER 31

"I'm going to be late," Jodi whined petulantly, but made no move to remove herself from Free's embrace.

"I think if you plead your case to your boss, she may be willing to let you stay," Free husked against her lips, his hands trailing over her back and down her bottom, hiking up the skirt she wore. Jodi sighed against his lips, but swatted at his hands, and he chuckled. He swatted her bottom playfully, then growled and pulled her close again for another deep kiss. When Jodi pulled away, Free pouted, which made Jodi laugh.

"I had the entire weekend off, Kit and Tess would kill me if I begged out on a Monday morning," Jodi said with a smirk. "Besides, you have chores to do."

"Killjoy," Free muttered, but winked. Jodi walked to the kitchen table, where she picked up the bags of baked goods they'd picked up at the store the day before. "May I make you dinner tonight?"

Pulling her purse over her shoulder, she smiled at him. "That would be lovely, thank you."

"What time can I expect you home?" Free asked, and he grinned, liking the way that sounded. Taking the bags from her, he carried them as he walked her out to her Jeep.

Jodi smiled shyly and murmured, "We close at six. I'll be back shortly after that."

She climbed into the driver's seat, and he closed the door gently. She started the car and rolled the window down. He rested one forearm on the windowsill and leaned in to kiss her once more. "I'll be here when you get back."

"You better be," Jodi whispered then blushed. "I'll see you later."

"Later, baby," he murmured and tapped the windowsill, straightening and stepping back. She waved as she pulled out of the driveway. His phone rang as her car disappeared, and he fished it out of his jeans pocket, answering it. "Hey, Red."

"Duuuuuuude," Roxy groaned dramatically from the other end of the phone, and he laughed. "I've been *dying*, waiting for an update. How did it go?"

Free laughed again, walking back up the porch steps and going back into the house, walking to the kitchen to pick up his coffee cup that he'd set down when Jodi had walked out of the bedroom dressed for work. He took a sip, then said, "The wedding was beautiful. Shane and Cassie are sitting on a warm beach somewhere drinking fruity cocktails out of a coconut, I'm sure."

Roxy's muttered curses made him grin widely. "You know that's not what I'm talking about! How did it go with Jodi?"

"Oh, that's what you were talking about?" Free teased, taking another drink of his coffee before sitting down at the dining table.

"You know damn well I want all the juicy details!" Roxy fumed.

"And you know that I don't kiss and tell," Free chuckled.

Roxy's squeal of glee made Free pull the phone away from his ear and he didn't return it until he was sure she was done. "Oh, I knew it, I knew it! Please just tell me y'all have been holed up in a bedroom somewhere for the last two days."

"Not just the bedroom," Free laughed.

Another resulting squee of joy from the other end of the phone made him roll his eyes. "Oh, this is just fantastic. I can't wait to meet her, Free."

"You'll love her," Free murmured, smiling.

"Have you decided what you're going to do?" Roxy asked softly. "Now that it's happened?"

Free took a deep breath, then exhaled slowly. "I don't know."

"Do you really think you'll be able to leave her now?" she asked.

"Red, I don't know. I don't know what this is yet," he muttered, running the fingers of his opposite hand through his hair, pulling the long strands away from his brow. "Texas has been home for seven years; I have commitments there."

He could almost sense her rolling her eyes. "You rent a house; I can take over the lease. You're an honest, hard worker. You can get a job anywhere."

"What about you?" Free snapped. "I'm just supposed to pack up and leave my best friend?"

"Nuh-uh, don't put that on me," Roxy countered. "You ran away from this girl, you left your brother, your best friend, your home. Now that you know it could work with you two—"

"I didn't say I know it could work between Jodi and myself," Free muttered. "Red, we've slept together a couple times. Whatever this is, it's still in its infancy. She's just coming out of a bad marriage; I don't know that she's even looking for anything permanent."

"I can't even handle how stupid you are sometimes," Roxy muttered in a derisive laugh. "You're just looking for an excuse to run again. If you fuck this up, I'll kick your ass myself. Just see where it goes, Free. Don't you think you deserve that after all this time?"

Free hated admitting that she was right, as usual. He was thoroughly enjoying Jodi's company, spending time with her was as easy as breathing. It was comfortable. He'd wanted this for as long as he could remember. Free had spent the majority of his adult life running from any kind of commitment, content to keep his feelings for Jodi to himself, buried in a dark corner. Now, his feelings for her had not only surfaced, but deepened in the last week, which terrified him, if he were being completely honest with himself. He felt at home for the first time in almost a decade. His impending departure in a matter of weeks hung like storm clouds in the distance, rolling closer each day.

He didn't want to leave, didn't want to leave Jodi. *Could* he stay?

Clearing his throat from the uncomfortable knot that had lodged there, he changed subjects and asked, "How are things there?"

"Meh, it's alright. Neal showed up at work. He didn't come in, just stood in the parking lot, and left before the police showed up. Bobby has come by every morning and evening to make sure everything is okay," Roxy said dismissively, though Free could tell there was a hint of trepidation in her voice. "It'll be fine, don't worry."

"Just be careful, please," Free said gently.

"Yeah, yeah," Roxy muttered. "Everybody is watching out for me. I'll be okay."

"Yeah, yeah," Free repeated, then, "I gotta run, Red. I need to get to Shane's to take care of the farm."

"Okay, I'll talk to you later," Roxy said softly. "Tell her you love her, see what happens then."

CHAPTER 32

Kit and Tess were waiting for her when Jodi showed up at the shop, carrying the bags of baked goods and the usual tray of coffee and tea drinks for their Monday morning get together.

Tessa came around the corner of the counter as soon as Jodi had let herself into the building, nearly jumping up and down in excitement. Her shoulder length blonde hair bounced as she came toward Jodi, taking the bag of baked goods from her hands.

"I'm sorry I'm late," Jodi laughed contritely, and Tessa shushed her quickly.

"I don't even care, I just want to know what happened with Mr. Sexy Cowboy!" Tess gushed, setting the bags down on the counter. Kit took the tray of drinks and passed them out, tossing the cardboard tray into the recycling behind the counter. "I wouldn't have blamed you if you didn't come in today!"

Jodi laughed, remembering the conversation with Free before leaving the house and blushing, which only made Tess and Kit giggle louder.

Kit's honey brown eyes danced mischievously. "You didn't want to leave the house today, did you?"

Jodi blushed darker, if that were possible, making Kit laugh. Stepping behind the counter and taking a drink of her iced coffee, she admitted with a smile, "Not even a little bit."

"Is he positively yummy in bed?" Tess asked, and Jodi gasped out an astonished laugh.

"I'm not answering that," Jodi laughed, blushing furiously again.

Tessa and Kit shared a look, and Tess said, "I'll take that as a yes."

"Would you two stop!" Jodi exclaimed on another laugh, clapping her hands to her flaming cheeks.

"Is that a hickey?" Kit asked, pointing to one spot just above Jodi's collarbone.

Jodi gasped, running to the nearest mirror to check. Sure enough, a slight discoloration marred her skin. She flushed again, remembering exactly when he'd left that love mark on her. She also knew of several others he'd left in places for his eyes only. Adjusting her shirt to hide the mark, she blushed again. She wasn't sure when she'd blushed so much in her adult life!

Kit smiled and said softly, "I'm just happy to see you happy, Jodi. You deserve it."

Jodi smiled in return. "Thank you. It still doesn't seem real."

Kit took a drink of her coffee, then checked the watch on her wrist. "Oh, I've got to run. I'll see you girls later this week!"

As Kit took her leave, Jodi and Tessa moved around the shop, setting out that week's new arrivals, putting together the dessert display, and preparing a large pot of coffee to brew.

At nine o'clock, Tessa turned on the lighted open sign in the window and unlocked the door. They chatted throughout the morning, until Tessa took her leave at one o'clock, as it was her turn for an early afternoon. It was a busy day, and before Jodi knew it, it was nearly six. Closing the shop just after six, Jodi made sure everything was ready for Tess in the morning before walking out and locking the shop behind her.

Feeling giddy, she walked briskly around the short block to the back parking lot to her Jeep, climbing in and starting it. She drove home, eager to see Free again. Pulling into the driveway, she felt butterflies take flight in her belly seeing his truck parked in front of her house.

She climbed out and headed up the steps of the porch, opening the front screen door and walking inside. It smelled heavenly. Country music played from the Bluetooth speaker she had in the kitchen, and she could hear Free singing along. When she rounded the corner of the living room into the kitchen, Free spotted her. He beamed a smile and set down the spoon he was using to stir some kind of red sauce, coming toward her.

Those damn butterflies still fluttered crazily in her belly, even as he reached her, sliding his arms around her and pulling her close for a scorching, deep kiss. When he pulled away, she was breathless, and she bit her lip to stop the moan that threatened to escape her. She was already wet.

Free's eyes darkened and he grinned sexily, coming back to grasp her hips in both of his large hands, angling his hips against hers, chuckling when she gasped when she felt him hard against her. "Dinner first, then dessert."

He released her and stepped back toward the stove, picking up the wooden spoon again and stirring the contents in one of the pots there.

Turning to set her purse down on the table, she smiled when she saw a bouquet of fresh flowers in the center of the table in a vase from under the sink. "These are beautiful, thank you."

She moved to stand behind him, sliding her arms around his waist and resting her cheek against the hardness of his back. Her hands clasped together at his waist, and he covered the backs of her hands with one of his, turning his head to look over his shoulder, whispering quietly, "You're beautiful, Jodi."

She pressed a kiss to his back, through his shirt, before pulling away.

"It smells wonderful," Jodi said appreciatively from beside him. "I don't think I've come home to an already cooked meal since I was at Mom and Dad's."

Free's lips tightened, but then he smiled over at her, setting the spoon down and motioning toward the fridge. "I went and got us more beer, and a bottle of wine. I wasn't sure what you'd like with this meal."

Jodi moved to where he had pointed, picking up a bottle of red wine. "This looks delicious."

Free laughed, smiling widely, and Jodi was once again struck with how incredibly handsome he was. He was wearing his usual fitted blue jeans that hugged every inch of his long legs, backside, and cupped his sex. A plain black t-shirt stretched across his chest and back. His dark hair looked soft, like he'd just gotten out of a shower not too long ago, and it curled slightly at the ends. The dark facial hair had become one of Jodi's favorite things about him. She loved to touch it while they lay together in bed.

"Open 'er up," Free said and smiled. "Though I may take a beer while I'm cooking."

Jodi reached into the refrigerator and retrieved a beer, uncapping it and handing it to him. He took it graciously before tipping it to his lips and taking a long swallow.

Jodi's body felt hot as she watched his throat work, swallowing the cold beer, his Adam's apple bobbing.

When his eyes met hers, he grinned knowingly. "Later, sweetheart. I promise."

Jodi blushed, turning to find a bottle opener, and then picking out two wine glasses from the cupboard. She moved around the kitchen, grabbing plates and cutlery to set the table. Jodi could smell garlic bread in the oven, and her mouth started to water.

Free pulled a large salad bowl out of the fridge, setting it on the table, before walking back to the stove where he picked up the pot that had spaghetti noodles boiling, bringing it to the sink to drain. He moved around the kitchen effortlessly, and as Jodi tried to help, he shooed her out of his way, saying, "Just pour yourself a glass of wine and relax, I've got this handled."

The music on the Bluetooth speaker continued to play, a mix of 90's and early 2000's country. They were serenaded by the legendary George Strait, the heavy twang of Reba, and the comedic melodies of Joe Diffy. Free sang along as he worked, making Jodi smile.

As Free set the finished meal on the table, he turned to her and held his hand out to her, which she took. He pulled her into his arms, tucking her against his chest as they swayed to a slow Garth Brooks song, one of Jodi's favorites.

"I've never slow danced in the kitchen before," Jodi murmured, tipping her face up to his.

Free shook his head, reaching up to tangle the fingers of one of his hands in her curls, and Jodi let him tilt her face toward his, where he pressed a soft kiss to her lips. "I'm really not a fan of this ex-husband of yours."

As the song ended, Free motioned to the table, "Come on, let's eat before it gets cold."

They sat catty-corner from each other, and as Free dished the meal onto their plates, Jodi poured herself another glass of wine, and asked with a tilt of the bottle if he would like one. He nodded with a smile and she poured a glass for him as well. A tossed salad, spaghetti with a Boulonnais sauce, handmade meatballs, and crunchy, flaky garlic bread completed the meal.

They dug in, and they chatted companionably. They each asked how the other's day had been. When their plates were empty and bellies full, Jodi leaned back in her chair and took another sip of her wine, swirling it around the globe of the glass, and said, "That was delicious, Free, thank you."

"You are most welcome, Jodi," Free said and smiled over at her, reaching out and clasping her hand in his. The sun was just beginning to lower behind the tops of the trees out the front windows, casting reddish-orange sun rays across the yard and through the windows into the house where they danced on the hardwood floors. He glanced out the back patio doors to the large back deck, where Jodi had several Adirondack chairs. Motioning with his head, he asked, "Do you want to take a drink out to the deck and sit with me for a bit?"

"I would love that," Jodi said and smiled. Standing, she cleared the plates from the table, taking them to the sink. Free rinsed the dishes and stacked everything in the dishwasher as Jodi poured herself another glass of wine and uncapped a fresh beer for him. Free slid the patio door open and Jodi walked out to the back deck, and he followed, closing the door behind him. They sat in the sturdy wooden chairs, and Jodi watched as Free ran his hands over the smooth finish on the arm rests. The sun had disappeared behind the tree line on the other side of the house, and in front of them the skyline darkened from dusty blue to navy, and hundreds of stars were starting to make their appearance. "Dad made these for me when I bought the house."

"I thought I recognized your dad's craftsmanship," Free murmured, smiling over at her. His hand reached out and slid over one of her thighs, resting there comfortably. Except, at the slightest touch from him, her body tingled, attuned to every move he made. He must have sensed the shift in her, because when his gaze met hers, his aquamarine eyes were hot.

His fingers trailed over her thighs until they parted, and she whispered, "I think I'm ready for dessert now."

Free sat up straighter in his chair at the same time that Jodi stood, coming to stand directly in front of him. He reached under the skirt she wore and pulled the flimsy, lacy panties she had on down her legs, tossing them aside. Working quickly at his belt and the buttons on his jeans, he freed himself from the tight jeans, and one side of Jodi's mouth tilted up in an appreciative smile at his readiness.

He reached for her then, but she surprised him when she dropped to her knees in front of him. He gasped sharply, as her breath misted over him. "Jodi, you don't—"

But she effectively silenced him when she took him into her mouth, her tongue swirling around the tip, then down the hard shaft. She took all of him, and he choked out a strangled sound, as his hands tangled into her curls. She reveled in the sounds he made from above her as she took all of him, again and again. She pressed her thighs tightly together, her own desire amplified by the way his body responded to her mouth on him.

"God damn," he growled from over her and tugged tight on her curls, pulling her off him, panting. His aquamarine gaze was hot as he stared into her own. His breathing was ragged. "Get up here."

She smiled and stood, her skirt riding up around her hips as he pulled her so that she straddled him, her knees on the smooth wood of the seat. Free's hands tangled once more into her hair, pulling her mouth to his and kissing her deeply, hungrily, and she moaned when his tongue spiraled into her mouth to taste all of her.

Raising up on her knees, she positioned herself above him and then slowly sank down onto his rock-hard cock, her head falling back as she sighed, "Oh, yes."

Free's hands bracketed her hips, his fingers digging into the soft flesh of her ass cheeks as she began to move over him. Their mouths met again fiercely, kissing deeply. Free's mouth fell from hers and he let his head fall back to rest against the back of the chair, his eyes raking over all of her as she moved over him. His hands tugged at the shirt at her waist, pulling it up and over her head, tossing it away and then cupping her breasts through the lacy bra she wore in his hands. One of Jodi's hands was braced behind her on his knee, the other clasped his shoulder for leverage as her thighs began to burn.

"Don't stop," Free growled through clenched teeth that showed up whiteley against his tanned face. "Don't stop until you come all over this cock."

Silvery moonlight illuminated his face for Jodi, and she cried out as her legs started to shake with her impending orgasm. Free reached between them, finding her clit with his fingers, and after a few strokes Jodi exploded like a firework. She felt more than heard

Free's growl of approval, and then his hands grasped her hips tightly again as he pounded upward into her, quickly coming to his own culmination with a fierce groan. Jodi fell forward onto his chest, burying her face in the side of his neck, her thighs trembling and her breathing ragged.

Free's fingers trailed along the curve of her spine as they both regained their breath. Jodi shivered; the night air cool against her naked skin. Free turned his head and pressed a kiss to her forehead, and Jodi smiled against the skin of his neck, satiated and content in Free's embrace.

After long minutes, Jodi gasped a soft moan and brought her eyes to his. He grinned wolfishly, shifting his hips beneath her even as he grew hard inside her again. "Ready for round two?"

CHAPTER 33

"Three eggs over easy, biscuits and gravy, a side of ham, and... ah let's throw on some wheat toast as well."

Free, flashing a smile at the unsuspecting waitress, closed his menu and handed it to her as she stood at the side of their booth. The poor girl stuttered, asking Jodi what she wanted, and after Jodi placed her order of French toast, the young woman hurried away, her cheeks flaming red.

"It's not fair, you know. How you dazzle women," Jodi teased, opening a single serve French vanilla creamer to add to her coffee.

Free rested his forearms on the laminate tabletop, leaning forward slightly and then grinned at her, making those damn butterflies that were never far away take flight. "Do I dazzle you, Jodi?"

"Routinely," Jodi breathed with a smile.

"Good," he whispered back, before leaning back in his booth seat and picking up his coffee cup to take a drink.

Free had woken early again, slipping out of bed and leaving the house before Jodi was awake to head to

Shane's for morning chores. When he returned, Jodi was awake and drinking a cup of coffee while watching reruns of *Friends*. He'd instructed her to get dressed, because he was taking her out for breakfast before her afternoon shift at the bookstore.

"By the way, Gram and Papa are having their annual Labor Day barbeque on Monday," Jodi said, raising her coffee to her lips and taking a sip. "The entire Storm and Kendall clan will be there. I'll never hear the end of it if we don't make an appearance. I can't deny Mom the chance to feed you. And I'm sure Dad will have his usual horseshoe tournament."

Free grinned, taking another drink of his own coffee. "Are you asking me out to a family function, Ms. Kendall?"

"I do believe that is what I'm attempting to do," Jodi teased, smiling. "Though I feel like you have an unfair advantage meeting the family; you already know everyone."

"I'd love to go," Free said and winked.

The waitress came by with a tray laden with food, and Free thanked the young woman, who blushed again as she set their plates down before them. Jodi giggled as the girl rushed away. "I told you."

"Well, it's a good thing I'm not trying to dazzle anyone except the beautiful woman sitting in front of me," Free whispered as he unwrapped his silverware, placing the napkin in his lap.

Jodi laughed. "I may have to fight for you. You've dazzled half the women in this diner already."

Grasping her hand in his, he pulled it to his lips to kiss the backs of her knuckles. "I'm all yours, baby."

When they finished their meal, Free paid and they exited the diner hand-in-hand. As he drove them back to Jodi's, one of his hands held hers captive while the other was draped loosely over the steering wheel. Jodi glanced at him from beneath her lashes, admiring his handsomeness. In this moment, she couldn't help but think how incredibly perfect her life was.

As they pulled into Jodi's driveway, she gasped, sitting straighter in her seat. "Are you fucking kidding me?"

Free braked the truck next to Jodi's Jeep, cutting the engine.

Scrambling out of the passenger seat, she closed the door of Free's truck and ran around to the front of her Jeep, where the hood was propped open. Jodi's mouth fell open and she looked over at Free as he came around the hood of his truck toward her.

The car battery was missing, and several of the hoses and wires had been cut.

Jodi stared down into the empty space where the battery should be for several long heartbeats. Clenching her fists so tight they hurt, her arms ramrod straight at her sides, she screamed, "Fucking asshole!"

Whirling away from her car, she stomped away several feet and then spun around, her breathing harsh. She paced back and forth several times, aware that Free was watching her closely. Tears stung her nose, and she stomped her foot angrily.

"I'm assuming you have an idea of who did this?" Free asked quietly, letting her have her moment of anger.

Jodi laughed, and it was an ugly sound. "Oh, yes."

"Your ex-husband?" Free guessed, his brows furrowing into a deep V.

Nodding, she crossed her arms over her chest. Blowing out her breath heavily, she shook her head in disbelief. "I thought I had escaped all of this."

"He's done this before?" Free asked, his voice low, and Jodi was surprised at the fury simmering just beneath the surface.

Swiping angrily at the tears that leaked out of her eyes and slid down her cheeks, she nodded. "Twice when we were married. This makes the third."

"Why did you marry this jackass, Jodi?" Free whispered, stepping forward until he stood directly in front of her. He placed his hands on her shoulders gently.

Jodi shook her head, whispering, "I don't want to—"

Free shook his head, too, clasping her shoulders in his hands so she couldn't hide from him. "No. I want to know. I'm cashing in on that promise to answer any question I have about this jackass."

She sighed deeply, letting her shoulders drop in defeat. "You want to know about my relationship with Josh?"

He nodded solemnly. "Yes, Jodi."

Jodi shook her head, blowing her breath out in frustration. He wanted to hear all the awfulness, he was going to get it, unfiltered. "I honestly don't know why I married him. I'll be the first to admit I was tired of being alone. I… I still had feelings for you," she admitted around a lump in her throat, and she thought she might die of embarrassment at the admission. She kept her eyes down, scared to look at him. "He was the first guy that made me feel like maybe I could… move on. I hadn't really dated much. I was woefully naïve. One of Dad's acquaintances introduced us one night, and I fell for the smoke screen that he presented. I don't think I ever really *loved* him, but I liked him. He was funny, seemed like a good person with friends that were very loyal, and seemed like he cared about me. He didn't so much ask me to marry him as much as it was a mutual agreement. We were married less than four months after meeting. Like I said, I was… woefully naïve."

Jodi laughed, though it wasn't a pretty sound, and she continued, "He was a good showman, very charismatic. I didn't see until then what he was really like; manipulative, cruel, jealous. He was looking for connections, anyone that could help him get a leg up. He wanted an entry into my dad's company, thought being a son-in-law would get him an automatic job and a big promotion. When Dad didn't even hire him, he was furious. He ended up choosing to go into real estate. He loved that he could still use my dad's name for clout."

Jodi took a deep breath, exhaling slowly before continuing. "I was working full time to get the bookstore up and running. Because he had put up a down payment for the store, he said it was my duty to pay for his real estate training. I was terribly unhappy, lonelier than ever. I realized I had made a huge mistake, but I didn't know how to get myself out of it. I was so embarrassed."

Digging the toe of her shoe into the gravel, she shrugged. Free was silent, letting her speak. "About nine months after we got married, I had decided to take a weekend off to myself to go to a writing convention downstate. Josh always hated my passion for writing. Said it took too much of my time, that he wouldn't allow me to publish because he didn't want to be associated with someone that writes 'smut'. When I told him I was going to the convention, he told me I couldn't go. He was convinced I was lying about where I was going and what I was doing, accused me of having an affair with some imaginary man. So, to try and stop me from going, he unhooked the car battery, and was beyond mad when he realized I'm not an idiot and could hook it back up. While he was out, I left for the convention. I was… punished… when I got home that Sunday evening. That's when he started taking the battery out completely. He'd hide it, wouldn't give it back until he'd given me the silent treatment for days, waited until I apologized."

"Shane said he put his hands on you," Free stated, his hands tightening on her shoulders slightly.

"Of course he told you," Jodi breathed, stepping away, forcing his hands to drop to his sides. "He never *hit* me, Free. He loves to be able to tell people he never hit me, because it was true. It was more… intimidation, than anything. Josh was almost always drunk. He'd back me into corners, lean over me if I was sitting, scream at me about how I never did enough for him, he complained that our sex life was a disappointment and that I didn't 'give it up' enough, how I clearly didn't know how lucky I was to be with someone that was such a great catch," Jodi laughed darkly. Free's jaw clenched tightly. "He hated that I had opened the bookshop, said it was a waste of time and money. When I told him I was going through with publishing in my own name, he was furious. My name, not my married name, but he was associated with it regardless. He screamed at me that I was going to humiliate him. He was more worried about what would happen to him, how his name and his job would be affected by something he saw as a shameful hobby his wife had. It was a compounded fight, because I had also become aware of an affair he was having, that he had habitually lied about until I had solid proof, and even then he tried to convince me I was crazy..."

Jodi trailed off when Free's hands tightened into fists at his sides. Shaking her head, she waved her hands dismissively. "I'm sorry, you don't need to hear this—"

"What happened then, Jodi?" he asked roughly.

Watching his face, she shrugged and whispered, "I told him to leave me alone, that I was going to bed and he needed to sober up and that we would talk about everything when he was clear headed. He just kept on, and I said that if he didn't leave me alone I was going to go to Mom and Dad's for the night until he calmed down. Josh took my car keys out of my purse and put them in his desk so I couldn't leave, and continued to scream at me. He backed me up against the bed. I kept telling him to leave me alone, to give me my keys back, but he just kept getting closer and more irate."

"When he pushed me, I'd had enough, and I reached for my phone to call my parents to come get me because I didn't want to stay in the house with him at that point," she continued, staring out over the field, her gaze unfocused. She shivered despite the heat of the day. "He flew into a rage; I'd never seen him so volatile. He snatched my phone out of my hand and threw it across the room, then grabbed me by the arms and pinned me to the bed, held me down with his knee in my abdomen. But he never *hit* me."

Jodi wrapped her arms around herself and shrugged, and she could see the tension building in Free. He nodded for her to continue, though his features were stony.

"I couldn't break his hold, I remember screaming for him to get off me, and then I managed to wriggle out from under him enough to try and use one leg to throw him off, though realistically I didn't get loose until he was ready to let me go. I ran, picked up my phone from the floor and went outside, ran halfway down the street to get away. I called the police, dispatch stayed on the line with me until the officers got there. When they arrived, he tried telling them I broke his ribs by kneeing him in the side, completely unprovoked. They didn't believe him; I had bruises on my arms and he didn't have a mark on him, and he was stinking drunk, though he tried to tell them he'd only had one beer. It's just what he does. Spins stories and tells lies to fit his narrative. They took him to jail for the night, but I was too scared to actually press charges."

Jodi watched as Free's jaw worked, though he stayed silent, letting her tell her story without interruption. "After that, I knew I needed out. My parents helped me move out that weekend, not that Dad was going to let me stay there after that. There wasn't anything I could fix, not that I wanted to. When I gave him the divorce papers a few weeks later, he shouted at me, called me a stupid bitch and a cunt, and told me I would never find someone that would put up with me the way he did..."

When Jodi finally raised her eyes to Free's, she was both nervous and awed at the fury that darkened his eyes and bunched his jaw.

"I'll kill him," he growled ominously.

Jodi shook her head slowly, her eyes softening. "He's not even worth it, Free."

Stepping forward, she slid her arms around his lean waist, resting her cheek against his chest. His arms encircled her, and she felt him sigh against the top of her head.

"How long were you separated before the divorce was final?" he asked.

Jodi took a breath in, taking the briefest of seconds to bury her nose in his chest, and allowing his now familiar scent to wash over her. He felt like home. She shrugged then, thinking. "We'd been married ten months when I filed and moved back in with Mom and Dad. That was last April, I think. Divorce took until this May when it was final. So, just over a year, and three months since then."

Free squeezed her gently, his fingers trailing over the skin of her back that was left bare from the tank top she wore. Pressing her forehead into his chest, she laughed sadly. "I'm sorry. I shouldn't have lost my temper like I did earlier."

He pulled away and looked down at her in astonishment. "Why are you apologizing? Jodi, the man came onto your property uninvited, stole your car battery and vandalized your vehicle. He clearly has a history of abusive behavior. You *should* be mad. You should be calling the police."

Jodi was shaking her head before he finished talking. "I don't have any proof that he did it."

Free stared at her for a long moment, and Jodi fidgeted nervously. "You're still scared of him, aren't you," he murmured, not so much a question as a statement.

Jodi shrugged again, and Free blew out a frustrated breath, releasing her and walking away several steps. He turned on his booted heel and placed his hands on his hips, watching her. She lowered her gaze to the ground sheepishly.

"What hold does this douche have on you, Jodi?"

Jodi sighed heavily and turned to her Jeep, lowering the hood with a metallic clunk, then dusted her hands off. She would have to call Shaun and Tristan to come do the repairs and bring a new battery, she thought to herself. She so badly didn't want to have this conversation with Free, but it seemed that he wasn't going to let it go.

"Jodi," he pressed.

"You want me to admit that I'm still scared? Yes, yes I am scared of him!" Jodi finally shouted, whipping around to face him again, her breathing harsh. "Where should I start, Free? Was what I just told you not enough of a reason? It's like he knows what I do as soon as I do it. It's unnerving the way he keeps tabs on me. He's allowed to move on and do whatever he wants with his life, but I'm not afforded the same privilege, because I humiliated him by getting him arrested and divorcing him so quickly. I am the villain in his story, he loves to play the victim, like he didn't do anything to me. I wounded his pride and poked holes in the façade that he works so hard to keep in place. Not only had he been committing adultery—sleeping with that girl you and I ran into at the store— that I didn't even find out about until a couple months ago— but after that ended, he started seeing someone new. This new girl was the affair I had found out about just before I gave him the divorce papers. He moved her in just weeks after I left, but I even think about *talking* to someone new and he has to be his douchey self and sabotage it. *That's* why he came to you as soon as he knew we were even potentially a thing. He likes to remind me he can manipulate my life any way he feels fit."

Jodi threw her arms wide, pointing to her house, her car. "He shows up here whenever he wants, makes passive aggressive comments about how I dress, how my weight fluctuates, who I'm seen in public with. *But*," she laughed maniacally, "probably my favorite way he exercises his control over me is this: When I was buying the building for the bookshop just after we got married, he made some sales pitch about how it would be smarter for us to put the deed in his name first, which then gave him majority ownership. I had been working on opening it for a year, before we even met. I was so stupid. He put some puny amount up for the down payment, and used that as a way to manipulate me, too, even though Dad and I were the ones that financed it. I fought to get sole ownership when we divorced, but he had a good lawyer. They left it as is. Not only do I have to pay him rent on *my* building for *my* business, but he also feels entitled enough to help himself inside after hours. Which, because he owns the building, isn't even illegal! And, to put the fucking icing on this cake, I don't even have any proof because he's smarter than I gave him credit for and stole my surveillance tapes last week!"

Letting her head fall back until it almost touched her shoulders, she closed her eyes, taking several deep, steadying breaths to calm herself. If this tirade didn't scare Free off, she would be amazed. Tears made her nose sting, and she fought them back.

"Is that what you wanted to hear, Free? All the different ways this man has terrorized me and continues to manipulate my life? Is that sufficient reason for me to still be afraid of this asshole?"

Free came to her then, wrapping her in a bear hug. "I can take care of him for you."

Jodi laughed, then took a deep breath in, letting it out slowly. "Dad has already offered, but thank you."

"You said he took the surveillance tapes. Do you have a new system in place yet?" Free asked, resting his chin against the top of her head. She remained settled against his chest, her arms tucked between them. She nodded.

"Yes, Warren came to the store and put in an all-new system. I'll catch him, it's just a matter of time. I don't know what good it will do me, but eventually I hope to be completely Joshua Murphy free... I keep asking him if I can buy him out of the property, but he refuses," she said, shrugging.

"I will do whatever I can to help you, Jodi," Free said, squeezing her.

But Jodi shook her head, looking up at him then. "No. If you do anything, it will only make it worse. Trust me. He knows how to play the game."

"And I'm not afraid of some piece of shit woman beater," Free snapped, though his eyes were gentle. "You have no reason to be scared of him anymore. I'm not going to let him do anything else to you."

Tucking her head back into his chest, she sighed sadly. She wished that she could believe him... but she knew this was only temporary. He would be gone in another couple weeks, and then she'd be left alone to pick up the pieces of her broken heart all over again when he left.

But, when Free tipped her chin up and lowered his mouth to hers, all thoughts of his impending departure flew from her mind.

CHAPTER 34

"Good morning."

Jodi opened one eye and grumbled unintelligibly, rolling over in bed so that she was laying on her stomach, burying her face in the pillow. "It's not even light out, yet."

"It's almost six," Free breathed close to her ear. His fingers trailed, feather light, over the curve of her shoulders, down her back, to the dip of her hips.

"You kept me up all night," Jodi whined petulantly into the pillow.

"I didn't hear you complaining earlier, or the time before that..." he breathed, palming one ass cheek in his hand before sliding his hand down between her thighs, which fell open with little prompting.

"I'm not complaining now..." she sighed, her hips moving against his hand. "Ooooh, yes. Please."

Free nipped at the meaty part of her shoulder, making her gasp. He shifted, moving so he was between her thighs, his front pressed to her back. "I like it when you say please."

Jodi murmured appreciatively and shifted slightly, allowing him to slide one forearm beneath her ribcage, his palm flat against her abdomen, tilting her hips toward his. He levered himself up on his other elbow, fisting the other hand into the pillow next to her head. Probing with the head of his hard cock, he found the entrance to her already slick and ready for him. Pushing inside until he was buried all the way in, he felt more than heard her low moan against his chest. He let his forehead drop to the curve of her shoulder.

Rolling his hips against the softness of her backside, he gritted his teeth and ground out, "Fuuuuck, I love how good you feel."

Arching her back to receive each of his thrusts, Jodi tossed her head, her sleep-tousled curls falling to one side, revealing half of her face where it was pressed into the bedsheet beneath her. Her cheeks were sleep flushed, her lips swollen and well-kissed. Her fingers fisted in the sheets and she moaned softly as she took all of him.

She was a goddess— his own personal Aphrodite.

Sliding his hand around her jaw from beneath her, he tilted her face up and back, forcing her to arch her back further, even as he continued to pump into her. It was an intoxicating sight. "God damn, Jodi, you're so fucking sexy."

She bit her lip and he growled low in his throat before capturing her mouth with his, kissing her thoroughly. Rocking into her, his tempo increased. Releasing her jaw and gripping the headboard in tense fingers, he let her fall back to the bedspread, and she sobbed, "Oh my god, Free, please!"

"That's it, sweetheart," he growled. "You're going to be a good girl and come for me, and then I'm going to pound you until I come, too."

"Yes, please," Jodi moaned, pressing into him harder, and he could feel her thighs start to tremble, her telltale sign that she was close. Free smiled darkly from behind her, then reached around her body until his fingers found her clit, flicking it back and forth until he felt her come hard around his cock, her cry of ecstasy music to his ears.

He pumped into her rhythmically, letting her enjoy the high, before he growled, "Hold on tight," and then pounded into her, quickly coming to his own intense climax.

Jodi panted beneath him, sucking air into her lungs like she'd forgotten how to breathe. He rolled off her to her side, gathering her into his arms and tucking her head beneath his chin, running his hands over her arms and back, even as she trembled. Reaching for the sheet, he pulled it up to cover her, worried he'd been too rough.

Her fingers trailed over his chest, shaking slightly. He captured her hand in his, bringing it to his lips. "Was that okay, Jodi?" he whispered against her fingers. "Did I hurt you?"

Taking a deep, shuddering breath, she shook her head, then finally raised her head so she could look up into his eyes. Her sapphire eyes were limpid and she let out a half laugh, saying breathlessly, "I had no idea it could be like this."

"Like what?" he asked softly, smoothing her hair away from her face. The sun had started to come up, the sky out of Jodi's bedroom window was brightening, casting pale light across her face as he watched her.

"Like *this*," Jodi whispered, her eyes searching his. "You're some kind of magician, I think. You pull orgasms out of me like bunnies out of a hat."

Free laughed out loud, throwing his head back, then leaned down to press his lips to hers gently.

"It's going to take some getting used to," Jodi murmured, tucking her head back under his chin, settling against him.

Free's brow furrowed, and he gripped her chin between his thumb and forefinger, tipping her face up so she was looking at him again. "Don't tell me that clown couldn't even get you off."

Jodi shrugged, and he was coming to recognize it as a defense mechanism. One side of her mouth tilted up slightly in a sad smile and she lowered her eyes from his shyly. "It was never a priority, so I guessed it was just normal not to."

Free hated this fool. He wasn't sure he would be able to do as Jodi wished and hold himself back if he ever ran into this jackass again. What a joke this clown was. Clearly the man hadn't had a clue what to do in bed to please a woman, or was too arrogant to believe he needed to.

Though, he admitted to himself, he took perverse pride in the knowledge that he was able to give Jodi the kind of pleasure she hadn't known in her marriage. He wasn't sure he would ever get enough of her.

Now that he knew what it was like with Jodi, he never wanted it to end. The thought of leaving in another couple weeks was painful, and he quickly pushed those thoughts from his mind. Right now, with her, was all he wanted to think about.

Smoothing his fingers over the hair at her temples, he settled his chin on the top of her head, at the same time tightening the arm around her shoulders, pulling her closer to his chest. "It's my pleasure, Jodi, I assure you."

CHAPTER 35

"I think castration is a great option."

Free tipped his beer in salute and nodded his head in agreement. "I support that statement."

Jodi rolled her eyes and laughed dryly. Shaun leaned over the open hood of Jodi's Jeep, inspecting the damage Josh had done the day before. Free had argued that he could do the repairs, but Jodi had told him no, that Shaun and Tristan would never forgive her if she let anyone else do her car repairs.

In trade, Free had insisted on taking her to work that morning and told her he would be back to pick her up when her shift was over. He had surprised her with dinner ready when they'd gotten back home after picking her up from work. Shaun and Tristan had shown up just as they were cleaning up dinner, ready with replacement parts. Warren had been out earlier in the day to install a security system with cameras as well, per Levi's instructions.

Shaun reached over and took a drink of the beer Free had offered her before setting it back down on the railing of the porch. While she was getting her things set up to do the repairs, Tristan asked, "Are you ever going to put up that porch swing Mom got you?"

Jodi nodded, taking a drink of her beer, too. "Sure, eventually."

"Porch swing?" Free asked.

"Yeah, Mom got me a porch swing as a gift when I moved in. I just haven't had the extra pair of hands to put it up," Jodi laughed.

Standing from where he sat on one of the porch steps, he waved his hand to Tris. "Come on, show me where it is. Jodi, where do you want it?"

"You really don't have to—" Jodi protested, but was cut off when Free leaned down to press a kiss to her mouth.

"Shush. Where do you want it?" Free asked.

One corner of Jodi's mouth tilted up and Free's eyes glinted with humor when he saw just where her filthy mind had taken her.

"Later," he husked quietly before straightening. Tristan and Freeman sauntered off toward the shed, where the swing was currently stored. The two came back a few minutes later, the large wooden porch swing suspended between them. They carried it up the porch steps, and Jodi retrieved the metal hooks from the drawer in the kitchen, bringing them out to Free. He walked over to his truck, reaching into the backseat to retrieve a well-worn bag of tools.

While Shaun started on the Jeep, Tristan and Free went to work hanging the swing where Jodi instructed. When it was suspended from the rafters of the covered porch, Free gestured toward it and Jodi laughed before sitting down, testing it out. The sun was beginning to set over the treetops in the distance, and Jodi smiled over at Free and her brother. "Thank you."

Tris nodded and grinned widely before heading down the steps toward Shaun, who had just called from where she was under the Jeep for a specific part. As Jodi's two siblings worked, Free came toward her and sat down on the swing next to her sighing appreciatively before draping his arm across her shoulders. "This is nice."

"Yes, it is. Thank you, again," Jodi murmured, settling into his side. He pecked a quick, chaste kiss to her lips. His booted feet pushed them back and forth gently. She was more content than she'd been in a long time. Happier than she'd been in a long time. She knew it was because of Free.

Love was blooming in her heart for him, just as she'd known it would, as she'd secretly feared it would. It had been a protected bud for so many years, she wasn't surprised it had finally begun to blossom under the warmth of his smile and inherent kindness. Slowly, but with each petal that unfolded, Jodi knew her heart would forever belong to the man sitting beside her. And it was going to break like hell when he left again.

"I swear to God the next time this man touches your car I'm going to murder him myself," Shaun called angrily from beneath the Jeep, her voice muffled. "I'm getting really tired of replacing perfectly fine car parts!"

Jodi and Free laughed, and Tris turned to them, asking, "Are you going to Gram and Pops this weekend?"

Jodi nodded, but it was Shaun who answered, her voice still muffled from under the vehicle. "I think Mom and Gram both would disown any one of us for missing a family BBQ."

"You're probably right," Jodi laughed.

"Should we bring anything?" Free asked, looking over at her, his arm still draped over her shoulders. His foot continued to push them back and forth gently.

Tris, Jodi, and Shaun all laughed. Shaun poked her head out from beneath the Jeep and called, "Are you kidding? Don't you remember any of the family gatherings you went to before you left? A BBQ at Gram and Papa's is an all-out shindig. They'll have enough food and booze for an army, lawn games, a bonfire, probably a band. Gram would be offended if you brought anything."

"Alright," Free laughed again, holding up his hands, palms out. He took a drink of his beer, then pointed to Jodi's. "Do you want another?"

Jodi shook her head, smiling over at him. "No, thank you. If you're going inside, I will take a water, if you don't mind?"

"No problem," he said, rising from the swing. Calling down to the other two, he asked, "Shaun, Tris, you guys want anything while I'm inside?"

"I'll take another beer," Shaun called.

"Me too," Tris joked.

"Come talk to me in about four years," Free chuckled. Then, winking over at Jodi, he said, "Three, if you don't tell your parents or Jodi."

"That would mean you have to stick around that long," Jodi quipped lightly. The weight of the words hung in the air between them, and Jodi wished she could take them back as soon as they left her mouth. She felt her cheeks warm with embarrassment.

"Maybe that's my plan," Free murmured with a grin before disappearing into the house.

CHAPTER 36

"Ready to go?"

Jodi nodded, taking one last look in the mirror, doing a half turn to check her reflection. She fussed with a stray curl that had escaped the loose braid she'd fashioned to the side so that it draped over one shoulder, but decided to leave it to frame her face. Sliding her freshly pedicured feet into leather sandals, she turned to find Free watching her from the doorway. His gaze was smoldering.

"No," Jodi laughed, pointing one finger at him. "We don't have time for that."

"I was ready ten minutes ago," he drawled from where he was leaning against the door frame, his hands in his front jeans pockets, pulling the fabric tight across his hips. Jodi swallowed hard, and he grinned wolfishly.

"Looking this good takes time," she teased, doing a mock curtsy. She wore a pair of light wash jeans that were well worn and molded to her shape, and she had cuffed them just above her ankle, capri style. A white racer back tank top left her tanned shoulders and back bare. A pair of cobalt blue Goodr sunglasses were perched on the top of her head, and they almost matched the blue of her eyes. A small, brown leather purse was on one shoulder.

"You could wear a potato sack and look stunning," Free stated, then reached out his hand for hers. She slipped her hand in his and smiled up at him, pausing as he leaned down to press a kiss to her mouth. He nipped her lip gently and Jodi's body betrayed her, going limp against him as she sighed wantonly. Free chuckled and smacked her bottom soundly. "Get, before you make us late."

"Me?" Jodi exclaimed, laughing. "How would I make us late?"

Free leaned down and drew his lips along her jawline, up to her ear, where he breathed, "Keep making that sound like when I bite your lip and find out."

Jodi's mouth fell open and Free laughed out loud at the look of astonishment on her face. He pressed a smacking kiss to her surprised mouth before leading her toward the door. They walked hand in hand down the porch steps and he opened the passenger door of his truck, assisting her up into the seat.

Jodi watched as he sauntered around the hood of the truck, and her mouth went dry as she took in the beauty of his body. He truly was the most handsome man she'd ever seen. And he was all hers.

He climbed in behind the wheel and glanced over at her as he shut the door with a thud. "That—" he growled and leaned over, gripping a handhold of her hair and hauling her over the console to meet him,

"—is not the way to get us out of here on time." His mouth plundered hers thoroughly, leaving her aching and wet and breathless when he finally released her mouth. "Stop looking at me like that or I will carry your sexy ass back into the house and we won't leave at all tonight."

Jodi bit her lip and smiled when he let her go, settling herself into the seat and buckling the seatbelt. "Yes, sir."

Free shook his head and laughed darkly. "Don't say that, either. I like that, too."

Jodi laughed huskily as he put the truck in gear and maneuvered them out of the driveway, heading in the direction of Hanna and Paul Storm's homestead. As they got close, colorful banners were hung from one towering maple tree to another on opposite sides of the driveway. Free's truck rumbled down the long, gravel driveway until they reached a fork, leading to the left under a canopy of maples where several dozen other vehicles were already parked.

Free exited the truck first, coming around the bed to open Jodi's door. Before she could hop out, he gripped her hips in his hands and lowered her slowly to the ground, letting her body slide down his, deliberately. Jodi's eyes raised to his, and his breathing was ragged as he stared down at her. Jodi watched as he opened his mouth to speak, but a car pulled up and parked close by, and he glanced around before smiling at her and taking her hand in his once more.

As they walked along the gravel driveway toward the sprawling farmhouse atop a small hill shaded mostly by more towering maples, oak, and birch, they could hear a band playing from somewhere around the backside of the house. Jodi laughed and said, "I told you they would have a band. And what do you want to bet that Gram tells you you're too skinny?"

Free rolled his eyes and linked his fingers with hers, pulling her hand up to kiss the back of it. Leaning down, he whispered in her ear, "If you're right, you have to give me five."

"Five what?" she whispered, already knowing the answer. Her eyes were wide with bewilderment at his boldness.

Free grinned down at her devilishly, winking. Jodi's heart thudded in her chest, and damn him, but she was aching again.

"I can't do five," she whispered breathily, panicking slightly.

Jodi felt as if every nerve in her body was going to jump out of her skin when he leaned down to breathe in her ear, "Is that a challenge?"

She swallowed hard and he chuckled, his breath tickling her neck. He straightened as they rounded the corner of the house. He squeezed her hand gently.

Tantalizing aromas wafted toward them as they came around the side of the house, where the majority of the Storm family and friends had gathered. A white-haired gentleman wearing blue jean overalls stood beside a giant metal BBQ pit where a whole pig was being roasted on a spit. Jodi smiled and waved when Paul Storm, her maternal grandfather, looked up from what he was doing and spotted her across the way. The

BBQ pit with the slowly turning pig sat on a concrete pad near a massive pole barn, where Jodi could see her mother and maternal grandmother inside, both fussing over hordes of side dishes and desserts. Hanna Storm had the same white hair as her husband of forty-seven years, pinned back into a clip, wisps floating around her round face.

Serenity saw them and smiled broadly, then wiped her hands on a dishtowel before making her way toward them. When she reached the two of them, she hugged Jodi and pecked a kiss to her cheek before turning to Free and pulling him into an embrace as well. Jodi blushed to the roots of her dark hair when her mother's keen eyes looked them both over, to the familiar way they touched each other.

Gram came up to them then, hugging Jodi tight and squeezing her hand in hers. She turned to Free and said excitedly, "Oh, how I've been dying to see this handsome face!"

Free laughed and leaned down to hug Hanna, pressing a kiss to her wrinkled cheek. "Not as much as I've been waiting to see your beautiful one."

Jodi watched as her grandmother's blue eyes, the same as hers and her mothers, sparkled. "Oh, stop it, you rascal!" Gram murmured with a laugh. Freeman had the ability to woo three generations of women in her family!

Gram held either side of Free's face in her hands and patted one of his cheeks gently. "You're too skinny. Come on, let's get you something to put on those bones."

When Gram had turned and headed with Serenity back to the pole barn, Jodi dared a glance at Free. He simply held one hand up, all five fingers splayed wide. *Five*, he mouthed, then grinned wolfishly.

CHAPTER 37

Jodi and Free hadn't made it more than a dozen steps before Shauntelle and Tommy descended upon them. Shaun and Jodi launched into a conversation about the sunglasses still perched on Jodi's head. Tommy held out a cold beer to Free, who took it and nodded, saying, "Thanks."

"We haven't really had the chance to introduce ourselves," Tommy said, cracking open his own beer. "I'm Tommy."

"Freeman," Free said and they shook hands. "You're Shaun's boyfriend, right?"

"Right," Tommy said, nodding, then took a sip of his beer. "I've heard about you from Shaun."

Free took a drink of his own beer and chuckled. "Good things, I hope."

Jodi and Shaun wandered into the pole barn after Jodi glanced back to say, "I'm going to grab a drink." Free smiled and nodded.

"How long have you and Shaun been together?" Free asked. He looked the younger man up and down, admitting that he was a handsome guy. He had sandy blonde hair that was long enough to touch the collar of his shirt and fall over his brow. His eyes were a whiskey brown. He had a construction worker build, strong and lean.

"Almost a year," Tommy replied, taking another drink of his beer.

Free nodded, watching as the younger of the two sisters poured two hefty cocktails. Lord have mercy, Jodi was going to be hammered in an hour if Shaun was in charge of the alcohol tonight. Free laughed, raising his beer in a salute. "She's a handful."

"That she is," Tommy laughed. "What about you and Jodi?"

Free had braced himself for that question. He knew it was going to be a recurring question over the course of the night, since it was no secret he and Jodi were... What *were* they? He felt like a besotted teen again. He hadn't been in any kind of real relationship in well over a decade.

"We're... figuring it out as we go," Free said simply. "It's still new."

"Well, I knew her when she was with that Josh tool," Tommy muttered and took another pull of his beer. "It's nice to see her smile again."

Free nodded, taking a self-conscious drink of his beer. He still wanted to pulverize Josh's face into nothing, despite Jodi's objections. He was glad to hear that the general opinion of Jodi's ex-husband was one of distaste. He didn't feel quite so bad about the loathing he felt for the man, learning that others shared the same feelings.

Paul Storm and Levi sidled over to them then, and Free extended his hand to the elder, shaking it firmly. "Free, how are you, son?" Paul asked, his green eyes twinkling.

"Good, sir," Free said and smiled. He had always liked Jodi's grandparents. They had taken him in just as Serenity and Levi had done. He'd never felt out of place when with this family, that was for certain. "How are you?"

"Oh, just fine, just fine indeed," Paul said, his voice gravelly. He gestured to the bruise that was fading beneath Free's left eye. "You getting into trouble already?"

Levi grinned at Free, who rolled his eyes and chuckled. "Courtesy of your daughter's husband."

Paul glanced between the two of them and shook his head with a low chuckle. "Damn bully."

"He deserved it," Levi grumbled roughly, though he grinned around a drink of his own beer. He cocked his head toward Jodi, who was laughing as she spoke animatedly with Shaun, Serenity, and Gram. "Thank you."

Free swallowed hard. "For what?" he asked roughly. Nerves made his heart thud erratically in his chest.

Levi's eyes were softer than Free remembered ever seeing them when he said gruffly, "For giving me my daughter back."

Paul harrumphed, sidling away, though Free saw the moisture in the older man's eyes as he turned away, toward the pole barn. Free avoided Levi and Tommy's eyes, the latter jumping like he'd been bit, taking a long drink of his beer and then coughing when it went down the wrong pipe. Levi pounded Tommy on the back roughly.

Pop and Gram met at the wide door of the pole barn and he reached up to ring a hand-crafted iron bell suspended from the wall. When the clanging quieted, the large group of guests stopped what they were doing and turned toward the two, who stood hand in hand.

Paul called gruffly through the gathered crowd, "Let's eat."

Jodi found Free moments later, her cheeks flushed and a wide smile on her face. She linked her arm with his, looking up at him, and he couldn't stop the hand that came up to tuck one of her errant strands of curls behind one ear. He allowed his fingers to linger along her cheek for an extended moment, reveling in the feel of her against him.

He didn't know how he was going to let her go.

But he did know he didn't want to.

CHAPTER 38

The local country band that was on a small stage played rousing renditions of classic favorites, keeping the guests entertained and on the large wooden dance floor that had been constructed in the backyard. A massive, already roaring fire had been built in the hand built fire pit. Folding chairs circled it, with family members and friends chatting. Children ran through the large yard, chasing each other, playing, and laughing. Jodi recognized several of her young cousins, but had yet to see her aunts or uncles.

Dinner had consisted of the roasted pig and chafing dishes filled to the brim with foods that Jodi knew to be all fresh from her grandparents' gardens; corn on the cob, potato salad, baked beans, mixed vegetables, and so many other options that Jodi and Free didn't have room on their plates to try. An entire table was laden with desserts: pies, cookies, fruit, and some decadent monstrosity that was made entirely of chocolate.

Jodi and Free sat together at one of the many wooden picnic tables that were arranged throughout the expansive yard. They were joined shortly by her parents, and Shaun and Tommy. Warren had left for his sophomore year of college the day before, despite Seren's pleas to wait a couple more days. Her brother Tristan was off in the distance with several other cousins and her uncle Spencer, tinkering with dirt bikes, and her sister Fallon was curled up in a hammock beneath one of the towering maple trees engrossed in a book.

Serenity's sister, Summer, found her way over to them, accompanied by her husband, Micah, who happened to be Levi's baby brother. Summer was the exact opposite of her older sister, with golden blonde hair and green eyes. Micah looked like a younger, clean shaven version of Levi, short dark hair and cobalt blue eyes. Their youngest trailed behind them, a towheaded little boy with blue eyes the same shade as Micah and Levi's.

As soon as the young boy saw Jodi he grinned and ran toward her, launching into her arms for a bear hug. Jodi squeezed him tight and kissed the top of his white-blonde head. "Hi, my little Benny boy!"

Ben held up a small toy car to show her, saying, "Jo-dee, I have a Lightning McQueen car! I want to race Tris!"

Jodi laughed and hugged the little boy tight. He had been a surprise pregnancy for her aunt and uncle, nearly ten years between Ben and their middle child, Kylee, who was nearly fifteen. Ben turned to look at Free, waving shyly. Free smiled back, and said gently, "Hi, I'm Freeman. Who are you?"

"I'm Benjamin Lee Kendall," he said, enunciating each word as if he'd been practicing. "I get to go to kindergarten soon!"

Free smiled at Jodi before turning his attention back to Ben. "Kindergarten? That's pretty important. Are you ready?"

"I think so," he said nervously.

Aunt Summer reached over to ruffle Ben's hair. "He's going to do great," she said encouragingly. Free stood then, in order to hug Summer and shake hands with Micah. "It's been too long, Free! We were so happy to hear you were home."

Jodi saw her aunt's eyes take in the two of them, together. Free's hand had been riding high on Jodi's thigh when the three of them had walked up. She was grateful her family had taken this new *whatever this was* between her and Free in stride. The age difference was a big deal to Free, but seemed to be a non-issue to everyone else. She hoped that helped Free resolve himself of any of the lingering guilt he may be feeling over their age gap.

Ben hopped off Jodi's lap when several other cousins zoomed past them, and he ran several feet away, then stopped short, turning back to his mother. "May I go play with Ross and Jake, please?"

Summer nodded, sitting down on one side of the picnic table as Shaun and Tommy stood, walking together toward the pole barn to get another round of drinks. "Go ahead. Only to the fence, though."

"He's adorable," Free laughed as he raced off.

Micah chuckled. "He's a hellion. Tanner and Kylee did not get into nearly as much mischief as he does on his own. Imagine my surprise when Summer told me a week before Kylee's tenth birthday that her period was late. I about had a heart attack."

Summer rolled her green eyes heavenward. "He acts like he doesn't know how babies are made."

Jodi stopped breathing for an extended heartbeat, her mouth going dry.

Babies. She knew how babies were made.

She hadn't even thought about the possibility of pregnancy. And she and Free had not taken any precautions.

Free must have had the same thought, his eyes slicing over to hers. His eyebrows were raised slightly. She shook her head, barely, lowering her eyes guiltily. She watched as he swallowed hard. She felt like her head was spinning.

The sun had begun its descent toward the horizon, casting the gathering in long shadows as the sun descended behind the tree line on the western edge of her grandparent's property. String lights that had been suspended from tree to tree began to glow as the shadows deepened. Free motioned with his head toward a grove of willow trees on the far side of the yard, and Jodi nodded. Her heart was in her throat.

They excused themselves, but ran into Shaun and Tommy as they exited the pole barn, fresh beers in Tommy's hand for himself and Free, and Shaun had taken the liberty of pouring Jodi another cocktail. Jodi accepted it and downed half of it, excruciatingly aware of Free's eyes on her. Shaun and Tommy wandered off toward the fire, while Jodi and Free continued toward the fence line beneath the massive willow tree.

They were silent for a long time as they stared out over the cornfield beyond the fence. "I didn't think to ask," Free finally whispered. "You're the first woman I've been with that I haven't used a condom with. It never even occurred to me."

"I stopped taking my birth control when Josh and I divorced. I had no interest in dating..." Jodi murmured. "I'm sorry."

"Don't apologize," Free said gently and gave her a crooked grin. "I'm as much at fault here. I'm sorry I didn't protect you."

Jodi wouldn't admit that the thought of a baby with Free wasn't a terrible one. Whatever *this* was, it was much too new, though. She didn't know what it was, yet, if it was anything. Or what his feelings for her were.

She did quick math in her head, counting back the days. "I can't promise for sure, but I think we're okay. I should know in about a week."

Free nodded, smiling gently at her again. He leaned down and pressed a kiss to her lips. "We will just be careful from now on." He winked at her. "Don't think I'm even close to being done with you yet, Jodi."

To make sure she understood exactly what he meant, he dipped his tongue into her mouth, at the same time running a hand up between her thighs. The drapery of the willows' low hanging boughs offered them enough privacy that no one would see what he was doing to her. Jodi sighed, but it turned into a moan when he nipped her lower lip with his sharp white teeth. His fingers played at her through her jeans and she groaned when he stopped.

"Shh," he whispered hoarsely, covering her mouth with his own again, kissing her until she was breathless. His chest heaved with each deep breath he took when he released her mouth finally. His lips moving against hers as he spoke, he whispered gruffly, "If you come right now, that doesn't count as one of my five."

Jodi thought she might die of the fire that consumed her at his words.

Free nipped her lip again and chuckled when her knees buckled slightly. "Let's go, you shameless hussy."

The sun was setting as they walked back toward the party, and if possible, more people had shown up for the festivities. The dance floor was nearly packed with line dancing couples, and Jodi smiled when she saw her parents and her grandparents twirling to a rendition of Alan Jackson's "Good Time".

Micah was tending the growing fire in the massive fire pit when Jodi and Free walked up. Free stepped over to assist in placing two large wooden pallets on the fire, which didn't take long to catch.

"Thank you," Micah said with a grin. "Tristan was supposed to be helping me but he got distracted." He nodded with his chin in the direction of the pole barn.

"Is that Cyndall?" Jodi asked, her eyes going wide with shock when they landed on the girl that her brother was talking to.

"His tongue is going to fall out of his head if he doesn't pull it back in," Free laughed. "She's not family, right?"

"Lord no," Jodi laughed. "Cyn is Tristan's best friend. She always leaves for the summer to visit her mom in North Carolina and comes home just before school starts in the fall. She didn't look like that when she left in June."

The girl in question grinned over at Tristan, who stumbled slightly. She reached up one hand to tuck a strand of auburn hair behind her ear. Her skin was deeply tanned, with hundreds of freckles bridging her nose and cheeks. Her sky-blue eyes were bright against her tanned skin. Jodi noticed she'd grown about four inches since the last time she'd seen her, and had filled out from the gangly, knobby kneed girl from before. Jodi had never seen her brother act this way around a girl. A car maybe, but never a girl.

"Poor sucker," Micah chuckled, shaking his head as he sat down in one of the many chairs circling the fire just as Summer joined them.

Jodi and Free chose a padded bench swing, Free's booted toe pushing them back and forth gently, his other ankle resting on his knee. The fire felt good against the coolness of the evening as dusk disappeared completely, the stars coming out full force.

With Jodi pressed against his side and Free's arm draped over her shoulders, his fingers were able to idly trail along the bare skin of her shoulder. It made goosebumps break out along her flesh and she was mortified when her nipples peaked at the contact. Jodi's hand rested on his jean clad leg, her fingertips playing with the stitched seam on the inside of his thigh.

"You're teasing me," he breathed against her temple, only loud enough for her to hear. Shivers ran down her body as his breath ruffled her hair. Fanning the flames of her desire, the fingers trailing along her arm moved upward to stroke the side of her neck, and Jodi's breathing quickened. She knew, behind the fly of his jeans, he was growing hard. She squeezed his thigh and smiled coyly when she heard his answering growl in her ear. "Jodi."

They sat that way for a long time, murmuring to each other in the firelight. Jodi was pleasantly buzzed, thanks in part to Shaun's heavy-handed pours in the cocktails she'd mixed, and in part to the ministrations of Freeman's hands on her skin. Her body thrummed with desire. It was never far from the surface now. It didn't take more than a few strokes of his fingers against her or one thorough kiss for her to be wet and wanting.

Jodi checked the time and groaned, she still had to open the store in the morning. It was going to be crazy after being closed for the holiday. Free must have understood, smiling and standing, giving her his hand to pull her up. They made their rounds of goodbyes, Jodi apologizing, explaining that it was going to be an early morning. They had almost made it to the driveway when Jodi heard Shaun call her name.

Her sister was walking fast toward her, and the look on the younger girl's face alarmed her. She stepped away from Free, meeting her sister several feet away. "What? What's the matter?"

Shaun grabbed Jodi by the hand and pulled her around a nearby tree trunk. Holding up her left hand, Jodi was left speechless at the small diamond that sparkled in the string lights above them.

CHAPTER 39

"Oh my god," Jodi breathed, looking up into her sister's face, a smile forming before it fell. "Why do you look like that?"

"I didn't know what to say. I don't remember saying yes. I—I don't remember anything after he asked. I blacked out," Shaun rambled, her eyes wide and frantic. "What do I do?"

Jodi laughed but stopped when she saw the panic in her sister's face. "Umm, I don't know. Take the night and think on it? What do you want to do?"

"I don't know," Shaun groaned, her tall frame sagging, whirling away and looking up at the starlit sky. She turned back to Jodi. "I like Tommy, you know I do. But—" her words seemed to stall, her mouth working with no sound coming out "—I didn't know this was coming."

Jodi didn't want to point out to Shaun that she had said 'like' not 'love'. That would be a conversation for a different time, perhaps when the shock had worn off.

"Oh God, here he comes," Shaun moaned, ducking behind Jodi, as if Jodi's five-foot two frame could hide her sister's five-foot eleven one. She seemed to realize it was futile, because she straightened and turned a forced smile on her new *fiancé* as he approached. "Hi."

"I didn't think you would run away from me," he murmured gently, stopping several feet away. Jodi inched sideways, slinking away. His eyes were gentle and understanding as he stared at Shaun. "I don't want you to say yes if you're not ready."

Jodi snuck away as silently as she could, leaving the two of them to talk. She walked swiftly toward Free, who was still standing where she'd left him, phone up to his ear. She heard him say, "Red, call me, I haven't heard from you in a while and I'm starting to worry" before hanging up and sliding his phone back into his pocket.

"Everything okay?" Jodi asked as she drew nearer.

He nodded. "Just checking in." He looked down at her, sliding his eyes over to where Shaun and Tommy were still hidden behind the trunk of the tree. "What was that about?"

Jodi laughed wryly and shook her head. "It's a long story, I'll fill you in later."

Free cut a wolfish grin over to her as he helped her up into the truck. "I'll fill *you* in, later."

Jodi laughed out loud and blushed. "You're insatiable."

"Yes, and you love it," he teased as he closed the door.

Free drove them home, and when he parked the truck and reached for her, all other thoughts except for him flew from her mind.

His mouth ravaged hers, kissing her thoroughly, his hands on either side of her face. He nipped at her bottom lip, making her squirm.

"I told you I want five. I expect you to count them out, Jodi," he growled through the dark. Jodi moaned throatily; the demand sexier than anything she'd ever heard. "Tell me you understand."

"Yes," she breathed against his lips, panting.

"Good girl," he growled, and then he was gone, sliding out of the truck. He damn near prowled around the hood of the truck to her door, opening it and lifting her out, letting her slide down his body, and Jodi sighed when she felt him hard against her.

Walking up the steps of the porch to the front door, he didn't touch her once. They walked through the door, stepping into the ebony darkness of the living room. He stalked toward her then, using his forefinger to tip her chin up so she was looking at him.

"Where should I take you, Jodi?" he whispered roughly. She had never been so turned on, this dominance thrilling. "Where should I make you give me the first one?"

"Oh my god," Jodi groaned, her body turning into a puddle.

Dragging the pad of his thumb across her lower lip, he grinned, his white teeth showing up in the darkness of the room. "Maybe the couch?" he rumbled. Her breaths came in soft puffs against the thumb still stroking her lip. "Mmm," he murmured, shaking his head. "Should I spread you out on the table, legs over my shoulders so I can feel your thighs shake when I make you come?"

"Holy fuck," Jodi moaned, reaching for him, but he clucked his tongue and stepped backwards before she could make contact. "Now who's the one teasing?" she whined petulantly.

"So impatient," Free chuckled darkly, sliding his hand up through the hair at the nape of her neck, pulling taut. He sighed when she caught her breath at the pleasurable pain. "I plan on taking my time with you tonight, Jodi. You're going to scream my name before we're done."

Before Jodi could make a sound, he swept her up into his arms, chest to chest, and she locked her legs around his hips, arms draped over his shoulders, as he carried her down the hallway into the bedroom. He didn't stop until he deposited her on the bed, immediately reaching for her sandals and sliding them off, letting them thud onto the carpeted floor. He made quick work of divesting her of her clothes, and when she lay naked on the bed, he shed his own, letting the articles drop where they may. His cock was rock hard at the junction of his thighs.

Jodi made to scoot up toward the pillows, but he growled a warning and grabbed her ankles, yanking her to the edge of the bed, where he dropped to his knees. Lifting first her right leg, he planted a hot, open-mouthed kiss to the tender skin on the inside of her thigh, before placing it over his shoulder. He did the same thing with her left leg, trailing kisses along that thigh before sucking gently, then laved the bruise left there with his tongue. He placed that leg over his other shoulder and Jodi knew it would not take long for him to draw that first one out of her.

Before his mouth made contact with that part of her that ached for him, he looked up her body, their gazes meeting, his aquamarine eyes fierce. "Remember to count, Jodi."

And then he began. One hand fisted into the bedding beneath her, the other sliding into Free's dark hair. This was heaven and hell all rolled into one, Jodi thought brokenly as his tongue manipulated her like a fine-tuned violin. And she was right, it didn't take him long to draw her to that edge of the first one, her legs shaking as he hurtled her over that precipice. She cried out, fisting her fingers into his hair as she came for him.

One hand swung out and slapped her ass cheek smartly and she moaned at the pleasure it caused, and he growled at her, "Count, Jodi."

"One," she moaned. "One."

"Good girl," he whispered, before his head disappeared between her still shaking thighs again. He didn't give her time to recover from the first tumult before starting once more, and Jodi thought she just might die from the pleasure. But lord was this one helluva way to go. It was moments later that she cried out, the second tearing through her like a train, her legs trembling violently where they rested on his shoulders still.

"Two," Jodi cried into the dark, her head tossing against the bedspread beneath her.

Free's hands moved over her body, caressing her ass where he'd laid that sharp slap, soothing. He raised his head to press his mouth to the inside of her right thigh, which still trembled in aftershocks. "Again, Jodi. We're not even close to being done."

"Fuuuucccckk," Jodi moaned as he replaced his mouth, this time adding one finger, then two. Growling his approval at the wetness that was there.

Suckling her clit like it was his favorite meal on earth, he used his fingers, finding that sweet spot inside, effectively shattering into a million pieces. Jodi was gasping for breath, a fine sheen of sweat making her body glisten, her legs shaking uncontrollably, as the third barreled through her, making her close around his fingers again and again.

"Three," she cried on a moan, her entire body on fire. Her hands trembled as she held on for dear life. "Three. Three."

Free waited until the last of the aftershocks rippled through her before standing, a beautiful, dark angel, his chest heaving like a bellows. Jodi admired him from where she lay trembling on the bed, her knees raised, feet on the bed.

He climbed onto the bed, kneeling between her thighs. He lifted her hips at the same time pulling a pillow from the head of the bed and sliding it under her, raising her hips. He draped her legs over his thighs, then those strong, capable hands gripped the meaty part of her hips as he speared into her, sliding all the way in in one long thrust. Jodi's eyes closed and she let her head roll against the bedspread, a throaty moan escaping her at the feel of him settled so deeply inside her.

"Open your eyes," he growled through the dark. She did as she was told, her eyes meeting his. His dark hair fell over his brow, and sweat made his skin shine. "Again."

And then he was moving, the hands on her hips gripping tightly, the muscles in his arms bunching as he used them to rock her onto him, over and over again. Jodi's hands clutched at the muscles of his forearms, over his magnificent chest, down his abdomen. "Oh my god, yes," she moaned as he pumped into her, filling her. She was so close…

"Come on, Jodi," he groaned, his teeth clenched tight. One of his hands left her hip, reaching down between their bodies to flick over her clit, once, twice, three times, before fireworks exploded through her once more, her legs once again trembling where they lay over his. "Yes, yes, Jodi. *Count.*"

"Four, four," she sobbed brokenly. Jodi's entire body was raw, her every nerve ending overwhelmed from the pleasure. She was sure if he tried to take a fifth, she would surely perish. Her breathing was harsh, her heart pounding, her body flushed. "I can't— I can't do five. I can't."

"Yes, you can, Jodi," he whispered, his body nestled inside hers, and she felt his cock surge when aftershocks pulsed around him. "Come here."

He stood, pulling her to her feet. She stumbled; her legs as wobbly as a newborn fawn. Jodi blushed seven shades of red when she realized where he was leading her; to the long, low dresser across the room. Their reflections peered back at them from the vanity mirror that sat atop it. Reaching around her from behind, watching her reflection, he cupped her breasts and rolled the already peaked nipples between his fingers. Her head fell back to rest against his chest, eyes drifting shut. Jodi moaned when his hardness pressed into her back, a reminder that they weren't finished yet.

Jodi's eyes opened when she felt his fingers at her throat, then they slid up until his fingers strummed along her lower lip again, love bitten and swollen now. His other arm wrapped around her from behind, his hand disappearing between her thighs, fingers sliding into her, and she felt the primal growl that rumbled his chest pressed against her back.

"You're so beautiful. So sexy," he breathed against her temple, still staring at her reflection. For the first time, she believed it. Her hair was a tousled mess of curls around her head, her eyes limpid, her body flushed from his loving. "Look at you."

When he gently pushed her forward until her forearms and chest rested against the smooth top of the dresser, her ass in the air, she went willingly. She rested her cheek against the coolness of the dresser, and shivered when his hands smoothed over her back. She felt him then, pressing against her, and she tilted her hips to grant him better access. The angle of her hips was perfect, he slid right in, all the way to the hilt. Jodi moaned into the dark, rolling her hips, taking him even further in.

He withdrew, almost to the tip, then slammed back in, nearly lifting her off her feet. She sobbed, "Yes, oh please." He did it again, and again. The dresser rocked beneath her at the force of his thrusts. She gasped sharply when he reached up and curled his fingers into her hair, pulling tight until she raised her head, her eyes meeting his in the mirror once more. He truly was magnificent, she thought dazedly. This dark prince that had captured her heart and body and soul.

"Do not close your eyes until I tell you to." The dark demand made her shiver. He rocked into her, his other hand creeping up to slide around her neck like a dark, forbidden necklace, squeezing just the slightest bit. It was the sexiest thing she'd ever seen, and as he continued to pump into her, she quickly hurtled toward that edge once again. Her legs ached as they began to shake anew. She knew that Free could feel it, feel her begin to tighten around his cock that was buried so deep inside her. She watched him in the mirror; his eyes were fierce, his jaw clenched tight, holding himself back with an iron will, waiting. Waiting for her. "Again, Jodi. I want my five."

Jodi bit her lip until it was almost painful, her trembling fingers curling into fists where they rested against the dresser beneath her, no choice but to follow his dark command. Her body was already so sensitive, each nerve ending zinging with electricity. The fingers at her throat tightened marginally, and with that, she shattered. A raw cry fell from her lips as she came, harder than before, her entire body convulsing even as he continued to pound into her from behind. Her eyes slid shut and he pulled tight on the hair his fingers were still tangled in.

"Look," Free snarled from behind her, and she opened them again, dazed and shaking as her climax continued to roll through her. "Count it, Jodi."

"Five," Jodi sobbed brokenly. "Please!"

His hands withdrew from around her throat and in her hair, settling on the meaty part of her hips. "Good girl," he growled, and she purred at the approval. "Such a good fucking girl. So beautiful. So perfect for me."

"Please, Free," Jodi begged. "Please."

Free smiled darkly at her through the mirror as he moved in and out of her. "I don't want to stop because you feel so good, but I want to fuck you until I come."

"Yes," Jodi begged, unsure which she was begging for. "Please, Free."

"Hold on, then, sweetheart," he murmured and let go of the iron hold he'd had on his release. He pounded into her, again and again, then pulled out just in time, as he came to his own roaring climax moments later. "Fuuucck."

Free curved his body over her back, resting against her for only a moment, before pressing a gentle kiss to the curve of her spine, even as their ragged breathing filled the room. He straightened, and when she made to stand, her legs gave out. He chuckled, scooping her into his arms effortlessly, padding over to the rumpled bed and lowering her down gently.

He tucked her under the covers, then slid beneath them beside her. Jodi felt weak, her body shaking still, as she rolled to curve her arm over his middle, resting her cheek against his broad chest. She could hear his heart hammering beneath her ear and smiled slightly, for she knew her own heart was doing the same in her chest. Free's arm draped around her shoulders, pulling her more securely into him. Jodi yawned broadly.

"Did I hurt you? Was I too rough?" he asked gently.

Jodi shook her head, yawning again. "You could never hurt me. It was wonderful."

Free pressed a kiss to her forehead, then rested his cheek against the top of her head as she snuggled into him. "So next time we'll go for six?"

Jodi pinched the skin on his side and he yelped in surprise, then chuckled, as she whispered tiredly, "I'm going to need like a week to recover." She yawned again and he smoothed a hand over her hair.

"Go to sleep," he whispered, and it was mere heartbeats later that she did just that.

CHAPTER 40

The hall was cast in shadows and seemed to go on in either direction for an eternity. Closed doors lined each wall, and she walked for what felt like hours. Each door was locked. Panic was setting in as she tried every door she passed. Fear gripped her chest, making her throat feel tight, her breath coming fast and shallow. She walked faster and faster until she was running.

Finally, a light. Still too far away. Her lungs and legs burned from running.

The light slowly came closer, until she slowed to a walk, her chest heaving. A door was cracked open, and a sliver of pale light arced across the polished floor. The shadows seemed to encroach on that small sliver of light, as if trying to will the door to close before she could reach it.

Her breathing was ragged in the complete silence of the corridor. Muffled voices drifted from the room and she could make out a male and female tone, but couldn't make out what was being said. The male voice was familiar, safe, and she knew she should recognize it, but couldn't. The woman's voice was unfamiliar, but soft, endearing.

Her heart was thundering in her ears too loud for her to hear what those voices were saying.

She inched closer to the crack in the door, fearful that whoever was in there would hear her. Terrified of what she would find when she opened the door. But she needed to know who was in there, speaking so softly.

"You're perfect for me, perfect. So beautiful…" the male voice whispered. "I've waited so long for you, for this…"

Her breathing hitched; she did know that voice. It was his. He had said those words to her, just hours ago. If she was out here, then who was he speaking to inside…?

She remained hidden out in the darkened hallway that still seemed to stretch interminably in either direction, those shadows licking at her as she got closer to the light, to the open door. Her heart continued to thunder, drowning out the woman's response. When she couldn't stand it any longer, she pushed the door open, those dark shadows curling around her feet, as if trying to pull her back even as she stepped inside.

Her eyes were drawn to a woman lying in a hospital bed, aglow in a small halo of light. The man was hidden in shadow, just beyond the circle of light.

The woman had vivid red hair and a beautiful, exotic face. In her arms she held a tiny, blanket wrapped bundle, and it moved.

She walked forward until she stood directly beside the bed, looking down into the tiny face of a newborn child. The beautiful baby had a head of dark hair that lay against the woman's naked breast.

A strong, work roughened hand reached out to touch the baby's soft cheek, a silver ring glinting in the aura of *light surrounding the woman and newborn. A wedding band. Those familiar, work roughed fingers moved upward to twine into the woman's vibrant hair. The woman looked up, smiling radiantly into the face of the man standing beside her.*

She looked up too, following the line of the man's arm until she could see his face.

The look of undiluted love on his face as he looked down at the new mother and child was enough to suck the air of her lungs like a vacuum. She cried out, but there was no sound, and she took an involuntary step back as if she'd been dealt a physical blow.

Free leaned down to press a tender kiss to the woman's lips, whispering adoringly, "I love you…"

Those shadows from the hallway swallowed her as she fell backward, a silent scream of terror escaping her as she passed through the floor and fell and fell and fell, the picture of pure bliss on Free's face haunting her as she tumbled endlessly through nothing…

Jodi jackknifed upright in bed, a strangled cry tearing from her throat. Tears streamed down her face as she gasped in lungful after lungful of air. The sheets were twisted around her legs, her body naked beneath the sheets. Free woke, startled, and he sat up, reaching for her in the dark.

"Jodi, what's wrong?" he asked, anxiety making his voice crack, as his hands scoured over her body, as if searching for a cause for her alarm. She was drenched in sweat, and she shivered from cold. Jodi's body shook as sobs wracked her. Panic tinged his voice as he beseeched, "Jodi, sweetheart, talk to me. *What's wrong?*"

"Ohhh," Jodi sobbed wretchedly, reaching for him blindly, burying her face in his chest as he gathered her into his arms, rocking her there gently. He scooped her close, moving her so she was in his lap, continuing to run his fingers over her hair, her face, her body. She cried into his chest for long minutes as he held her.

"You're okay, sweetheart," he whispered gently against her temple. His voice was a soothing balm against the terror and heartache that had flooded her. "It was just a nightmare. I'm right here. You're okay."

"Don't go," Jodi whimpered, tears still trailing down her cheeks. "Don't leave me. Please."

"Oh, sweetheart, I'm right here," Free whispered back, smoothing her hair away from her face. "You're okay."

Jodi shook her head, turning in his arms. Frantic, she wanted— *needed*— to assure herself he was there and that he was still hers, at least for now. She reached for his mouth with her own. Her body was tired and deliciously sore from earlier. Her legs ached and the junction of her thighs was tender, but she didn't care, she needed him now.

Free's mouth settled on hers, gently at first, but he must have sensed the urgency behind her kiss, because within a heartbeat he growled and twisted her around so that she could place her legs on either side of his hips. Jodi felt him, already hard, against her belly. Raising herself up, she moved over him and impaled herself on his steely length. Jodi felt more than heard the savage groan as it rumbled through his chest as she began to move, riding him. He grasped her hips, his hands none too gentle, as he delved deeper into her.

It was quick and almost brutal in its intensity. He used his strength to pound upward into her, and Jodi's arms locked around his neck, her legs burning, but still, she didn't stop. His mouth ravaged hers, and when she threw her head back in rapture as she came hard around him, that magical mouth ravaged her throat, leaving love marks on the tender skin there. Jodi sobbed his name, holding on as tightly as her unravelling body would allow. A growl caught in Free's throat, and he shuddered a heartbeat before hauling her off him, groaning as he came, jetting onto her skin.

Jodi slumped against him, her hair cascading over his shoulder where her head lay against his sweat slicked skin. She pressed kisses to the side of his neck, her fingers trailing along the smoothness of his chest, playing with the hair that dusted his upper chest and torso. One of Free's hands sank into the curls at the back of her neck, cupping the back of her head gently even as he panted raggedly into the darkness. The other hand squeezed the meaty part of her hip where it connected with her ass, then soothed, feather light across her skin.

As their breathing returned to normal, Free turned his head and pressed a lingering kiss to her temple, then tipped her face up to kiss her mouth tenderly, belying the ferocity of their coupling from moments ago. They exchanged breaths and fleeting, air light kisses, staring into each other's eyes, the only light a sliver of glittering moonlight that filtered in through the window across the room. Jodi ached to say the words she felt on the tip of her tongue with every fiber of her being, but lacked the courage.

Instead, she drew the words with her fingers along the skin of his chest, directly over his heart. It was all the courage she could muster in the inky shadows of the room.

Jodi swallowed hard and whispered so quietly it was merely breath, her lips still grazing his, "I need you."

Pressing another achingly tender kiss to her lips, Jodi could barely hear him when he whispered back through the night that surrounded them like a cloak, "I need you, too."

CHAPTER 41

The Tuesday after Labor Day was pure chaos at the bookstore, just as Jodi had guessed it would be. They had closed for the holiday, allowing Jodi, Tessa, and Kit to each spend the day with their families and friends. Free had driven Jodi to work, insisting on making sure the shop was secure after the long holiday before the three women went in.

Jodi had carried in the beverage tray of coffee and tea while Free checked the entire interior of the building, Tess right behind her with a large box of freshly baked goods. They had immediately gotten started unboxing the treats, and Kit came flying in through the door moments later with breakfast sandwiches from down the way.

Free's phone rang, and Jodi watched him answer it, frowning when no one responded on the other end. He hung the phone up and tucked it back into his pocket. He ducked his head and kissed her quickly, then took his leave.

The three women sipped their beverages and ate the breakfast sandwiches between tasks and conversations about their weekends.

Tessa was in the front of the shop with a customer, and Jodi and Kit were unpacking a box of new releases when the other woman stopped and stared at Jodi for a long moment. She straightened and Jodi looked up, wide eyed. "What?"

"You're in love with him, aren't you?" she whispered quietly.

Jodi rolled her eyes, but her heart fluttered at hearing the words out loud. She hadn't allowed herself to say them, even to herself, out loud. "I like him."

But Kit shook her caramel-colored hair, her soft honey brown eyes keen as always. "No, this is more."

Jodi straightened, though she ducked her head, fidgeting with the row of buttons down her blouse. "I know," she whispered forlornly.

Kit laughed gently, reaching out to touch Jodi's shoulder. "Is that such a bad thing?"

Jodi raised and lowered her shoulders quickly, then let her head fall back until she stared at the ceiling, willing the tears she felt building not to fall. Last night had been… intense. Something had shifted between them, and she wasn't sure what, yet. Free had looked at her this morning before he left with an intensity that startled her. An intensity that she felt, too.

"Even if I do, he's leaving in a week," Jodi whispered dejectedly. "I… I had a nightmare last night. It was… awful." Taking a deep breath in and letting it out slowly, she looked over at her friend. "I was married, and never felt for him the way I do for Free. What if he leaves and I never feel this way again?"

"Have you told him how you feel?" Kit asked gently.

Jodi shook her head with a vehement, "No."

"Do you think he feels the same way?" Kit questioned.

Jodi swallowed and shrugged her shoulders again. "I know he feels something, but I don't know what, exactly. Obviously, there is an attraction…" Jodi said and blushed to the roots of her hair, remembering the delicious things he'd done to her last night. "We have a lot of fun. It's simple, easy, when we're together." Turning to place a stack of books on one of the shelves behind her, she said quietly, "But what if it's just curiosity? We had this thing that happened so long ago between us, what if he just wanted to know what it was like? Just idle curiosity while he's stuck here with nothing else to do? And what if— what if I'm not worth it, in the end?"

Kit sighed heavily, looking her friend up and down. "Is it so hard for you to believe that someone might actually like you, really like you, even love you, for *you*? *Just you*? With no ulterior motive behind it?" Without waiting for Jodi to answer, Kit continued, "I know Josh did a number on your self-confidence, but girl, *I'm telling you*; the way that man looks at you… phew. My guess is he's been in love with you just as long as you've been in love with him."

Kit's phone rang then, and she dug it out of her back pocket before excusing herself to the back of the stockroom to answer it. When she came back, she grimaced. "I'm so sorry, I have to run. My apartment is flooding."

"Oh no!" Jodi exclaimed. "Go, go! We will be fine!"

Kit rushed out moments later, and the remainder of the day flew by in a whirlwind of customers, orders, and deliveries. By the time Jodi and Tessa turned off the lighted Open sign and locked the doors, they each slumped against the nearest solid object and laughed, thankful the hectic day was over. Even Tessa's typically infallible red lipstick was looking a little lackluster by the end of the day.

Free met them there about twenty minutes later, waiting on a bench in the park until they exited the building. He stood when he saw them, and sauntered over to Jodi, reaching for her hand. Jodi's body zinged at the simplest contact from him. They walked Tess to her car, hand-in-hand, before walking the block to the truck. Ever the gentleman, he opened the passenger door for her, assisting her up into the seat, before closing the door and rounding the truck to climb in behind the wheel.

He had prepared a delicious dinner of grilled steak and roasted vegetables, and the kitchen smelled heavenly when they walked in. The evening was mild, and they decided to eat out on the back porch. Jodi brought Free a beer, and he took it with a thank you and a smacking kiss.

"A girl could get used to this," Jodi teased as they sat side by side in the Adirondack chairs that they had christened the week before.

Free grinned over at her as he took a bite of the perfectly cooked steak. "Happy to be of service, my dear."

They were different, though. Jodi sensed that shift between them that she'd felt this morning, and last night. His hands lingered on her body longer than normal, his lips stayed pressed to hers for heartbeats longer, his eyes locked with hers more frequently. That night as they'd laid in bed on their sides, he'd tucked her back against his front. He'd pressed into her from behind, sinking into her. It was slow and unhurried, so different from the night before. He rocked them both to climaxes, coming together as he pressed kisses to her back, her shoulders. Jodi blushed as he removed the condom and put it in the trash in the bathroom. He'd then tucked her back against him, wrapping his arms around her, and minutes later she knew by his slow, even breathing against her neck that he was asleep. Jodi lay awake for a long time, sadness creeping in and tinging the warm glow that she had allowed herself to feel with him.

They didn't talk about it, but she was excruciatingly aware that each day that passed, that dreaded day of his leaving drew nearer. She hated it.

CHAPTER 42

Jodi woke with a start, sitting up and looking around the sun brightened room. Rubbing the sleep from her eyes, she listened, trying to figure out what had woken her so suddenly.

A knock on the door.

The other side of the bed was empty. Free must have left to go to Shane's, as he usually did in the mornings. She glanced at the clock and was surprised to see how late it was. Midmorning sun shone through the windows.

Another knock, more impatient this time.

Tossing the blankets off, she threw her legs over the side of the bed and picked up the closest article of clothing she could find; Free's discarded t-shirt from last night. It fell halfway down her thighs. Another banging knock from the front door. She glanced at her reflection in the mirror over the dresser, blushing furiously at the memory of Free standing behind her, inside her. Her hair was a mess, but it would have to do.

Padding down the hallway, another knock. Opening the door just a hair, she wished she would have stayed in bed.

His insolent hazel gaze raked over her state of undress, clearly wearing a shirt that did not belong to her, her hair tousled from Free's hands. His eyes found the love mark on her neck and scoffed.

"Classy," he sneered derisively.

"What do you want, Josh?" Jodi snapped, torn between using the door as a shield and crossing her arms over her unrestrained breasts beneath the shirt, aware that the majority of her legs were bare. But then she squared her shoulders and refused to back down. Why should she be ashamed?

He shrugged, then showed his teeth in what was supposed to be a snarky grin. "Idle curiosity."

The words tripped something in her mind, but fury won out and she bristled with anger. "Why can't you leave me alone? Huh? And stop with the 'your wife' bullshit. We're divorced. Period."

Josh shrugged again, leaning his shoulder against the door frame, his hands in his pockets. He crossed his ankles casually. It made Jodi want to kick in his knee, that she knew he had injured trying to waterski two summers ago.

"I'm just wondering how long this can last," he murmured innocently. "He's leaving soon, right? I wouldn't stick around longer than necessary, either."

"How—"

"I mean, I just can't help but wonder if maybe this cowboy is just using you," he continued, cutting her off. He spread one hand across his chest in feigned worry. "He's here, nothing else to do to pass the time. What better way to make a couple weeks pass than start a quick fling? It was easy enough, wasn't it? You always were easy."

Tears stung her eyes, and she opened her mouth to speak, but again he cut her off.

"And, I would hate to see you, you know, *fall in love* with someone that doesn't reciprocate those feelings. You've *got* to wonder why none of your relationships have worked out, Jodi. There's not too many guys that are going to be willing to deal with all that—" he waved vaguely toward her as a whole. "I told you before you left that you'd be hard pressed to find someone that's going to put up with your shit."

Jodi's heart hammered in her chest, her eyes stinging with unshed tears. *How? How* did he know all of this, *any* of this? She had only talked about this with Kit, at the store—

She gasped, her eyes flying to his. "You bugged my store." Rage, pure, unfiltered rage, boiled through her veins. *That's* how he always knew everything, almost as it happened. "You bugged my store to spy on me!"

Josh merely smiled. "Prove it."

"Get out!" Jodi screamed, her arms ramrod straight at her sides. She was shaking, her fury barely contained. "Leave!"

Josh laughed then, taking several steps backward toward the porch stairs. He grimaced sarcastically, which made her all the angrier. "Good luck keeping a man with that anger problem."

Jodi picked up a heavy potted plant that sat next to the front door and chucked it at him. He laughed harder, as it missed him by several feet, shattering on the wooden slats of the porch. Shards of porcelain, soil, and flowers spilled everywhere.

He pranced down the stairs and slid into his car, waving insolently as he pulled away from the house.

Jodi fell to her knees on the porch, wretched sobs wracking her from the very depths of her soul. He had found her fears and used them against her. She would never be free of him. Of his manipulation. Of his abuse.

She cried until her throat was hoarse, her eyes swollen from the tears.

She called in to beg out of work for the evening, giving Tess an excuse about a bad migraine. Her friend assured it was okay, and that she hoped she felt better soon, before hanging up.

Jodi cleaned up the mess that she'd made with the plant, picking up the broken pieces of the pretty blue painted pot and sweeping the soil and flowers into a bowl until she could get a replacement.

She called her father, telling him everything, everything he didn't already know, though much of it he did. The tampered locks, the missing tapes, the vandalized vehicle, the taps he as good as admitted were hiding in the store. All of it was Josh. She had no doubt in her mind. Levi swore succinctly and promised he would take care of it.

She then curled up in the corner of the couch, pulling a thick, fuzzy blanket up around her chin, as a chill settled over her, despite the warm day. Her eyes were puffy and burned from her tears. She closed her eyes, her entire being utterly exhausted.

But still, her mind wouldn't shut off. What if he was right? She *did* have a lot of baggage. Why would anyone want to be with someone with so many issues?

She heard Free's truck pull into the driveway a time later, but she didn't have the motivation to move. When he came in through the door, he called her name, worry ringing in his voice. She was supposed to be at work. He found her seconds later on the couch, rounding it to come sit on the edge beside her.

"Jodi? Jodi, are you okay?" Free whispered. He pressed the back of his hand to her forehead. "Jodi, sweetheart, why aren't you at work? Is something wrong?"

When she opened her eyes and finally looked up at him, she noted the alarm on his face with her bloodshot eyes and pale face. She nodded though. "I'm fine. Just a headache."

But Free simply lifted her out of the corner of the couch, turning and sitting down, pulling her into his lap.

She curled into him, breathing in his now familiar scent. Fresh tears started and her lip trembled. How was she supposed to let him leave in a few days when she loved him so much?

CHAPTER 43

"Shane and Cassie will be home Saturday afternoon," Free said, running his fingers through Jodi's hair where her head lay on his chest. He wasn't sure what was wrong, and Jodi wouldn't tell him. He knew it wasn't as simple as a headache. Her usually brilliant blue eyes were sad, her face lacking its typical glow. He'd gotten back from doing chores to find her on the couch, which had worried him. When he'd finally seen her, that worry had increased tenfold. Her fingers fisted into his shirt, but she didn't say anything. "They want us to go out for drinks with them, to celebrate."

Jodi nodded, just barely.

"Please tell me what's wrong," he whispered. "Have I done something to upset you?"

Jodi shook her head then. "No, of course not," she whispered back, burying her face in his chest once more. "I'm sorry I'm not feeling like myself today."

"Can I help?" he asked gently.

She finally looked up, not entirely meeting his eyes. They were so sad, so morose. She reached up and let her fingertips flit over his facial hair, as he'd learned that she liked to do. He caught her hand in his and pressed a gentle kiss to the center of her palm. She smiled, though it didn't quite reach her eyes, but almost. He would take it.

"What would you like for dinner? Since I get you for the whole evening," he murmured, "how about a hot bath in that big ol' bathtub you've got in there?"

Jodi smiled again, getting a little closer. "Only if you join me."

"Try and stop me," he smiled down at her. How had this girl stolen his heart so thoroughly? he wondered as he stared into the sapphire blue eyes that had become so dear to him.

His decision had been made the other night, after Jodi had woken from whatever terror that had haunted her in sleep. Leaving her wasn't only impossible, but the thought cut him to the core. When she had whispered 'I need you' so quietly he'd almost not heard her, it had been the honest truth when he'd whispered back the same words to her. Whatever this was, wherever this could lead them, he had to find out.

He loved her. Irrevocably. He probably had the entire time. He wasn't sure how to tell her, though, or if she felt the same way.

Early evening sun filtered in through the windows, dancing along the shiny wooden floors, dust floating through the sun rays. And with her smiling once again, that little light beginning to return to her eyes, he kissed her mouth. "I need to shower. I smell like barn animals."

Jodi nuzzled her nose into the hollow of his throat, breathing deeply, then letting her breath out slowly. "You smell wonderful."

Free laughed out loud, shaking his head. "You need your senses checked then."

Jodi whined when he made to stand, holding on tighter. "Please don't go yet," she murmured quietly. It was the second time she had said similar words in the last several days. He squeezed her tightly and kissed her languidly.

"I'm just showering. I'll be right back, I promise," he said and winked, setting her back down on the couch. "Ten minutes, tops."

When he came back after showering hurriedly and filling the jacuzzi tub, she was no longer on the couch. He found her in the kitchen, wearing only his t-shirt, her legs bare to high thigh, her breasts bouncing beneath the soft, faded fabric. She was flitting through the kitchen, placing crackers, fruit, sliced deli meats, and cheese on a platter. A bottle of red wine was opened, two glasses waiting beside it. When she heard him, she turned, and he was grateful that her smile was once again true, reaching her eyes.

She gestured toward the spread on the tray shyly. "I thought this would go well with a bubble bath."

Yep, his decision had definitely been made. Leaving this woman would kill him on the inside.

Before the sappy grin that tugged at his lips gave him away, he picked up the bottle of wine and two glasses. "Lead the way."

They luxuriated in the hot water, feeding each other bites off the tray of food, and between the wine and the hot water, they were feeling relaxed and happy. They sat facing each other at opposite ends of the tub, bubbles floating on the water between them. He said something and Jodi laughed out loud, throwing her head back. She had piled her curls high up on the top of her head, and the heat from the water had left stray tendrils curling wildly around her face.

She took a sip of her wine, smiling languidly over at him. "Thank you," she said quietly.

"What for?" he asked, tilting his head. This was the most domicile thing he'd ever done with a woman. Freeman Thorp, in a bubble bath, drinking wine? But he loved it. Because he loved her.

She shrugged, causing the water to lap at the edges of the tub, over her breasts. His eyes darkened at the sight. She was so beautiful.

"For this," she said, gesturing to the space between them. "For cheering me up."

He found her foot under the water, near his thigh, and squeezed it gently. "Anytime, Jodi."

And he meant it.

CHAPTER 44

"We're going to be late."

"I can't reach my toothbrush," Free whined.

Jodi gave him a sidelong glance at him over her shoulder, his chest pressed against her back. Her arms were above her head, securing her curls up with a decorative clip as she stood in front of the mirror in the bathroom. She glanced down her body, where each of his hands cupped a breast, his fingers idly playing with her nipples.

"Mmm, Free," she sighed, letting her head drop back onto his shoulder. "That sounds like a you problem."

"Your tits just fell into them," he teased, nuzzling the side of her neck with his nose, pressing hot kisses along her jaw. "It's not my fault."

"You're horrible," she breathed, letting her hands fall to cover his. "Stooopp," she cried softly, stilling his fingers. "They're so sensitive."

"I'm sorry," he murmured, pressing his palms to them, lifting them. "I didn't realize."

Jodi blushed furiously. She knew he had noticed the evidence in the trash can earlier in the day. She nodded. At least they knew she wasn't pregnant.

Free's phone rang from the bedroom. He kissed her soundly before padding into the bedroom to answer it. She heard him say, "Hey, yeah, we're almost ready. Meet you there in half an hour?"

When he came back into the bathroom, she was just finishing her hair. She had deftly applied her makeup while he'd been in the shower. "That was Shane. They're on their way into town."

Jodi nodded in the mirror. "I just have to get dressed and then I'll be ready."

Free disappeared back out the door, and she heard him shuffling around the bedroom. By the time she exited the bathroom, he was dressed in his typical jeans and a heathered gray t-shirt. His ball cap was in his hand, and as he reached up to put it on his head, he caught sight of her. He whistled long and low, his arm stilling halfway to his head.

"Damn," he breathed. Jodi blushed again and offered a small curtsy.

She had chosen a form fitting little black dress. It was simple in design, with a halter neckline that connected at the back of her neck and down her spine, racerback style, leaving large swaths of tanned skin on her shoulders bare. It hit mid-thigh, leaving her legs bare. Low heeled, black sandals adorned her feet. Turquoise and silver jewelry completed the outfit, and she had a black jacket over her arm, in case it got cold later in the evening.

"You're breathtaking," he whispered in awe. She blushed again.

"Thank you," she said appreciatively. She nodded to the black hat in his hand, that still hadn't made it to his head. "Have I ever told you how much I like when you wear that hat backwards?"

He grinned lopsidedly, reaching up to put it on finally. "No, but I'm glad you like it. The cowboy hat can be cumbersome sometimes."

"Don't get me wrong, I love the cowboy hat, too," Jodi said and smiled broadly. "But this is... sexy... in a way I wasn't expecting. The same with your beard. I was never a beard girl, until I saw you on my porch two weeks ago. All of a sudden, my main character needed a beard, too."

"Oh really?" he asked. She nodded, smiling. "I'll have to remember that," he growled and she laughed. He reached out his hand for hers. "Ready?"

"Yes," she said, placing her hand in his. They drove into town, pulling into the parking lot of the dive bar Free had brought her to that first night. He took her hand and they walked through the parking lot toward the door.

The place was jam packed, a band playing loudly. The billiard tables were all occupied, and the bar was three people deep. But Kyle the bartender saw them as they walked in, over the other patrons' heads, nodding to them in greeting. In minutes, they each had beers in hand, sliding away to find an empty table, waiting for Shane and Cassie to arrive.

It was noisy and hard to hear each other over the crowd, but Jodi smiled, happy to be with Free, in what might be one of their final evenings together. They still hadn't talked about it. And she wouldn't tonight. She wanted to enjoy this.

Shane and Cassie found them, and Jodi jumped out of her seat to hug them both. They each looked sun kissed and gloriously happy, if a little exhausted from travel. Cassie wore a kelly green sundress that floated around her legs, showcasing her tropical tan. Shane had a tan line on his face from wearing sunglasses for the last two weeks in the tropical sun. Free and Shane hugged, congratulations were exchanged, and as they sat the newlyweds launched into a tale of how their luggage had been lost for the first two days of their trip. By the time drinks had been dispersed, Jodi and Free were rolling with laughter.

Jodi saw the look that Shane passed between her and Free, no surprise showing on his or Cassie's faces. Free must have told him. He simply smiled at her, reaching out and squeezing her shoulder gently. She nodded and smiled in return.

Sheila and Brad were there again, as usual. They joined the table and Sheila regaled them all with the story of the tiny morel, using her pinkie nail for reference. Free shook his head and grinned, taking a long pull of his beer, emptying it. When Sheila noticed, she stood and hollered over the crowd, "Shots!"

Jodi was rolling in her seat. Before she knew it, a tray full of shots and fresh drinks had been delivered to their table, the shots each adorned with a wedge of lime and a salt shaker in the middle. "Cheers," Sheila crowed, downing her shot.

Jodi smiled at Free and they clinked their shots together in a cheers before downing them. Jodi lifted the slice of lime toward her mouth, but Free caught her wrist, bringing the lime to his own mouth and sucking on it. Jodi gasped, white hot desire ricocheting through her as his tongue laved at the lime between her fingertips. When he released her wrist, he leaned forward, grasping the back of her neck in his hand, and pulled her toward him for a scorching, open mouthed kiss. Her body thrummed. As his mouth left hers, he remained leaning close. He slid his thumb over her bottom lip, his eyes searching hers fervently.

The cacophony of the bar surrounded them, people laughing, shouting, the music blaring. And despite the noise around them, it was as if they were the only two there. Her eyes never left his, his thumb still on her lip, stroking softly. She had just enough liquid courage in her system to make her brave, and she whispered, "I love you."

CHAPTER 45

Jodi thought her heart was going to pound out of her chest. She couldn't believe she'd just said it out loud. Free's eyes widened as her words processed, and she closed her eyes, suddenly terrified of what he would say. When she opened them, he was still staring at her, though a smile tugged at his lips.

As he opened his mouth, Shane snarled loud enough to bring their attention around to him. He had risen from his chair, his body taut. "Can we help you?"

Jodi and Free looked toward what had caught his attention, and Jodi blanched. Free shot to his feet, taking a step between Jodi and Josh, who had just walked up to their table. Jodi stood too, placing a hand on Free's bicep, though she remained half behind him. His body was tense with rage.

"What do you want, Josh?" Jodi asked around Free, thankful for the noisy room. She didn't want a scene.

"Idle curiosity," he said, the same as before, and Jodi's teeth ground together in anger. He crossed his arms over his chest where he stood just a couple feet away from their group. He turned to Free. "Did she tell you I came to see her the other day?"

To Free's credit, he hid the surprise well, his only tell was a stiffening underneath her fingers that still clutched his bicep. Warning bells went off in her head. She knew what Josh was doing, what he was trying to do. But Free didn't.

"I'm guessing that's a no?" he asked, bouncing his hazel eyes from her to Free and back again. Jodi made to step around Free, but he moved his arm to keep her as far away from Josh as possible. Josh's eyes landed on hers. "So am I right?"

"Go away," Jodi snapped. She knew the glaze in his eyes, knew he was drunk and looking to cause trouble. And she was terrified that Free would give him exactly what he wanted. Tugging at Free's arm, she begged, "Free, let's go, please. He's looking for a fight. Please, let's go home. Please."

Free looked down into her eyes, and the anger in his own softened as she stared into them. He nodded. "Okay."

"Hey, when you're done fucking her out of boredom—"

The words had barely left Josh's mouth before Free's fist connected with the side of his face.

"No!" Jodi cried, reaching for Free, but it was too late. He grabbed a hold of Josh's shirtfront and pulled his arm back, punching him again. And again. The crunch of bone could be heard even over the noise in the bar. Blood poured from Josh's nose, broken, and it splattered Free's knuckles and the toes of Jodi's shoes.

"Free, stop! Stop!" she screamed, flinging herself between them, pushing Free back with all her strength. Shane got Free in a barrel hold, pinning his arms down and hauling him backward. His hat fell off, clattering onto the floor in the scuffle.

"Stop!" Shane shouted to Free, who was struggling against the hold. Jodi pressed her hands to his heaving chest. "Don't."

They had drawn quite the crowd, a wide circle forming around them, and the band had stopped playing. Kyle was doing his best to subdue the throng.

Josh stumbled away, covering his face that now gushed blood down his chin, dotting the floor. He spat blood at Free's feet and smiled.

It had all happened in mere moments. A heartbeat.

Jodi watched in dismay as two police officers stepped through the door of the bar, understanding dawning clear as day, as the two made their way over to the group of them. Tears ran down Jodi's cheeks. He had planned it. The whole thing.

Free saw the two uniformed officers making their way toward them and he immediately quit struggling against Shane's hold. He dropped his chin until it almost touched his chest, squeezing his eyes shut and letting a vile expletive fall off his lips. Shane released him from the barrel hold and Jodi sobbed, her hands flat on Free's chest, shaking her head as the officers approached them.

"Please, he didn't do it on p-purpose," Jodi said between sobs. She pointed to Josh, who was putting on a show of pain several feet away, "He pr-provoked him. Pl-please."

"Jodi," Free said gently, tilting her face up so she was looking at him. Tears continued to track down her cheeks. He smiled sadly. "It's okay. I threw the first punch." He sighed and nodded to the officers, one that stood near them and one that was standing talking to Josh, who was gesturing wildly toward Free now. "This is how it goes."

"No," Jodi sobbed, shaking her head again. "He knew what he was doing. He wanted you to hit him."

"I know."

Jodi sucked in a shaky breath. "This isn't fair. Josh did this on purpose. They could let you go—"

Again, Free smiled sadly and shook his head. Shane leaned toward them, saying somberly, "He's over there talking about pressing charges for assault. Jodi, honey, we have to let them take him. We're lucky they're not coming in like gangbusters."

"No," Jodi whispered emphatically. "No."

"Sir, please turn around and put your hands behind your back," the one officer said to him after an unspoken cue from his partner. Free nodded solemnly. Jodi sobbed again, reaching for him, but Shane pulled her back. Cassie stood several feet away, visibly shaken.

"No!" she cried, finally turning to her ex-husband. "Please! Josh, don't do this! Josh, stop this!"

Her pleas fell on deaf ears, as she knew they would. Free turned his back, putting his arms out wide before bringing them back, palms out. The officer pulled a pair of heavy handcuffs off his belt and cinched them to Free's wrists, while giving him the speech about his rights. He looked over at her as the officer began to herd him toward the exit. "It's okay," he said gently, which only caused more tears to fall down her cheeks.

As he was taken outside, Jodi, Shane, and Cassie followed. It broke her heart to watch as he was put into the back of the cruiser, the blue and red lights flashing in the dome atop the car. This was her fault.

Josh stepped out of the bar then, walking toward them. She snarled at him, hatred for him oozing out of every pore. "You're an ass, you know that? Was any of this necessary? Why? Why, damn you?!"

Shane put his hand on her elbow, trying to lead her away from Josh. She shrugged out of his hand and pointed one finger up into Josh's face. Trembling, she whispered, "I have my proof. Drop the charges, or I take everything I have to the police tomorrow."

"If you had anything solid you wouldn't wait until tomorrow," Josh scoffed arrogantly.

He knew they hadn't found it. He knew she was grasping at straws, and she hated him all the more for it. She and her dad had searched high and low to no avail. Jodi merely squared her shoulders. "Drop the charges, Josh."

Josh slid his hands into his pockets and shrugged. "Nah. I think he'll look good in orange, don't you?"

If Shane hadn't grabbed Jodi around the waist when he did, she would have launched straight at Josh and scratched his eyes out of his smug face.

Josh laughed darkly. "Are you trying to join him in there tonight, Jodi?"

Jodi seethed, still trying her best to break free of Shane's grasp.

"Get in the car," Shane muttered in her ear, pointing Jodi in the direction of their car. "I don't have the bail money for both of you."

Jodi climbed into the back of Shane and Cassie's car while Shane went back inside to pay their tab. Josh left shortly after; his work was finished for the night.

When Shane returned, he had Free's truck keys and his ball cap in his hand. He held them both out to Jodi, which made fresh tears sting her eyes. "Do you want me to drive you home?"

"I'm okay," she whispered, fingering the brim of the hat. The chaos of the last half an hour had sobered her. "I just want to go home."

"Well, let me follow you to the driveway, at least," Shane said gently. Jodi nodded before walking to Free's truck and climbing in behind the wheel. It was the first time she'd driven it, and it felt foreign, wrong. Free was supposed to be driving them home. The truck rumbled to life, and she drove the short way home, waving to Shane and Cassie as she pulled into the long driveway.

Parking next to the Jeep, she scrubbed her hands over her face before climbing out. She had made it up the steps and almost to the front door when she realized something was off. Reaching inside the door after unlocking it, she flipped on the exterior light switch, but nothing happened. She tried the switch again, but the light didn't turn on. Pulling her phone out of her purse, she turned on the flashlight app and gasped.

Her exterior light fixture had been smashed to pieces. Twisted metal and severed wires hung from where it was suspended from the ceiling of the covered porch.

Something crunched beneath her shoes, and when she moved the flashlight downward, she saw broken glass glittering everywhere. As she looked up, she saw bright red spray paint marring her living room windows and siding. *Slut* and *Whore* were amongst the slurs hastily sprayed on, the paint dripping down the siding and onto the porch.

And then Jodi smiled, despite the absolute train wreck the evening had been.

Because Josh had unwittingly given her all the proof she needed; all of it caught on cameras he clearly had no clue were there, hiding in plain sight.

CHAPTER 46

"They won't let us post bail until tomorrow morning," Shane said over the phone. "Because it's a weekend, and it was an assault charge."

"I'm working on that," Jodi said, tucking the phone between her ear and shoulder. Her parents were sitting at the kitchen counter, reams of paperwork and Levi's laptop opened to the raw footage from the night before. A compilation of everything they had taken with them to the police station earlier. "Josh will drop the charges."

Her eyes burned from the tears and lack of sleep the night before. She had called Levi first thing that morning, and he and Serenity had come over right away. Levi had wanted to go straight to Josh's condo when he saw the red lettering on Jodi's house, but she had convinced him to wait. They needed to let the police handle it, needed him to cooperate. If they beat the hell out of him again, it would do them no good. If this was going to work the way Jodi needed it to, they had to do it right.

"I hope you're right, Jo-Jo," Shane said quietly from the other end of the line.

"He will drop the charges," Jodi repeated, smiling. She had felt a deadweight lift off her shoulders when the officer and lawyer they'd spoken with that morning had told her they had everything they needed. Her lawyer had assured her that not only would the charges against Free be dropped, but that Josh would have to forfeit his stake in the bookshop, making it hers finally. Her lawyer had admitted that he probably wouldn't do any jail time, but a restraining order had been filed nonetheless. She could at last see the light at the end of the tunnel. A life free of Joshua Murphy.

Now, she just needed Freeman back.

Levi and Serenity took their leave shortly after, though her mother was fretful after witnessing the damage done to the house. The yellow crime scene ribbon that the police had used blocked off the section of her porch that had been vandalized jarred her. Levi had already contacted a friend to come out and replace the windows and repaint the siding, with a promise that it would be done by midweek. A tech friend of Warren's had been called, and the teen had promised to come by the shop and do a thorough sweep to find the wiretap. The news of the bug seemed to upset Seren the most. Her mother had pleaded with Jodi to come stay at the house, to which Levi said wasn't a bad idea. Jodi grudgingly accepted, packing a small overnight bag.

She and Fallon stayed up later than they should have watching a soapy, sappy romcom, until Serenity had come in to remind Fallon she still had school in the morning.

Jodi tossed and turned in her old bed, the walls still the same periwinkle blue she had painted them during high school. Unable to sleep, she wandered the house, finally ending up in Levi's den. She switched on one of the dim lamps, running her fingers along the many books on the shelves, the soft felt of the billiard table that sat in the middle of the room. Taking a crystal highball glass down from one shelf, she poured herself a finger of whisky. Taking a sip, she relished the burn as it went down.

"You okay?" Levi rumbled from the shadows of the doorway. She didn't jump, not surprised he'd found her there. He'd always known when one of them was out of bed.

Jodi nodded, crossing her arms over her chest, the highball glass in one hand. "I'm sorry I made such a mess of things, Dad. I never meant to embarrass you and Mom like this."

Levi grumbled something unintelligible as he shuffled into the room. He took a matching highball down and poured himself a hefty portion before turning to look at her.

"You think your mom and I are embarrassed of you?" Levi asked, his deep voice rumbling over her. Jodi nodded, swirling the contents of her glass. "Jodi, your mom and I couldn't be prouder of who you've become, what you've accomplished."

"Free is in jail because of me," Jodi whispered, casting her eyes downward.

"Free is in jail because Josh is a tool," Levi quipped dryly.

"But it's because of me. I wouldn't blame him if he packs his bags and leaves straight away tomorrow morning," Jodi whispered, her throat closing on the words. Tears threatened and she blinked rapidly to dispel them. She took a drink of the whisky, grateful for the burn as it went down. She wanted to feel something other than the tears stinging her nose, her eyes. She had told Free she loved him. But what if—what if it wasn't good enough?

Levi offered her a half grin behind his beard. He extended his hand to her and she hesitated for a moment before taking it, setting her glass down. He pulled her into his side, dropping a kiss to the crown of her curly head. "I don't think you have anything to worry about, sweetheart."

Jodi laughed sadly. "You're supposed to say that; you're my dad."

"Any man that is going to be scared off by an overnight stay in jail isn't worth your time anyway. I don't think Free is that skittish. That is not, however, a suggestion to find a habitual criminal," Levi said gruffly and Jodi huffed a wry chuckle. "He did it *for* you. Not because of you. You've known for a long time that he would do anything to protect you. I knew it. I didn't necessarily like it, but I knew it was there."

Jodi sighed, inhaling deeply the scent of pine, maple, and cedar that always seemed to cling to him, a souvenir from work every day. "Like I said, you're supposed to say that because you're my dad."

Levi chuckled and kissed the crown of her head again. "Go to bed. We'll see how everything plays out in the morning."

Jodi nodded, squeezing him tightly around his broad chest one more time before stepping away. "Good night, Dad."

"Good night," Levi said.

As Jodi made it to the door, he called softly, "Hey, Jodi?"

She stopped, turning at the door. "Yeah?"

"Next time you decide to get into my good whisky, invite me down first."

Jodi laughed, rolling her eyes. "Okay."

Tucking herself back into the old, familiar bed, Jodi was asleep almost as soon as her head hit the pillow.

CHAPTER 47

Jodi had called both Tessa and Kit to fill them in on what had transpired over the weekend, everything down to the suspected bug somewhere in the store. They knew a tech guy would be stopping by sometime during the day to locate it and remove it. When they arrived at the shop, mum was the word, lest Josh caught wind of what they were doing.

The young man came in an hour later with minimal gear, which surprised Jodi. Levi and a police officer met him there. Jodi felt sick to her stomach as she watched from across the room, as he found six individual wire taps spread throughout the building. When at last he felt they had found them all, the attending officer bagged them for evidence. Levi was furious.

She checked her phone regularly, waiting for a call, a text, anything, from Free or Shane that he was being released. After what felt like a lifetime of waiting, her phone finally rang, and she nearly tripped over herself running to the back of the stockroom to answer it.

"Shane?" she answered, out of breath from sprinting to the back. "Is he out?"

"Not yet, but soon," Shane said from the other end of the line. "I've been waiting outside of the courthouse for three hours." He paused, then said, "They just brought Josh in. Is this what you were talking about last night?"

"I didn't want to say much, because I didn't want to jinx it," Jodi said. "Josh will drop the charges, I promise."

"I'll call you when I get word he's being released," Shane said, though Jodi could swear she heard a smile in his voice from the other end of the line. "Talk to you in a bit."

Jodi waited. And waited. With no call.

Finally, just after four in the afternoon, a text message came through from Shane.

He's out, I just dropped him off at your place.

Jodi sagged with relief. Tessa assured her she would be fine to close by herself, and Jodi rushed home, spraying gravel as she drove down the long driveway. When she pulled up to the house, he was already there, sitting on the porch swing.

She parked hastily and climbed out of the Jeep, rounding the hood and flying up the steps. He stood, taking several steps toward her. He was wearing the same clothes from Saturday night.

They stopped, leaving about three feet between them. Jodi let her eyes rove over him, assuring herself he was okay.

"Hi," was all she could bring herself to say. So much had happened. And what she had told him right before it all...

"Hi," he said back, his voice low. His aqua gaze traveled over her, warming her.

They stood awkwardly for a long moment, before she motioned toward the house, "You could have gone inside."

Free shrugged. "I didn't mind waiting outside. The sun felt good."

Tears stung her eyes. "I'm so sorry, Free."

He shook his head then, finally taking a step toward her, placing his hands on her shoulders gently. "Don't. Don't apologize. I knew he wanted a fight. I knew what would happen. It felt good to clock his ass."

Jodi laughed, reaching out to spread her fingers over his chest, feeling his heartbeat beneath her palm.

Free motioned toward the red paint that marred her house and windows. "Is that why I was told the charges were being dropped?"

"Yes," Jodi murmured, her eyes searching his. "Among other things. I can tell you about it."

Free raised one hand to cup the side of her cheek. "I think there's a lot that we need to talk about."

Jodi nodded, a million butterflies taking flight and dive bombing her stomach. He swept his thumb over her bottom lip once before pulling away.

"First, I would like to take a shower. And charge my phone since it died sometime over the weekend. That's why I didn't call you myself," he said and smiled. Jodi led him into the house, stopping at the living room.

He leaned down and kissed her once, twice. "I'll be out in a few."

Jodi nodded, heading into the kitchen. She was terrified of the conversation that was coming. She'd been brave the other night but was quaking with fear now.

She figured he had to be starving, her own stomach rumbling. She set about making a quick dinner, simple sandwiches. When he didn't return, she padded down the hallway and into the bedroom.

He hadn't made it to the shower. Instead, he lay on the pillows, snoring softly. His boots lay on the floor beside him, one leg still draped over the edge of the bed. Jodi smiled before reaching for a throw blanket on the nearby chair and spreading it over him gently. Jodi went back to the kitchen, wrapping the sandwiches for later before joining him in the bedroom.

Curling up beside him, she herself was asleep in minutes.

They must have slept for several hours, because when Jodi woke, the sky outside of her window was shadowed. The sun had set and dusk was settling across the skyline. When she looked over, Free was gone.

She sat up, searching the room. His boots still lay on the floor where he'd left them. Then she heard the shower running in the bathroom through the closed door and let out a sigh of relief.

Jodi climbed out of bed, pulling the clothes she'd worn to work off and leaving them in the basket by the door. She pulled on a pair of black leggings, and then found a comfy gray top that hung off one shoulder. She let her hair down from the confines of the topknot she'd had it in, massaging her scalp with her fingertips.

She left the bedroom, returning to the kitchen, pulling the sandwiches out of the refrigerator. She plated the sandwiches, along with potato chips, and a hefty spoonful of macaroni salad.

She had just closed the fridge after grabbing two beers when she heard a timid knock on the door.

Puzzled, she set the bottles on the counter, then rounded the corner of the kitchen, walking through the living room. It was well after nine at night, who would be here this late?

Trepidation slowed her footsteps. Was Josh still in custody, or had he been released? Would it be the police waiting on the other side of the door?

She reached the door and called through, "Who is it?"

A pause, and then a soft voice called back through the still closed door. "My name is Roxy. I'm looking for Free."

CHAPTER 48

Jodi opened the door, reaching for the porch light out of habit before she remembered it was damaged. The porch was deeply shadowed, making it difficult to make out the woman's features in the dark.

The woman shifted from one foot to the other nervously. "I'm so sorry it's late. I'm trying to find Free. Shane said I could find him here?"

"Uhh," Jodi stuttered, thrown off guard. "Yeah, he's here. He's taking a shower," she uttered lamely, pulling the door open slightly wider and taking a half step aside. When she did, the light from the lamp in the living room that Jodi had turned on earlier illuminated the woman's hair first, which Jodi noted was a vivid red, the same from her nightmare. Then, the light hit her face, and Jodi's hand flew to her mouth to stifle the gasp of shock that escaped her. Her mouth worked, but nothing came out, and a half a heartbeat later she heard Free round the corner from the hallway. She could smell his bodywash as he got closer.

"I didn't think we were expecting company," Free said as he walked toward her.

She half turned toward him as he reached her, words still stuck in her throat. Her eyes followed him as he rounded the door, his gaze falling upon the woman still standing in the doorway. A broad, genuine smile lit his face a half second before a deep V formed on his brow.

"What the hell happened!" he snapped, stepping around Jodi and pulling the woman through the door into the living room, and as they did, the light revealed more of the woman's face, which made Jodi queasy. "Did Neal do this?"

Dark bruises covered the left side of her face, obscuring her eye and cheekbone, and her lip was split. The eye that was blackened was swollen nearly shut. Stunned, Jodi moved on autopilot, closing the door as Free led the woman to the couch, sitting her down and lowering himself to the seat directly next to her. His hands moved over her, tipping her chin up so he could look at her face more fully, then over her shoulders and arms that were also covered in angry dark purple and blue bruises. Jodi stood awkwardly by the door, wringing the hem of her shirt between her fingers. Tears ran down the woman's cheeks, which Free swiped away with his thumbs, all the while talking to her gently.

"I tried to call," the woman was saying, "but it kept going to voicemail—"

"I know, I've been… busy," Free murmured, taking her hands in his. Jodi's throat closed as anxiety clawed at her. The familiarity between them, the way they sat together, the way Free touched her, left Jodi with a knot in her stomach that made her feel ill. It was the same way he touched *her*, comforted *her*. Jodi knew, without a doubt, she was Free's lover. Jodi felt sick to her stomach, felt like her heart was going to claw its way out of her throat. She felt like an intruder in her own home as she stood by watching them together.

Neither Free nor the woman, Roxy, she had said her name was, looked up when Jodi stepped outside onto the porch, closing the door behind her. She walked over and sat down on the hanging porch swing, the one that Free had helped install. Jodi stared out over the field. There was only a sliver of moon visible in the night sky, and it cast just a hint of silvery light upon the tops of the trees across the field. Occasionally, she could hear a car pass on the road in the distance beyond the tree line. The tall field grass swayed in the breeze as she sat in the darkness.

Her heart was breaking, and she hated herself for it. For how incredibly stupid she'd been the last few weeks.

After what felt like an eternity, Jodi heard the front door open and then heavy footsteps on the wooden planks of the porch. He had put on his boots.

She turned her head just as he reached her, and he crouched down in front of her. He reached for her hands, but she pulled them away before he could touch her, and another deep V formed on his brow. His hair was nearly dry and looked soft in the moonlight that glinted on the top of his head.

"Jodi… I have to go," he said quietly, staring up at her from where he knelt.

"I figured."

"Red needs my help," he murmured slowly, and she knew he was trying to gauge her emotions.

Jodi closed her eyes for a brief second, then snorted derisively before she could stop herself. "Right. *That's* Red. The Red that I asked about, and you said it was 'just a friend'. You didn't mention that she's a woman," Jodi muttered sourly, and Free lowered his gaze guiltily. Jodi nodded, knowing her gut had been right after all. Her chest felt like it was being squeezed by a bench vice. Her voice trembled when she stated, "You didn't tell me because she's someone you've slept with."

"Jodi—"

"Don't…" she warned bitingly, "…don't lie to me, please." Jodi stood abruptly, stepping around him where he crouched. She took several steps away before turning to look at him again. He straightened from where he'd been kneeling, staring at her stoically in the darkness. "I have eyes. I can see that you and she are… familiar… with each other."

"Red and I are just friends," Free said slowly, his voice low.

"Do not stand there and tell me you haven't slept with her!" Jodi exclaimed sharply.

"Alright, yes, dammit!" Free shouted then, spreading his arms wide, palms up, before letting them fall to his sides in defeat. "Yes. I have slept with Red. A lot. I've also slept with a lot of other women, Jodi. What was

I supposed to do? Be celibate for my entire adult life on the off chance I'd ever see you again?"

Her head snapped back as if she'd been physically hit, and she sucked in her breath sharply. "That's not fair, Free."

Free heaved a sigh, raising his shoulders and then letting his palms slap against the outside of his thighs. "I can't change my past any more than you can change yours, Jodi. Crucifying me for living my life as I did—"

"Oh for the love of—" Jodi snapped, striding away from him, then turning back to look at him, hands on her hips. "Don't. Don't do that. This isn't high school. I don't give a damn that you've slept with other women, Free. I'm not a prude."

"Yet here you are, pissed at me for having sex with another woman!" Free snapped.

"That's not what this is about, and you damn well know it!" Jodi shouted. "We're adults, and I do understand what that comes with. However, I don't have to like the fact that you lied about who she was. And even though we are adults and I do understand, I don't have to appreciate having her paraded in front of my face, especially in my own house!"

Free nodded a small concession, before saying, "You're right. I shouldn't have hidden who she is to me. But I didn't lie to you." He held up his hand when she started to interrupt, and she clicked her teeth shut. "She *is* a friend. One that needed help, and when she couldn't get in touch with me, she came here to find me. She tried to get a hold of me all weekend, but I was sitting in jail for assaulting your ex-husband,"

Free snapped, and the bitterness in his voice stung her to the core. She reeled for a moment, staring at him in stunned silence.

"So you do blame me," Jodi finally said, shaking her head miserably.

"No," Free snapped, blowing out a frustrated breath. "No, I don't blame you, Jodi. But you're mad at me for a friend coming to find me because she was scared. What was I supposed to do when she showed up? Just send her away? You know I can't do that."

She knew, because he had always protected her, saved her, whenever he could. Of course he would be the same way with… others. Jodi knew he was right, but it just made her angrier. She had allowed herself to feel… special… and she felt like an idiot for it.

Jealousy, anger, and pain all rolled like a kaleidoscope through her, shifting from one emotion to the next in one continuous blur. "Is she your—" Jodi's throat closed around the words, choking her. She swallowed hard, willing the tears she felt welling in her eyes not to fall. "—is she your girlfriend?"

"No," Free said quietly, taking a step toward her, but Jodi backed away. Free stopped and raised his shoulders in a helpless shrug. "No, Jodi, Red and I are not and have not ever been in a romantic relationship." Jodi crossed her arms over her chest, in an attempt to hold herself together against the crushing ache in her chest. His eyes were gentle as he continued, "She is just a friend, one that I happened to have slept with. Sex with her was literally that… just sex. Nothing else, I promise you." He took another tentative step toward her, whispering beseechingly, "Nothing like the last few weeks have been with you, Jodi."

"Don't," Jodi whispered miserably, dropping her gaze to the wooden planks beneath her bare feet. Her traitorous mind had already conjured up mental images of him doing the same things to Roxy that he had done to her, and she wanted to scream. "Don't do that. I get that this—" she motioned between them with her hand, her chest aching and tears threatening her eyes, "—was just a fling."

Free's mouth tightened, his jaw taut. "You said you didn't want a fling."

"I didn't," Jodi snapped, hugging herself tighter. "But we both knew going into this that it was temporary."

He stared at her, his eyes unreadable, his jaw tight.

"You said you love me," Free whispered.

"And you're leaving!" Jodi cried, pointing toward the house where Roxy still waited. "You're leaving, so what does it matter? Just go!"

"You of all people should understand why I have to!" Free bellowed, spreading his arms wide in frustration.

"So go!" Jodi shouted back, gesturing toward the truck in the driveway. She was a wounded animal backed into a corner; her emotions took over and she reacted defensively, lashing out in anger. "I'm not stopping you!"

Free blew out his breath and stomped away from her, and when he turned back to Jodi the look on his face was ferocious. Growling, he snapped, "Just because I have to leave for now, does not mean that this was just a fling for me, Jodi."

"Don't," she whispered sternly. The tears that had been stinging her nose and threatening her eyes finally fell and she swiped at them angrily. "Please don't do that."

"No," Free snarled, striding forward until only a few feet separated them. Pointing one accusing finger in her direction, he snapped, "You don't get to say you love me and then turn around and say this was just a fling. You and I both know that's not what this was."

"Wasn't it?" Jodi snapped, raising her chin defiantly.

"No, and you know it," Free said fiercely. "You're running scared. You let that douchebag of an ex-husband convince you no one is going to want you, but he's wrong. You're scared and pushing me away, like a coward."

"*I'm* a coward?" Jodi gasped, astonishment and outrage battling for supremacy. "That's something, coming from the man that ran away and didn't come back!"

"I wasn't about to fuck my best friend's daughter, who was barely eighteen years old!" he roared, and Jodi could tell he had finally lost control of the temper he was fighting to hold in. He stormed away, each angry footfall thundering against the wood porch. He spun on his booted heel to face her. "*Fuck*, Jodi! Why do you continue to make me out to be the bad guy when I just tried to do the right thing? You were *eighteen* goddammit!"

Jodi watched wide eyed as his chest heaved, and when his eyes came back to hers, her stomach felt like it fell to the floor as he came striding toward her. She backed away, but he was quicker. His arm shot out and wrapped around her waist, hauling her high and hard against his body, and she landed against him, knocking the air out of her lungs. The fingers of his other hand fisted into the curls at the nape of her neck, and she cried out softly when he pulled, forcing her head back until she was looking up at him.

His chest still heaved, his breath hitting her in the face, and his eyes were fierce as he stared down at her. As much as she wanted to fight against his hold, this ferocity turned her on more.

"Do you have *any* idea how hard it was to walk away from you back then? It *killed* me, Jodi," he growled, his lips moving dangerously close to her own, the fingers in her hair tightening just the slightest, bringing her mouth ever closer to his. "Because I wanted you, just like this, and I hated myself for it."

Jodi gasped, breathless, every inch of her body on fire where it pressed against his. His eyes were the fiercest aquamarine blaze she'd ever seen as he stared down into her own.

He panted against her lips as he continued, "But if you think I'm going to let you go now, you obviously don't know the hold you have on me. I told you weeks ago I was just getting started, and I damn well meant it," he snarled, a half second before his mouth came crashing down on hers.

Jodi's arms wrapped around his waist, her fingers curling into fists in the fabric of his shirt against his back. He kissed her roughly for long moments, his tongue tangling with her own. Free's mouth released hers long enough to nip at her bottom lip sharply, which made her gasp. White hot desire ricocheted through her, her lower body aching for him even as his mouth crashed back down onto hers. The fingers tangled in the hair at the back of her head tightened, arching her neck as he deepened the kiss, effectively stealing her breath and making her brain go fuzzy with need.

And then he released her just as suddenly as the embrace began.

She stumbled backward several steps, her legs trembling, her mind still muddled from the intensity of his kiss.

His chest heaved like a bellows as he stared at her, his fingers drifting down to the fly of his jeans, and her eyes flicked downward involuntarily, even though she already knew how their kiss had affected him. Her body was on fire, too. Her eyes flew back up to his and she swallowed hard as he growled, "I'm coming back."

But Jodi was stubborn, her pride hurt, and despite everything he'd just said, he still hadn't said those three words back to her. She raised her chin, willing her lips not to tremble as she said with more bravado than she felt, "I won't hold my breath."

She knew she'd cut him to the quick, his eyes as foreboding as the sea just before a storm, and a dark half chuckle escaped him. Fury seemed to radiate off him as he turned and stalked into the house, the screen door slapping smartly behind him.

Jodi squeezed her eyes shut, the ache in her chest making it nearly impossible to draw a breath. Heartache and adrenaline coursed through her, and she started to hyperventilate. She refused to let anymore tears fall; wouldn't let him see them. Raised voices from inside the house drifted out to her, though she couldn't make out what was being said between the two.

The red headed bombshell, Roxy, exited, standing awkwardly just outside the front door. Free walked out moments later, his few belongings that had found their way into Jodi's house over the last few weeks thrown unceremoniously into a plastic grocery bag. He stalked down the stairs to the truck, flinging the door open roughly. Roxy took a few steps toward Jodi, who raised her chin stubbornly.

"I know you must hate me right now," the woman said, her voice steady, "and I don't blame you in the slightest. I— Free's the best friend I have, and he's the only one my piece of shit ex is scared of. I didn't know what else to do, didn't know where to go, after..." Jodi's anger melted at the pain and fear on the woman's face, recognizing it from her own. One side of Roxy's battered mouth tilted up in a rueful smile. "I never meant to cause trouble coming here. I've known Free for a long time, and I've never heard him, seen him, as happy as he is here. I know he's a stubborn jackass, but please don't be angry with him for too long."

Free barked at Roxy from the truck, and she looked over at him, holding up one finger as if to tell him to wait. She turned back to Jodi. "I know my past with Free isn't purely platonic, but he and I are just friends. That part of our... friendship... has been over for a long time." Jodi nodded stiffly, and Roxy continued as Free barked at her again to hurry up. Roxy gave him a withering look and he grunted something unintelligible before slamming the truck door closed. The redhead turned back to her, smiling sadly again. "I've waited a really long time to meet you. I hope that maybe someday we can be friends. I know you're angry with him right now, but I hope you realize how special you are to Freeman."

Jodi inhaled unsteadily, crossing her arms over her middle tightly. She nodded again. Roxy gave her another half-smile, before turning and taking the first few steps down the stairs. She turned back to Jodi and said gently, "I'm sorry, again. I'm glad I got to finally meet you, Jodi," and then she was down the stairs and climbing up into the truck beside Free.

He didn't look at her as he put the truck in reverse and backed away from Jodi's house, then put it in gear and slowly rumbled away, down her driveway. The tail lights shone brilliant red in the darkness, and they blurred with Jodi's tears as she finally let them fall as they disappeared around the tree line drive.

CHAPTER 49

"I can get us ice cream?"

Jodi rolled her head on the pillow to look over at Shaun, who lay with her in the bed, her cheek laying on her stacked hands. Jodi's eyes stung with fresh tears, and she took a deep breath, holding it in for ten seconds before exhaling slowly. Jodi shook her head though, and said quietly, her throat hoarse from crying, "Just lay with me, please."

Jodi had called her sister, tried to talk through her sobs, after Free had left. Shaun had been there within fifteen minutes, fresh out of bed still wearing a pair of flannel pj shorts and tank top, and hair piled high in a messy bun. She had pulled Jodi up from the couch where she'd found her and held her as she'd cried wretchedly. Finally, when Jodi's tears had slowed, she had changed into lounge pants and a loose, long sleeved shirt, and the two girls had climbed into Jodi's large bed. Jodi had given Shaun a short version of what happened, though she hadn't been able to ebb the flow of tears that had started again. She'd finished

331

the retelling, and Shaun had instinctively known Jodi didn't want advice or vitriol, instead just laying with her in the quiet of the room.

"How about some whisky?"

Jodi laughed, shaking her head again. "My head already hurts enough." She rolled onto her side to face Shaun, stacking her hands beneath her cheek the same way.

"What happened with La Douche?" Shaun asked.

Jodi heaved a sigh before beginning. "He's in a whole heap of legal trouble. He admitted to everything, the vandalisms, bugging the shop, stealing the video surveillance. They cut him some kind of deal to cooperate. He dropped the charges against Free," her throat closed when she whispered his name, "and he had to sign over the bookshop to myself and Tessa. He isn't allowed near me or the shop, or he will be violating his probation. He's getting off pretty easy, but at least it's finally over. I'll take it as a win."

Shaun nodded against her stacked hands. "I still think castration should be an option."

Jodi laughed. "He doesn't know how to use it anyway."

Shaun made a face of disgust and Jodi chuckled again. Jodi motioned to Shaun's stacked hands, the left that was home to the small diamond band. "Tell me what happened with Tommy last weekend."

Her sister shrugged, though Jodi saw the involuntary movement of her left hand, as if Shaun had remembered the small diamond ring that was settled on her finger. "I said yes. It still feels strange, like it wasn't me that said it. It makes sense though. I know Tommy loves me."

Jodi's brows pulled into a V as she stared at her sister. Her beautiful, exotic, fire-willed sister. Agreeing to a marriage proposal because 'it makes sense'. She hated to admit it, but maybe Free had been right… there was that chemistry, that spark, lacking between her sister and her new fiancé. That fire that burned within her sister would be snuffed out, choked into smoke, without someone willing to fan it and keep it smoldering. She liked Tommy Chandler well enough, but he was kind of a wet blanket, almost smothering in his adoration. Shaun needed someone to test her, push her, instead of coddling her.

Perhaps they would talk about it later, when the newness of the engagement had worn off. When Jodi's entire being didn't feel it had been run through a woodchipper, when heartache wasn't still suffocating her.

"You guys will figure it out," she said instead, smiling gently.

"Tommy is driving Zoey insane," Shaun said then, heaving a sigh. "He's been… overwhelmingly protective of her. I know he's only trying to help. With everything that happened, and their mom passing… Zoey's struggling. But she's trying."

"Does she still have nightmares?" Jodi asked.

Shaun nodded sadly. "Not as often anymore, but yes. She was diagnosed with PTSD, but she said that therapy is helping. And her work is something that keeps her going. She's stronger than she gives herself credit for."

Shaun was quiet for a long time and Jodi closed her eyes in the semi darkness of the room. They'd left one dim lamp on across the room, which cast half the room in shadows.

"What are you going to do?" her sister asked gently, and Jodi's eyes opened, gazing into the blue eyes that were so like her own. Jodi shrugged.

"I don't know," she answered honestly. "I was just so jealous. She's probably one of the most beautiful women I've ever seen in my life," Jodi laughed ruefully. Shaun smiled. "She actually seemed really nice. I understand why he had to go. Shaun, this girl's face... I can't imagine the pain and fear she must have felt, scared enough to fly halfway across the country to get away. Whoever did that to her... I hope they get him."

"Do you think he'll come back, like he said?" Shaun asked.

"I don't know that either," Jodi whispered. She sighed. "I said really hurtful things. I wouldn't blame him if he doesn't."

"Well, I think he'd be an idiot not to come back," Shaun said and yawned broadly.

Jodi smiled sadly and glanced at the clock, groaning. It was after midnight. She climbed out of the bed, crossing the room to turn off the lamp before climbing back into the bed, pulling the covers up to her chin. "Go to sleep."

Shaun nodded, yawning again loudly. "You first."

Jodi grinned in the dark. "Bossy."

Shaun's eyes closed, but Jodi could see her smile through the dark. "Don't forget it."

CHAPTER 50

"Why don't you take the afternoon off?"

Jodi looked over at Tessa, who's gaze was surveying her face warily. Everyone had been treating her like glass for nearly three weeks, and it was starting to grate on Jodi's nerves.

Three weeks since Freeman had left. It seemed like a lifetime and only hours at the same time. Jodi snapped, "I'm fine, Tess. You can stop acting like I'm going to break any second."

Her friend pursed her red lips and pushed her glasses back up her nose, her eyes narrowing. "You don't have to be rude, Jodi. We're just worried about you."

"Well, don't," Jodi griped, turning away from the blonde. "I don't need everyone looking at me like that."

"Like what? Like we care?" Tessa snapped, hands on her hips. Today, she wore a calf length black skirt with a slit up to her thigh, and a Red Hot Chili Peppers band tee that was knotted at her waist, a pair of red low top converse on her feet.

"No," Jodi grated, turning and taking the same stance as she continued, "like you all pity me. I'm fine."

Her friend laughed darkly. "This isn't pity, Jodi. And you're not fine. When was the last time you slept? When was the last time you ate? When was the last time you put anything in your system other than *coffee*?"

Jodi chewed on her lip. "I got drunk on tequila last night."

Tessa rolled her eyes, throwing out one hip as she crossed her arms over her middle. "Is that why you look like shit today? Because you're hungover?"

"I'm fine," Jodi repeated sourly.

"And I'm the Queen of England," Tessa snapped, though she turned away from Jodi. "Go home and sleep. Get something, *anything*, to eat."

"I don't need babysitters," Jodi muttered bitterly to her friends back.

"Obviously you do!" Tessa bit out over her shoulder as she walked away. She made a half turn and snapped, "Because whatever *this* is—" she waved at Jodi as a whole, "—needs to stop. Either call him or get over it. I'm tired of walking on eggshells around you and I'm tired of worrying myself sick over you. I understand that you're sad, and I hate that I can't help you. But starving yourself and refusing to sleep isn't doing you any good either."

Jodi's eyes pricked with tears, the words harsh, but true.

"Go home," Tessa repeated as the bell over the door of the shop rang, signaling that a customer had just entered. Tess walked up the narrow aisle between bookshelves, welcoming the customer when she got close.

Jodi walked to the front, where Tessa was showing the customer a row of books, regaling them with details of the new series they'd just put out that morning. She picked up her purse and slid it over her head, then nodded to Tess, who gave her a small smile and nodded back. She left through the front door, starting the walk around the block to her Jeep.

Jodi dug her phone out of her purse and found Free's number, staring at it for a long time, trying to garner the courage to press the call button. Three weeks and not a word from him, no call, no message, just crickets.

But she was a chicken, a cowardly little chicken, so she pressed the back button and dialed the familiar number.

Serenity answered on the third ring. "Hi, sweetheart. Why aren't you at work? Are you okay?"

"I'm fine," Jodi lied as she walked slowly. Late September had arrived, the air outside mild enough to warrant a long-sleeved shirt when in the shade, but warm enough in the sun to warm her bones. The leaves on the trees all around had begun their slow change into bright yellows, golden oranges, and crimson reds. Downtown shopping had slowed as fall arrived, the summer vacationers having returned to wherever they came from, leaving the locals to their hometown once again. The sidewalks were nearly empty even on a Saturday compared to the hustle of the summer months. "Tessa kicked me out for the afternoon."

Jodi sensed her mothers concern even through the silence on the other end of the line. She sighed. She hadn't realized how worried everyone was, and she felt a twinge of guilt.

"Why don't you come over? We can have lunch," her mother suggested softly, her voice gentle, no trace of judgment or pity in it.

Jodi smiled and said, "Okay. I'll be there in a few."

She made the short drive and then climbed out of her Jeep after parking next to Serenity's car in the driveway. She climbed the steps to the wide front porch and walked through the front door, finding her mother in the kitchen. A large pot of homemade butternut squash and sweet potato soup simmered on the stove, which smelled heavenly, making Jodi's stomach growl. She hadn't realized just how hungry she was.

Seren must have heard it, because she laughed, then pointed to one of the barstools on the other side of the kitchen counter. "Sit down, I was just about to ladle it up."

She walked to the kitchen door, calling up the wide staircase beyond to Fallon, who flounced down moments later, before stepping toward the stove.

Fallon swung into the seat directly beside Jodi, and she watched her mom as she wandered through the kitchen, ladling up three heaping bowls of her favorite fall soup. Today she wore a pair of loose linen pants in an olive green, with an oversized, chunky sweater that dipped off one narrow shoulder. Her long, dark hair had been secured with a claw clip on the back of her head, tendrils framing her face where they'd escaped the clip.

Jodi never failed to appreciate how beautiful her mother was and knew her father did as well. Seren sliced up a fresh loaf of bread, then brought the three bowls and the platter of bread to the island counter where Jodi sat.

She dug in, dancing slightly in her seat. It was delicious.

As they ate, Jodi asked Fallon how the first few weeks of high school were going. Fallon regaled her and their mother with wild tales that had Jodi laughing, which felt good.

After they'd finished the meal, Fallon cleared away their bowls and the platter that had once held the bread and mentioned algebra homework that was due the following Monday. She disappeared through the kitchen door and Jodi heard her climb the stairs to her bedroom.

Jodi sighed, leaning back in the comfortable bar chair. When she did, she noticed a bucket of cleaning supplies on the ground by the door. "What's that for?"

Her mother motioned outside, toward the barn with the loft apartment. "Your dad has a new hire coming into town tomorrow, we told him he can stay in the loft until he finds something more permanent. It hasn't been rented in a while and I need to go in there and get it cleaned up." She stood, walking over to the bucket of supplies and held out a pair of cleaning gloves. "I could use an extra pair of hands, if you're looking for something to kill time."

Jodi chuckled. "Sure, Mom."

The two of them stepped out of the front door, walking together the distance that stood between the main house and the barn. A flight of stairs ran up the exterior of the barn, up to the loft apartment above it.

As Jodi and Serenity entered, memories flooded Jodi. She hadn't been back in since the night Free had kissed her that first time, since the night he'd left so long ago. The curtains were drawn over the few windows along the only outward facing wall, and heavy sheets had been placed over the couch and the bed after it had been made clear that Free wasn't returning.

She still remembered the way he'd looked at her, as if in agony, even as he'd pulled her to him, crushing her mouth beneath his in that first, fiery kiss. The way his body had felt against her, the way his hands felt as they moved over her. She'd thought then that she'd die of this new desire he'd awakened. How little had she known of what wonderfully sinful things he could do to her.

Tears stung her nose again, and she covered it by pretending the dust had gotten to her as they peeled the sheets off the couch and bed.

"Have you tried reaching out to him?" her mother asked softly as they worked.

Jodi jolted out of her reverie, shaking her head. "I figured he didn't want to hear from me."

"What makes you think that?"

Jodi shrugged as she sprayed an all-purpose cleaner over the counters, then picked up a rag cloth and scrubbed. "He hasn't called, either."

"Maybe he thinks you're still upset with him," Serenity murmured from where she was cleaning the inside of the refrigerator. Jodi had told her mother about the fight, everything that he had said, everything that she had said. Admitted that she'd told him how she felt and that he hadn't reciprocated. Her mother turned to look at her, setting down the cloth she was using. "Jodi, I don't want you to miss out on something like this because of pride. I didn't say anything when you started dating Josh, and I regret it every day. I knew you didn't love him, but you seemed content. I can't stand by and let you and Free throw this second chance away."

Jodi fought the tears that stung her eyes. "This was just a fling, something to kill time while he was stuck in town. I think him not reaching out at all says enough. It's the same as last time."

But Serenity smiled over the small, cracked table that stood between them. "Jodi, sweetheart, Freeman looks at you the same way your father looks at me. Nobody looks at someone like that for 'just a fling'."

Jodi turned away, going back to scrubbing the countertops, so that her mother couldn't see how badly she wanted to believe those words.

CHAPTER 51

Jodi groaned into her pillow, willing whoever was knocking on her door to go away. She raised her head enough to look over at the clock, wrinkling her nose at the time displayed there. Sunday mornings were her only day to sleep in, and whoever was at her door was interrupting that.

When the knocking didn't stop, she swore in annoyance and climbed out of bed, pulling on a long-sleeved wrap over her pjs. Padding barefoot down the hallway, she rubbed the sleep from her eyes and opened the door. Her hair was a mess piled on top of her head, but she didn't care as she glared daggers at the man standing on her porch.

"Morning," Levi drawled as he leaned against the doorjamb. Jodi made a face. Her father chuckled, his eyes crinkling in the corners. "Got any coffee?"

"Don't you have coffee at home? I was sleeping," Jodi whined petulantly, crossing her arms over her middle, but she stepped aside grudgingly, letting her dad lumber inside.

He chuckled deeply and the sound soothed Jodi in a way nothing else did. Levi had always been the one man that she compared everyone else to, even Free. His gruff exterior masked the gentle giant that she knew he was. He had kissed her bruises, bandaged her scrapes, and hugged away any fears as she'd grown up. Her heartache was his heartache, she knew. She had watched him treat her mother with dignity and respect, had taught her and her sisters to demand nothing less— which she had completely ignored with her marriage to Josh. She loved her dad deeply and respected him just as much.

Jodi led the way to the kitchen, where her dad had settled himself into one of the wooden barstools at the small counter. Jodi started the coffee to percolate, having gotten it ready the night before so all she had to do was start it when she'd awoken. She crossed to the cabinet and pulled down two coffee cups, setting them down to wait for the coffee.

When it was ready, she poured a steaming cup and passed it to her father, black and hotter than hell, just the way he liked it. He murmured his thanks and took a scalding sip. Jodi rolled her eyes and poured a small amount of French vanilla creamer into the bottom of her cup before filling it the rest of the way with coffee.

Jodi leaned her hips against the counter across from where he sat. "What brings you over this early? I know it's not just for coffee."

Levi smirked around another sip of his coffee. "Can't a father come visit his oldest daughter?"

"At seven-thirty in the morning?" Jodi griped, throwing him a sidelong glance.

He set down the mug and wrapped his large, work roughened fingers around it, making it look tiny in his hands. "I'm just worried about you, sweetheart."

Jodi rolled her eyes heavenward. "I wish you all would stop."

Levi harrumphed and eyed her shrewdly. He ignored her last statement, saying, "Why don't you take a break from moping and come over for dinner tonight?"

"I'm not moping," Jodi muttered sourly, crossing her arms over her stomach, the one still holding the steaming cup of coffee stopping halfway to her mouth.

"Mmhmm," was all Levi said.

"We've been busy at the shop. And I'm tired," Jodi snapped irritably, raising and lowering her shoulders in a half shrug. "I haven't been sleeping well."

"Obviously."

Jodi's jaw dropped. "Rude."

But Levi just took a sip of his coffee, then held it out to her in a silent request for a refill. She rolled her eyes, setting her cup down on the counter with a thud before turning and picking up the carafe, bringing it over to him and refilling his nearly empty cup. She returned it to the hot plate and picked up her coffee again, once again leaning her hips against the counter. Her legs were bare from her lounge shorts, her feet crossed at the ankles.

When he had taken another drink, he set his cup down and said, "That new hire will be in today. Why don't you come out and say hello?"

Jodi blew out an exasperated breath then, throwing one hip out in annoyance. "Did you seriously come out here at seven-thirty in the morning on a Sunday to play matchmaker?"

Levi held up his hands in an innocent gesture, though Jodi could see the mirth in his cobalt blue eyes. "I just said come out and say hello."

"Mmhmm," Jodi murmured dubiously, eyeing her father shrewdly.

Levi raised his dark brows and smiled out of the corner of his mouth. "Just come by the house, even if you don't stay for dinner. Let Mom fuss over you, send a plate home with you. She's worried about you."

"I'm fine," Jodi whispered, though she knew it was far from the truth. Then, at the dubious glare her father sent her way, she amended grudgingly, "I will be fine."

His eyes softened then. "I know you will," he said gently. He drained his coffee and stood, striding over to the sink where he set the empty cup. He turned to her then. "We'll see you around six."

Jodi sighed in defeat, a wry half smile tiling up one corner of her mouth. It wasn't up for debate. "Okay. I'll see you at six."

She walked with him back to the front door, where he stopped and patted her shoulder awkwardly before lumbering out the door.

CHAPTER 52

Jodi took a long, scalding shower, letting her tears mix with the water as it streamed down her face. The last two days had been emotionally draining; the argument with Tess, cleaning out Free's old apartment for some new guy to move into, and now having her father— *her father, of all people*— playing fucking matchmaker with this new guy. As if her heart wasn't still laying, shattered, at her feet.

She was angry; at herself, at Freeman. She had *known* what would happen if she'd let herself lower her walls for Free when he'd shown back up. She'd *known* with every damn bone in her body, just how hard she would fall. Had known it would leave an aching, raw void in her life when he ultimately disappeared again. How impossibly broken her heart would be. Even though he had said he would come back. She had been an idiot, a great big dumb idiot, to even halfway believe the words that had come out of his mouth.

When she stepped out of the shower, she towel dried quickly, wrapping the fluffy towel around her body and another around her hair. Padding into the bedroom, she stood in front of the dresser for a long time, staring at the clothes in the first drawer she opened.

She ran her fingers over a plain black t-shirt that she had tucked back into the corner, one of Free's that had been left behind in his hasty departure. She had found it several days later, shoved halfway under the bed after stripping the sheets in a fit of rage and tears, the scent of him on her sheets and on the pillowcase too much for her shattered heart.

Taking the shirt out now, she held it to her face. When she'd found it, she'd balled it up and made to throw it into the trash out of anger, but she hadn't been able to. Instead, she'd folded it up and tucked it away into the top drawer of her dresser. She hadn't had the heart to wash it, along with the sheets, to remove the scent of him that still clung to the worn fabric, though it seemed to fade with each day that passed.

Tucking it back into the corner of the drawer, she closed it. Eventually she would get rid of it, but that was a task for another day.

The late September afternoon was mild, cool enough that Jodi decided on a pair of black leggings, opting for comfort, and paired them with a buttery soft, taupe colored long sleeved top that dipped low enough in the back to cover the curve of her bottom.

She applied simple make-up, just enough to disguise the dark circles under her blue eyes and put a smidge of color into her pale cheeks. She shook her curls out of the towel, fingering through a curl cream into her tresses, and then let it air dry in riotous ringlets around her face and down her shoulders.

Staring at herself in the mirror, she sighed, and slid her feet into plain black flats. It was the best she had the motivation to do.

Jodi drove the familiar roads to her parent's house, pulling into the long, sloping driveway that led to the expansive ranch house. Beyond the drive, she could see the loft apartment over the pole-barn, an unfamiliar dark blue pickup truck and a small u-haul trailer hitched to it parked alongside the barn. Sadness crept over Jodi as she imagined a stranger living in that small apartment.

Pulling up beside her parent's vehicles parked by the garage, she turned off the Jeep and climbed out, just as Serenity came out of the front door, wearing her usual well fitted blue jeans and a chunky knitted sweater, a dish towel tucked into one of the belt loops at her waist. Seren met Jodi on the porch as the younger woman climbed the steps to the long, wide covered front porch that was dotted with her father's handcrafted Adirondack chairs. Levi joined them moments later, stepping out and letting the screen door slap behind him. He stood with his hands in the front pockets of his jeans.

Her mother clucked her tongue and Jodi cringed inwardly. She had hoped her mother wouldn't mention her appearance, and had been thankful she hadn't brought it up the day before. She was well aware she looked... rough. Not like the vibrant, radiant woman from a month ago. Damn Freeman Thorp.

"I hope you're hungry," Seren murmured. "Did you even eat anything after lunch yesterday?"

"You sound like Gram," Jodi muttered dryly, though she didn't fight the gentle hug her mother gave her. When she pulled back, she said, "I ate a light breakfast this morning."

Levi cleared his throat. "Coffee doesn't count as a meal, Jodi."

Jodi stuck her tongue out at him and he smirked. Jodi motioned toward the strange blue truck and trailer beyond by the pole-barn. "So, who's the new guy?"

Seren smiled and nodded her head in the direction Jodi just had. "Why don't we go say hello before dinner?"

Jodi cringed, outwardly this time, making a face of aversion. "Oh, Mom, not you, too."

"What?" Seren asked innocently, much as her father had earlier that morning, though her mothers blue eyes shone with something akin to mischief. Jodi's own eyes narrowed when her parents shared a furtive glance. Seren stepped down the stairs with Jodi in tow, who let her shoulders sag, knowing enough that arguing would be futile. Seren squeezed her shoulders between her hands gently, as Levi followed, several steps behind. "Just go say hi. It won't kill you."

Jodi disagreed wholeheartedly, worried it just might. The thought of an introduction to some new beau her parents were trying to throw at her made anxiety claw at her chest.

As if to make sure Jodi didn't bolt in the opposite direction, Seren linked her arm with Jodi's as they walked the path toward the pole-barn. With about twenty feet to the main entrance of the barn and the flight of stairs that ran up the exterior to the apartment above, Serenity disengaged her arm from Jodi's, though Jodi didn't notice, as the new renter stepped out of the large barn door, dusting off his hands.

His aquamarine gaze met her stunned one, and he stopped. Jodi's mouth hung open slightly in shock, her heart thundering in her ears.

She swung her head around to her parents, who stood ten or so feet behind her. Levi hugged Serenity's shoulders in his large hands as her mother smiled radiantly, her hands clasped tightly together beneath her chin, tears forming in her eyes. Levi raised his dark eyebrows once, then harrumphed something unintelligible before steering Serenity away, wandering back toward the house. Leaving the two of them alone.

Jodi turned back to face Free, who was taking slow, measured steps toward her. His eyes traveled over all of her, and he slid his palms into the back pockets of his jeans as he stopped about five feet away from where she still stood rooted to the spot.

"Hi," was all he said, his eyes searching hers warily.

Still too stunned to speak, Jodi stared at him. He looked remarkably the same, his hair a touch longer as it touched the collar of his shirt at the back of his neck beneath the black cowboy hat that sat on his head. His facial hair was trimmed short, and he wore his typical well fitted blue jeans and had paired it today with a black button down shirt, the top two buttons left undone. The long sleeves were rolled up to his forearms, and a black carhartt work vest hung open over his chest, a concession to the mild temperature.

He continued forward, small steps at a time, until he stood within arm's reach. He was close enough that she could smell him, that mix of cedarwood and citrus that she had missed so much in the last weeks.

Jodi wrung her hands in front of her, twisting her fingers together nervously. "You didn't call," she finally whispered.

Free nodded, his eyes never leaving hers. "I know. I didn't know if you wanted me to."

Jodi ducked her head, taking a much-needed break from those intense blue-green eyes. She motioned lamely toward the truck and u-haul to their right. "What—what are you doing here?"

"Moving in," he said, one corner of his mouth tilting up just the slightest. Jodi's heart tripped over itself, but the look she gave him was withering. He shrugged, pulling his hands out of his back pockets. "I told you I was coming back. I'm sorry it took so long."

Jodi took a shuddering breath in as the words hit her. Anguish flashed in his eyes at the undiluted pain she knew she was unsuccessful at masking, and he took another step toward her, until she had to tilt her head back to look up at him.

If she just extended her hands the slightest, she could touch him. Her fingers ached with the temptation to slide her palms up his abdomen, over his chest, beneath the open folds of the vest. So she kept them clasped tightly in front of her.

"You're not sleeping," he stated quietly, his dark brows dipping into a worried V as his gaze studied her face.

Jodi shrugged but didn't say anything to confirm or deny his claim. She'd bite her own tongue before admitting how hurt she still was.

Damn him, but tears stung her nose despite her best effort, and she ducked her head quickly before he could see the tears well in her eyes. The way he'd left, the radio silence over the last three weeks. Her admission that evening right before her world fell apart...

But he had seen, and he husked, "Jodi," at the same time reaching up and tipping her chin up so she was forced to look at him again. At the first touch of his skin to hers, Jodi's lip began to quiver against her volition. His palm slid to cup her cheek, feather light, just as the first tear fell and he breathed miserably, "Oh sweetheart, don't. I'm sorry. I... I was an ass. I was overwhelmed, concerned about Red when she showed up in the state she was in, frustrated with the timing, and then you were so angry with me..." Jodi's breath shuddered in brokenly and he smoothed his thumb over her cheekbone, picking up the tears that escaped. "I know I should have told you who Red was and what our past included. I selfishly wanted that time with you for just us, and I didn't want to bring up any more trouble than what we already had to contend with. When I told you there was never anything romantic between us, it was the truth, Jodi. She's a friend. *Just* a friend. I promise you," he whispered beseechingly, cupping the other side of her face with his other hand, capturing her eyes with his, "I have never, in my whole entire life, felt like this, like I do with you, for anyone else. I love you, Jodi, and I should have said it before I left. *I love you.* I have loved you for so long I don't remember a time that I didn't."

Tears fell unrestrained from her eyes, her lip wobbling in earnest now. Jodi's hands came up and clasped his forearms with her fingers, his hands still holding her face.

"You told me you love me," he whispered, his face lowering to hers, until mere breath separated them. She stared up into those aqua depths that held her own gaze captive. "Please tell me I'm not too late."

A half laugh, half sob escaped her as she shook her head, still clasped between his hands, and she reached for his mouth with her own, closing the distance between them. Their mouths melded, tongues tangling. Jodi's body hummed, melting, as he kissed her long and hard and slow. When they finally pulled apart, Jodi knew he was just as breathless as she was.

Free sipped feather light kisses across her cheeks, then back down to her mouth where he settled hungrily. Jodi slid her hands up the outside of his arms and around his back, and his hands moved, one up through the back of her hair to cup the back of her head, the other down around her waist, pressing her close. When his mouth finally left hers, he gathered her into his arms, tucking her as close to his body as physically possible. Butterflies had once again taken flight in her belly, and they jolted as she felt him, hard and ready, against her middle. Jodi inhaled deeply the scent of him, burying her nose in his chest, and splayed her hands wide on the hard planes of his back.

"I love you," Jodi whispered, leaning back just enough to raise her head to look up at him. His left arm remained clasped around her, but his right hand came up to let his fingers brush the curls away from her cheek, his thumb picking up the remaining tears that lingered there. "I always have, Free. Always."

His fingers continued to brush the curls away from her face, and at her words he beamed a smile down at her, his eyes crinkling at the corners. "I hope you understand I plan on spending the rest of every single day that I have left with you, Jodi Kendall."

Jodi smiled radiantly up at him, reaching up to touch his bewhiskered cheek with her fingertips. "Took you long enough," she whispered, before sliding her hand up around his neck to pull his mouth back down to hers.

Jodi squeaked in surprise, then laughed gustily when he reached down, quick as a viper, and hauled her up into his arms, chest to chest. His hands gripped her bottom fully, splaying wide, and she wrapped her legs around his lean waist, her arms draping around his neck, and leaned into their kiss fully. He began to walk, heading toward the stairs leading up to the loft apartment.

And then his teeth nipped her bottom lip and all other thoughts except for his body against hers fled her mind. Jodi tugged his hat off with one hand and tunneled the fingers of her other hand through his dark hair, her mouth melding with his as he climbed the stairs effortlessly with her still in his arms. His hat dangled from her fingers at his back.

Jodi didn't know how he did it, her brain too muddled with desire, but the next second they were inside the small apartment, and he was striding toward the bed against the far wall. Jodi dropped the hat to the floor with a thud as she broke their kiss long enough to pull her shirt over her head and let it fall to the floor, too. She reveled in the sight of him before her, still held in his arms. She reached around her back, unhooking her bra and tossing it to the floor to meet her top.

Free groaned deeply as his white-hot gaze traveled over her nakedness before him, and she felt it rumble between her legs. He lowered her down to the bedspread that she and Seren had washed and remade the day before. Jodi blushed, realizing that her parents were in on this scheme, but then his mouth was on her breasts, and she failed to care about anything but the feel of him.

He stood then, peeling the black vest down his arms and popping the buttons off his own shirt in his haste to remove it, his breathing ragged. He toed his boots off one at a time, his gaze hot on her as she lay on the bed, her entire body thrumming with need. She needed him.

Free reached for her leggings, peeling them and her panties down her legs, leaving her naked before him. His eyes were luminous, his need matching hers. He unclasped his belt and then the top button, pulling the zipper down until he could slide his jeans down his hard thighs. His cock raged against the confines of his boxer briefs, and Jodi moaned at the sight of him. It was a half a breath later and he was just as naked as she was, and she reached for him as he knelt on the bed, directly between her thighs.

Her fingers found him, impossibly hard and oh so ready for her. Free braced himself above her on his hands on either side of her body as she guided him in. He sank fully into her, not wasting a breath, clenching his teeth as she took every glorious inch of him. His mouth met hers, ferociously, but he didn't move inside her.

Jodi's hands tunneled into his hair, and when he pulled away, he stared down into her eyes, at the same time pulling out to the tip, slowly, so slowly that Jodi gasped.

"I love you," Free breathed, and whatever control he had been holding onto snapped. He growled gutturally and pounded into her, again and again. Jodi moaned brokenly, her head tilting back in pleasure. Jodi repeated it, chanted it, as he rocked into her.

"You're mine," Free breathed raggedly, his lips only inches from her own. "Say it, Jodi."

Jodi let her fingers drift over his bewhiskered cheek, her fingernail scratching his full lower lip lightly. He groaned, his body bucking wildly. She knew he was close, because she was already shimmering on the edge, too. But still he waited.

"I'm yours," Jodi whispered. She moved her hand down to his chest, splaying her palm flat against the left side of his chest, where she could feel his heart hammering. "And you're mine."

Free pounded into her, calling her name as he came inside her, at the same time that she exploded, tightening around him. Free groaned, rolling them to their sides, while remaining locked inside her. Aftershocks pulsed through her, squeezing him, and he shuddered at each one. His fingers flit over her cheek, her hair, touching every inch of her bare skin, his eyes never leaving hers.

Jodi smiled at him, tracing her fingers over his chest, writing the same words she'd traced out weeks before. "I…love…you…" she breathed as she traced each word against his skin.

Free grabbed her hand, bringing it to his mouth and kissing the palm ardently, which made Jodi quiver with renewed desire.

"This is where it all started," he murmured, their bodies still intertwined. She stared at him, realizing the same thing. "Here, in this room. Seems fitting that we're back here."

"What's next?" Jodi whispered, her eyes searching his.

Free smiled against her fingers that were still pressed to his lips. He kissed them lightly, before pulling them away to breathe reverently, "Forever, my love. Forever is next."

ACKNOWLEDGMENTS

Mom, you were my first and always my biggest fan. Without your love and support this wouldn't have been possible! You knew when I was fifteen that I would be here one day, even when I doubted it myself. I love you!

Nick, thank you for letting me hide away at my desk for hours—and sometimes days—on end. Thank you for messaging me that my breakfast, lunch, or dinner was waiting for me when I was ready for it, because you knew I wouldn't even think about eating (thank you, Chef). Thank you for your unwavering support, faith, and enthusiasm for this passion of mine. Without you and the love you give me, I wouldn't have started writing again. My forever Prince Charming, I love you.

Erin. Sissy. You are the best big sister a girl could ask for. You and that amazing group of ladies in NC have been such a blessing and the best cheerleaders! "Oh, Danielle Baker? Yeah, that's my sister!" I love you, Sissy!

Haley, Kim, and Jenna; Thank you to this wonderful group of fellow authors that I have had the pleasure of being on this journey with! Haley, thank you for always being a critical and willing sounding board, and the Tessa to my Jodi! Kim, I'm so glad I met you and feel fortunate to be traversing this new journey with you! Jenna, your advice dating back nearly twenty yeas has been invaluable! Thank you, ladies!

Stasha, you told me almost twenty years ago that you would edit for me when I was ready. I can't believe we got here! Thank you for being there through the very rough first draft all those years ago, to the newly polished draft we finished. Thank you for helping me get here and believing in me that I could!

Katia, Tania, and the team with Miblart, thank you for the wonderful cover art, you took exactly what was in my mind and made it come to life! I look forward to what we can come up with for my future works!

To all the people that are not named but have beta read, listened to me venting or joined in my excitement over each new milestone, and all those that have rooted for me in this scary and enthralling journey, thank you!

Lastly, to all my readers old and new, this has only been possible because of the love and support you've shown me and these characters. I hope you love reading their story as much as I've loved writing it. I look forward to introducing you to MANY more! Thank you!

MEET THE AUTHOR!

Danielle Baker, romance author of *Love Unbound*, was born and raised in the beautiful city of Petoskey, nestled on the crystalline shores of Lake Michigan. She is married to the love of her life, Nicholas, and they have four children between them. Danielle's love of writing began while she was in high school. She wrote a slew of short stories and had written three novels by the time she graduated. Life got busy and writing was put on hold for many years while she started her family. At the urging of her mother, sister, and husband, Danielle was given the boost she needed to "get back in the saddle" and keep reaching for her lifelong dream of becoming a published author. When Danielle isn't working, writing, or spending time with her family, she can be found with a cup of coffee in one hand and a book in the other.

Chase Manning gritted his teeth, sweat pouring from his brow as he pushed up, again, again, again. Resting the dumbbell bar on the hooks, he exhaled as he sat up, letting his body relax after the rigorous set. He reached over and grabbed the water bottle to his left, taking a long pull, then splashed some over his face, pushing the black lock of hair back that had fallen over his brow.

The gym was about half full, a smattering of men and women on different work out machines throughout the long room. He rested his elbows on his spread knees, hands holding the water bottle dangling between them. His upper body was completely bare, having taken off his shirt an hour ago. He rolled his shoulders, stretching the muscles there, before pushing himself to his feet.

He crossed the room to a leg press machine, added weights, and then sat down. He was halfway through his first set when he realized a young woman was staring at him fixedly in one of the many mirrors that ran along the entire back wall of the gym. She had faltered on the treadmill as she watched him; thigh muscles bunching, calf muscles straining, as he counted out his reps. When she caught him staring at her, she quickly averted her gaze, the ponytail her blonde hair was in swinging over her shoulder. He chuckled to himself. She was pretty.

When he'd finally managed to make it through the rotation of machines he typically used, he was sweating, his breathing none too steady. He did a series of cool down exercises, and then made a beeline to the locker room, removing his gym shoes, where he pulled on a pair of grey sweatpants overtop of his shorts, then tugged a long-sleeved black shirt over his head. He stuffed his feet into his street shoes, before exiting the locker room.

The woman that had been watching him earlier was just outside the locker room door, and she made a show of bumping into him to catch his attention. He grinned down at her, from a long way up. At six foot five, he was taller than the average man, let alone the woman that couldn't have stood taller than five foot seven.

He let her apologize coyly, again flashing that grin he knew was disarming, before excusing himself from around her and heading toward the exit and out into the November cold.

Maybe he'd see her there again.

He'd only been in town a couple hours, but had needed to get a workout in before meeting up with his best friend, the brother he'd chosen for himself after having gotten a gaggle of little sisters instead. All of whom had tried their hand at setting him up with their friends, or friends of friends.

Busy bodies, all of them.

The chill in the late November air felt good against his flushed skin. He could have gone to the station, he supposed, gone in and gotten acquainted, but he'd welcomed the old, familiar gym he'd frequented years ago.

He climbed into his car and shut the door, tossing his gym bag into the back seat, and digging his keys out of his pocket. Starting the car, he adjusted the thermostat to defog the windshield before setting off into the familiar streets.

It was a short drive through town, and it wasn't long before he pulled into the driveway of the house that he had spent almost as much time at as a kid as his own. He turned off the car and climbed out. He had just reached into the backseat to grab the duffel bag with his street clothes when the front door of the house opened and Tommy stepped out, coming down the concrete path toward him.

Chase grinned, straightening, and extended his right hand. Tommy grinned back, taking that hand in his own and they drew together to lightly bump chests, their own way of embracing. Tommy stood several inches shorter than him, and his sandy blonde hair was cut short, almost buzzed. "What's up, dude?"

Chase rolled one shoulder in a shrug as he hoisted his duffel bag over it, letting it hang over his back as they started the short walk back to the house. "Just livin' the dream."

Tommy shot him a side-eyed glance. "Is that why you moved back? Livin' the dream?"

"Meh," Chase muttered and rolled his shoulder in that same casual shrug. "Needed a change of scenery."

As the two of them made it to the door, Tommy stopped and turned toward him. The wind whipped around them, stirring up a pile of fallen leaves and twirling them in a mini tornado around their feet. "I know you're gonna want to give Zoey a hug when you get inside," he said, and Chase narrowed his eyes on the shorter man as he continued, "but I need you to give her some space, okay?"

"Sure," Chase said slowly, eyeing Tommy uncertainly. "Is she okay?"

"She's fine," Tommy said, a bit unevenly. Chase knew his friend, and trusted his professional instincts, enough to know something was up. Tommy put his hand on the doorknob and opened it, saying roughly, "I know you haven't been home in a while. A lot has... changed."

As they entered, Chase couldn't help but smile at the familiar kitchen, smaller and a bit more cramped than was comfortable, but cozy and bright. He remembered the first time he'd banged his head on the hanging light from the middle of the ceiling; he'd grown several inches one summer and hadn't realized just how tall he'd gotten until he'd tried to walk under the light as usual and had caught the top of his head on it as he walked by. He'd been all gangly arms and legs for months.

When his eyes fell on a small pamphlet pinned to the door of the refrigerator, he cursed under his breath. Of course.

"I'm sorry I didn't make it up to say good-bye to your mom," he said solemnly, nodding with his chin to the funeral program with a black and white photo of their mother, Lena.

Tommy glanced at it and nodded. "It's okay. She would have understood." He crossed to the fridge, opening it. "Want a beer?"

"Absolutely," Chase said, accepting the cold beer Tommy held out to him. "Can I bum a shower though? I stink."

Tommy nodded around a drink of his own beer. "You know where it is. Bedroom at the end of the hall has been made up for you, too."

"Thanks," he said and ducked his head through the low archway that led from the kitchen to the living room, and the stairs to the second floor. He climbed them two at a time, easily finding his way to the bathroom. He glanced at the door that used to be Zoey's when they'd been young. She was six years younger, just a kid when they'd graduated and he'd headed off to the police academy downstate.

Shutting the bathroom door, he quickly shucked his clothes, turning on the shower taps to get the water heating. He dug out a towel from the cabinet in the far corner, then stepped into the steaming shower that was much too short for his six five frame.

Setting the beer on the window sill after taking a long drink, he ducked his head under the spray and rinsed his hair, lathering it with shampoo and washed his body of the sweat from his workout.

Ducking his head under the too short shower head again, he rinsed his hair. Cut short on the sides but left long on top, too long, he was sure he'd be informed it needed a cut before next week.

Tommy had asked him why he'd moved back. He wasn't sure he was ready to tell that story, not yet.

Nightmares still haunted him, sometimes even when he just closed his eyes. He could still see her. He hadn't been able to save her, and it had haunted him ever since. He'd needed to get away, start fresh.

Finishing the beer in one swallow, he climbed out of the shower, towel drying off swiftly. Realizing he'd left his duffel bag down in the kitchen, he slung the towel around his hips, securing it by tucking the end in. He exited the bathroom and was halfway down the hall when he realized Zoey's bedroom door was open, cracked about six inches. The sun had set and beyond the windows of her bedroom the sky was darkening, the only light in the room one dim lamp. As he made to walk past, his head turned and he peeked into the bedroom just for a heartbeat, but what he saw stopped him in his tracks.

Zoey was sitting in a padded gliding chair that had been positioned in the corner of the room. Her legs were crossed, one over the other, her top foot dangling, the other rocking gently, pushing against the carpeted floor.

But what had stopped him dead was the golden head that lay against her bare breast, a tiny hand that flailed in the air, as if trying to grab a hold of something invisible hanging above it. Zoey's dark golden hair fell in a curtain across her face, obscuring her, as she crooned softly to the babe in her arms.

Chase wasn't sure if he'd made a noise, but her head whipped around, as if sensing his presence. Her eyes went wide, but she didn't move.

Chase nearly tripped on himself as he rushed away from the door and down the stairs, stumbling into the kitchen, still naked save the towel slung around his hips.

Tommy looked up from where he sat at the small dining table. When he saw Chase's face, Tommy opened his mouth to speak, but Chase was quicker.

"She had a baby?"

Tommy nodded, standing.

"With who?" Chase demanded, that same old protective instinct he had with all of his sisters kicking in.

The look on Tommy's face was pained. "Some douchebag." Chase's mouth tightened, but he waited for Tommy to continue. "She was assaulted, Chase. Some dickhead college kid."

Blood roared in Chase's ears. "She was *what*? When?"

"Last year," Tommy said, sliding his hands into the pockets of his jeans. "Like I said… a lot has changed. She's changed. She's… still healing. Mentally."

Chase scrubbed a hand over his face, blowing out his breath. "What happened?"

Tommy shook his head. "I only know the bare minimum; she hasn't wanted to talk about it. I haven't pushed her. I'm not sure I want to know the details." The skin on Tommy's face went taut and paled slightly.

"What the fuck," Chase breathed, dropping his chin almost to his chest. When he did, he realized he was still in a towel, and swore again. "Is she… is she okay? Physically?"

Tommy nodded, shrugging one shoulder. "She doesn't have any permanent injuries, if that's what you're asking."

"Why didn't you say anything?" he asked, while he rifled through his duffel bag until he found a pair of sweatpants, pulling them on under the towel before hanging it over the nearest dining chair. He pushed his fingers through the longer locks on the top of his head, pulling the still damp strands away from his brow. He squeezed his eyes shut, but quickly opened them, memories assailing him.

Tommy crossed the small kitchen to the refrigerator, opening it, and grabbed two beers out of it. He held one up to Chase, who shook his head no. Tommy put one back, but opened the second.

Again, Chase asked, "Why didn't you say anything?"

Tommy opened his mouth to speak, but a small voice from behind him answered.

"Because I asked him not to."